EMERALD PROMISE

SARAH URQUHART

EMERALD PROMISE is a work of fiction. Names, characters, and places are products of the author's imagination or used fictitiously. Any resemblance to locales or persons, living or dead, is coincidental.

Cover design by Untold Designs

This book is a steamy, small town, shifter romance and is for mature audiences only. It contains sexually explicit scenes and adult language that may be offensive to some readers.

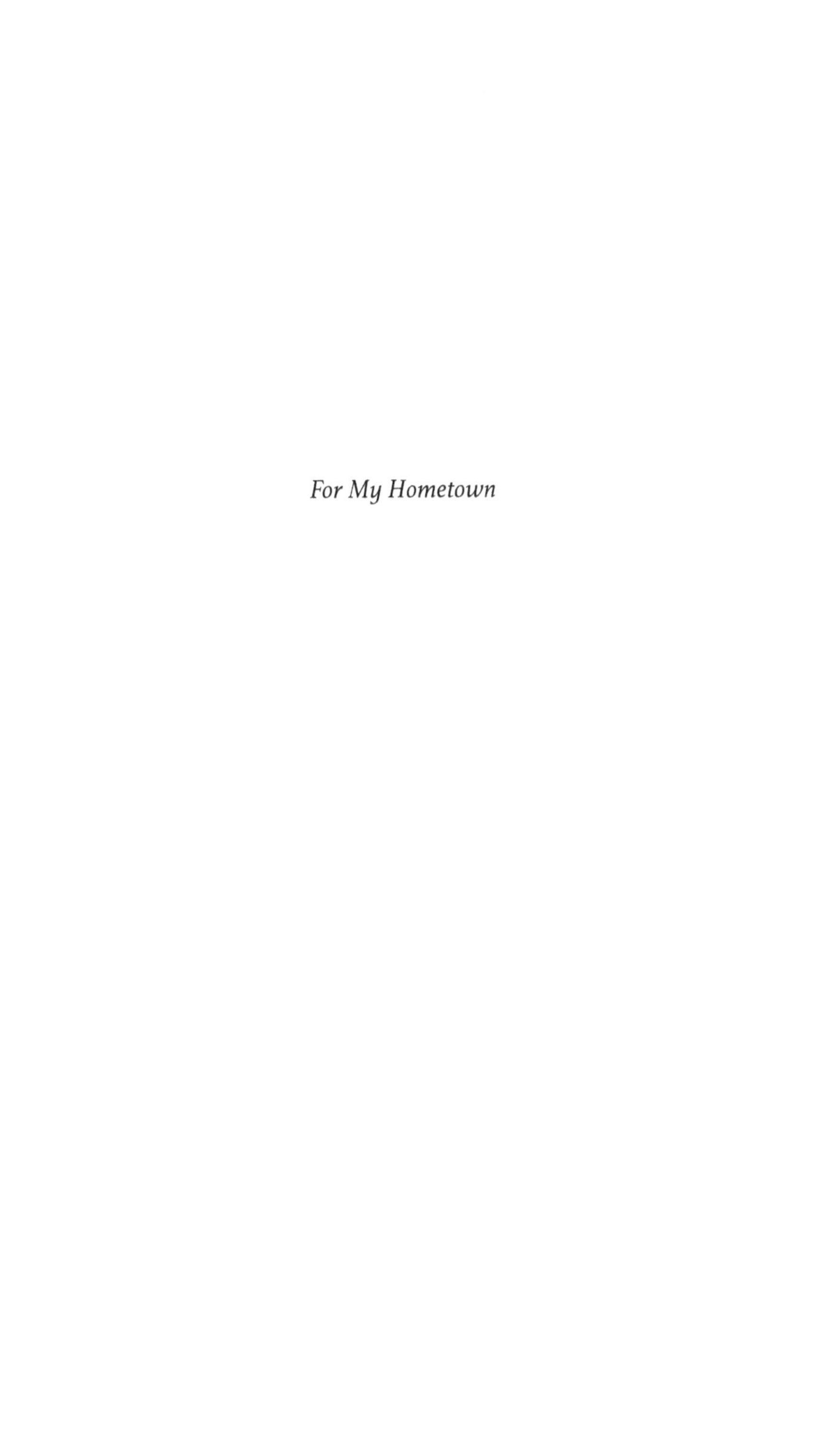

For My Hometown

ACKNOWLEDGMENTS

Life interfered a few times while working on this book. So the ones I need to thank the most are those that helped me through and helped in any way they could to make sure I could keep working. They gave me the encouragement, the breaks, the shoulders. Thanks to them, this book still released this summer, despite the delays. Thank you to each and everyone one of you.

And as always, no release is possible without the ladies in the sprint room, my beta readers, and my husband. Thank you for everything you do.

PROLOGUE

"No, you're lame!" Caiden shoved his brother Wyatt to the ground. He hadn't expected the return attack when he turned away. His face hit the dirt between the patchy grass on the lawn. Curling his lips inward, his face contorted into what his mom called his fight face. Wyatt wasn't that much older that he got to push him around whenever he wanted. They were born the same year. Caiden pushed up from the ground. Bending his knees and angling his shoulders, he charged, but the stillness of Wyatt and Dakota made him pause.

"What was that, Wyatt?" Their little sister gripped his arm.

"I don't know, Dakota."

Caiden stood on the other side of his sister. "Did you see something?"

"Not really. Something moved those bushes." Wyatt threw a weak arm out to point. "It kind of whistled too." Caiden watched with them, doubting them when nothing happened. But then a whistle rose, getting louder, and the bush jiggled like a shaking puppy.

"Let's go see what it is." Caiden inched forward, knowing Wyatt would follow. A tiny hand wrapped around his wrist. He stopped. Dakota had a grip on him and an identical one on Wyatt.

"Dad said not to go in there." Dakota had always been a daddy's girl. She never did anything to make their dad mad.

Caiden met Wyatt's gaze, an unspoken agreement that they were going anyway. They pried their sister's hands from their wrists.

"Then you can stay here." Wyatt patted her on the shoulder. He followed Caiden. Sure their dad would be mad, but it wasn't like he'd ban them from playing outside. Everything would be fine. They'd just peek on what was in the bush and Caiden could go back to beating on his brother.

"Guys!" Running feet followed Dakota's whine. At almost four, she was still little enough she didn't like being left alone. Ever. She always followed Caiden and Wyatt. Caiden rolled his eyes.

Wyatt pointed to Caiden, then to one side of the bush as he moved to the other. With a single nod, they both grabbed the bush to move their side out of the way. Nothing fled or tried to bury deeper in the foliage. Wyatt shrugged and turned back.

"There." Caiden waved to get his brother's attention. Another bush further in made the same movement and the same sound. They crept closer, each taking a side. This time, when they yanked on the bush, a faint green blur rushed away. It was too fast to get a look at what it was.

"Did you see that?" Wyatt stared after it.

"Yeah." The word a harsh hush from Caiden's throat.

"Come on, guys. We need to go back." Dakota bounced from foot to foot.

"You go back, Dakota." Caiden stepped forward and

ignored his sister, fascinated by what they were about to find. They ran in the direction of the green something. The distance between them and Dakota grew. Another trail of green rushed across the ground, and they chased after it.

"Slow down!" Dakota hadn't stayed behind, and Caiden hadn't believed she would.

They ignored her. The green flashed in and out of sight. Caiden's lungs struggled, starting a low burn. They came to an open clearing. Wyatt panted in tune beside him. Out from the trees on the other side, slithered their prey. Faint green wind lifted the twigs and leaves up off the ground to let them fall again.

"What is it?" Caiden asked his older brother, looking for reassurance.

"I don't know." His head shook while he followed the wind.

It moved around, up and down, twirling back and forth, blurring the forest behind it. A voice in the back of Caiden's mind told him they should go back now. This was way too far into the woods, and they didn't know what they were looking at. But neither of them moved.

Dakota caught up. She grabbed onto Caiden's shirt to catch herself.

"What's that?" The wind froze at her higher voice as if startled, like an animal perking its ears. It dashed off up into the trees.

"Come on." Wyatt put a hand on their sister and nodded at Caiden. "We should go."

Small grunts and the crunch of wrestling on the ground had them turning back. Two bear cubs tumbled into the clearing. Jaws open and paws flailing in a play fight. They hadn't moved until one cub noticed they were there.

"We really need to get out of here now. The mama bear

won't be far and she won't like us this close to her cubs." Wyatt tried to back them up. Caiden and Dakota didn't argue. Wyatt had an arm stretched out in front of Caiden, and Caiden had an arm in front of Dakota. The siblings backed up with cautious steps. Their steps slowed when the green tinted wind came back and played with the cubs. Small, fat paws swung in the air, distorting the green.

But then the wind changed course and charged at them, lunging over Caiden's and Wyatt's heads and toward their sister. It pushed their sister away from them.

"Caiden! Wyatt!" They tried to chase after her, but it came back and shoved them toward the bear cubs.

"It's okay! Just go home, Dakota." Caiden called back to her, then looked at Wyatt and shrugged. The wind was too strong. What more could they do?

The wind started playing with the cubs again. Wyatt gripped Caiden's sleeve and pulled. They backed up, hoping it wouldn't notice. But it did, and so did the cubs. The cubs jumped around their feet, smiles opening their snouts. Their prancing paws hit the ground with soft thuds. Caiden twisted and turned to keep up with them. The wind joined in.

"Wyatt? What's going on?" Sure, they had been born in the same year, but there were times Caiden was happy he had an older brother.

Wyatt didn't have an answer for him. His hand tightened around Caiden's arm, rough points of pain sinking into the muscle. Wyatt's eyes searched the trees, not paying attention to the cubs or wind. He copied his brother—waiting for the mama bear to show up and attack.

The wind turned warmer as it circled behind them.

"I don't feel good, Wyatt." Caiden gritted his teeth to hold back tears like he did when he was sick. The fear of knowing he was about to throw up and doing everything he could to avoid it.

"Me either."

The warmth seeped into Caiden's skin, cementing an ache in his bones. He had the urge to roll his shoulders and stretch his back like he did when getting out of bed in the mornings before collapsing on the couch to watch cartoons. The cubs played at their feet while the wind encased them in a translucent cocoon.

Wyatt's hand let go of his shirt just as the ache grew through him. His joints moved and rolled, despite Caiden tensing his muscles against the sensation.

Caiden groaned, an echo after his brother. He looked at Wyatt, hunched forward in pain. Whatever Caiden was experiencing, his brother was, too.

The ache expanded outward to the surface of his skin. Nausea filled his belly and his vision swam until suddenly everything in front of him held clarity. He shut his eyes to force the nausea down, caused by the sudden change.

Moments later, fresh warmth replaced the ache. Caiden lay on the ground, scared to open his eyes.

What's happened to us? The voice was Wyatt's, but it carried more like an echo.

Opening his eyes, he saw the two cubs that had been playing at their feet, rolling together again in the grass. Beside him sat a third cub with wide green eyes that raked over Caiden. He jumped up and stumbled back, tripping over something. When he checked to see what it was, it was his own paws.

We're bears, Caiden. He'd never heard that tone from Wyatt before, shaky and high, like the sound Dakota made before she cried after she fell.

Caiden stood, stretching his claws into the ground for balance. *What do we do?*

I don't know.

The cubs turned their heads, looking back at them upside down. They rolled to their feet and charged toward Caiden and Wyatt. Taking them to the ground, the wild cubs forcing them into wrestling matches. Caiden struggled to get his feet in the right places to push against the cub or to gain his footing. Wyatt seemed to have the same problem. When the cubs realized they didn't know how to play, they hopped off.

Caiden moved closer to his brother, their fur at their sides intertwining.

We can't go home like this, can we? Their parents or their sister wouldn't recognize them.

No. We follow them. Wyatt took an unsteady step forward. The cubs lifted their heads, excitement lighting their green eyes. As soon as both Wyatt and Caiden had taken several steps, the cubs pounced, tackling them again to force them to play.

1

———

Maggie turned her head down, tired of swiveling it back and forth to keep up with the conversations. The heat in the air was dissipating as the evening took hold.

"You burnt the burgers, doc." Zachary peered over Asher's shoulder at the barbecue.

"No. They're fine." He shoved his shoulder into Zachary's chest and flipped the next burger. If they weren't burnt, they would be soon. Maggie breathed in the faint, charred scent. But it wasn't her place to correct Asher.

"Take mine off now." Zachary thrust an empty paper plate toward Asher.

"And mine." Nathan followed.

Mine, too, Maggie thought. But she stayed where she was, attempting to shape herself against the picnic table. Her grey shirt camouflaged well against the aged colour of the wood. Ezaray and Holly dragged her along, claiming she'd kept herself hidden too often. For months, they'd visited, took her for lunch and coffee. Once in a while, they'd bring Gwen and Shaye along, but Maggie always cut those outings short—sometimes finding the four women overwhelming when all together. Now she sat in Asher's yard with not only the four other women, but their husbands and fiancés as well.

She knew there had been a time she enjoyed having friends, but those memories faded into dreams a long time ago.

"Really? You two want to complain about *my* cooking?" Asher took criticism with an ease that Maggie envied. His calm, jovial spirit attracted everyone around him. They all looked to him as if he was their leader.

"I don't have to cook to know what tastes good." Zachary grabbed another spatula and reached over to get his own burger from the barbecue.

Zachary wasn't wrong. She hadn't learned how to do much in the kitchen, but she'd discovered some strong dislikes in food since arriving in Alder Ridge.

At first, she'd only made slow progress. Space and peace had filled the last several months, giving Maggie the time to grow on her own. Everyone had been encouraging and friendly, helping her get used to what a normal life should be like. A job, friends, responsibilities. She was no longer nervous in crowds, worrying about what strangers would see when they looked at her. And a knock on her door didn't send her into a visible panic attack. Maggie felt her old self stirring within, starving inside her. Nobody pushed her to go past her limits, or what they thought were her limits. But Maggie wasn't sure what to do next.

Tires crunching over gravel that kicked up to ping against metal heralded a pickup truck speeding toward Asher's. The truck slid, creating skid marks as the driver slammed on the brakes, stopping an inch from the other vehicles.

"Asher!" the driver yelled as he jumped out, leaving the

door swinging open. Most of the group ran toward him, all stopping at different times, spreading themselves out. Maggie kept herself still at the table, although her curiosity had her leaning her head around the others. She couldn't get more than a glimpse of the man or the vehicle past all the bodies.

"What is it?" Asher stood closest to the new truck.

"A bear. He's been shot. I patched him up, so he'd survive the drive, but he needs a vet at the moment, not a doctor." A doctor. She knew that voice. A voice that sometimes echoed in her nightmares as a calming tone. He'd never hurt her, but she hadn't realized then that he'd been someone she could trust. Stretching her neck further she saw the doctor, a man that had worked for her step-brother, but had also helped them all escape the hell her step-brother had created.

But he'd brought a bear? The doctor brought a bear with a gunshot wound to a vet? Maggie gripped the seat of the table and hunched her shoulders. She'd only be in the way if she moved.

Asher opened the tailgate of the truck while the others lifted a tarp that covered the back. "Back the truck up to the deck."

The doctor got back behind the wheel. The others moved out of the way to give him room to drive across the lawn.

Asher waited on the steps. "Help me get him out. We'll need to get him stable."

Four of the men there worked together to pull the bear from the back, straining and struggling to get him up the stairs. The bear's head faced her as they pulled him from the truck. His eyes remained closed, hiding in his brown fur. Why weren't they concerned he'd wake up any second and attack? Seeing a bear, even an unconscious and injured one, made her want to back away.

They set him on the deck. Gwen had run inside and returned with a black bag, giving them space to settle the bear before handing the bag to Asher.

Asher's voice carried as he made the diagnosis, but she was too far away to hear it all.

"… bullet hit the bone. It's still in there." Bears were common in Maggie's hometown. She was certain that in a case like this they'd put the bear down. Holly's fiancé, Anthony, was a Fish and Wildlife Officer. Yet he stood there with his hands on Holly's shoulders, not saying what needed to be done.

Maggie didn't understand, and she was too far away. She pinched her lips between her fingers, fighting with herself. One hand gripped the table tighter to keep herself there, and the other pushed against the top to make her move. Pulling in a breath through her nose, she huffed it out when her butt didn't lift off the bench. Trying again, she stood. Years of practice kept her steps slow and quiet. She'd learned how to place her feet down when she walked to create the least amount of noise or disruption.

The closer she got, the more she heard.

"I'll need as many of you present as possible for the surgery. He's already started to heal around the bullet. I need to do this now. But I can only guess how much anesthesia I'll need. It's not as if I've ever had to perform surgery on one of our kind." Asher didn't look at any of them as he continued to work on the bear. Maggie moved around the truck. She stood behind the other women, but she adjusted to give herself a clear view of what was happening on the deck.

"How long have you been driving with him?" Zachary stood beside the doctor.

"Four hours, but I wasn't going slow."

"Do you know what happened?" Nathan had crouched on the opposite side of the bear from Asher.

"Not the specifics. I saw it from the sky. How the hunter got the drop on him, I'm not sure. He was running, not well, and the hunter gave chase, determined. The bear ran toward the road and the hunter stopped following him."

The sky? She hadn't thought the doctor had a hobby. Piloting wouldn't have been her first guess.

"That was a risky move. If someone else had found him, he would have been put down." Anthony confirmed what Maggie had thought. So why weren't they suggesting that now? And why did he drive him four hours to find a vet? There had to have been several veterinarians between wherever he came from and here.

"The outcome was looking the same no matter which way he went. He'd been slowing down. I stopped him before he broke through the trees. I did the best I could there, then *kindly borrowed* a vehicle. I drove for about an hour before I stopped and treated him better, then came straight here. I even found clothes hidden under the front seat." The doctor pulled on the shirt that hung loosely around his torso.

His story was a puzzle with missing pieces, but she was the only one that seemed concerned with filling them in. The others all understood everything he said. Flying with no clothes and able to see a bear through the canopy of the trees. The bear was their sole focus. What was so special about this bear that would have all these people gathering to save his life? Stepping to the right, she wanted to get a better look at him.

"Maggie." Ezaray spoke suddenly over the top of

everyone else and came to her side. All nine sets of eyes landed on her. A nervous instinct saying that the attention on her would get her hurt pulled at her spine, forcing her to take several steps back. "We can take you home. I doubt you want to see all of this." Ezaray scrunched her nose, but her voice pitched with the sound of a polite lie.

"I need Zachary here." Asher never stopped preparing for the surgery.

"Zee and I can take you home." Holly left Anthony's side and joined Ezaray beside Maggie.

Maggie only nodded, but she tried to get one last look at the bear while she walked between Holly and Ezaray. Questions gripped the tip of her tongue, ready to fly, but they wanted her gone so they could talk freely again.

THE URGE TO run rocked through Caiden's limbs, but no more than a twitch stretched his paws. Pain sliced through his flesh under his skin. Strange scents filled his nose. He wasn't home. But shifters surrounded him. Two wolves, a bear, and a hawk. The hawk. The scent was familiar. He'd been running, fighting through the pain shooting through his upper body. The hawk stopped him from running into the road. Once he'd stopped, the adrenaline slowed its transmission through his blood. His flight instinct screamed through his mind, but he'd passed out after that. Caiden remembered the panic as his eyes had closed.

Voices hummed around him. He tried to focus—feeling the wood surface beneath him, the dryness of his mouth. He counted the unfamiliar scents surrounding him. There were more than the fours shifters. Others that carried an odd, wild scent. He thought he smelled an owl nearby, not close like the others. Unconsciousness tugged at him again. Struggling to hold on, he breathed deep. A euphoric scent drifted through the others, faint and distant, but it shot straight to his head.

"I need you ready to hold him." Male voices were right above him.

"Let's go." Females were there, but drifting away. He breathed in again to pinpoint the scent, but dizziness collided with the pain and nothing he did stopped his muscles from relaxing against the wood as darkness tightened its grip.

Spikes of pain interrupted his memories, pulling him in and out. Each time he regained consciousness, he tried to open his eyes. He got as much as slits of vision that showed deck railings and the legs of two men. Caiden couldn't smell his brother. The familiar scents of the lodge, of home, the mountains, weren't there.

When next he woke, the sky was dark and filled with the stars. The pain had subsided, but an ache tightened his front leg. He tried to move, to brace himself with his front paws, but collapsed back to the wood with a grunt.

"The big guy's awake." Someone moved behind him. Caiden lifted his head. With narrowed eyes, he watched two men get up from wooden chairs, throwing blankets to the side. He inhaled the distinct scent of shifters. Broken memories filtered into his mind. The hawk. Waking, surrounded by shifters. It was a hawk and another bear that walked toward him now. The bear tapped on a door as he passed.

"How are you feeling?" The hawk crouched in front of Caiden, squeezing himself between his front paws and the deck railing. Caiden stared back. How the hell did the hawk expect him to answer? "Your eyes are clear. I'd say you're out of the woods. But Asher will be down in a minute."

As if on cue, footsteps sounded on stairs from inside the house. The door swung open and the strong scent of wolf wafted over the deck with a breeze. He assumed this was Asher.

"Well, that's a good sign." Asher motioned the hawk away and took his spot. He met Caiden's eyes. "Don't bite me."

Caiden didn't have a reason to, for now. He might not know where he was, but these shifters saved him. Asher touched his front leg and Caiden growled. The involuntary rumble spiked in the top of his chest and vibrated his gritting teeth. Pain stretched outward from his touch.

"Sorry. But you're healing. You won't be able to shift for a few days. It's best to let this heal as much as possible first. Then the magic can finish it with a shift." Asher took his hands away and stood to lean against the railing. "Do you remember what happened?"

Did he remember? He'd been out for a run after a particularly busy rush at the restaurant, letting his bear free. He hadn't called Wyatt to come, and Caiden hadn't met up with Theo, his animal pair, yet. Forest debris crunching, heavy, short breaths—they were his only warning. The wind had been blowing over his fur toward the heavy breather until it was too late for Caiden to realize what was happening. Then pain sliced his front leg. Yeah, he remembered.

He met Asher's eyes and nodded. Then he looked at the hawk who'd stopped his run toward the road to lose the hunter. Caiden had two choices, face the hunter chasing him while injured, or take a chance that whoever he ran into in town was his brother or one of his cousins.

Caiden nodded at the hawk, his eyes closing. He owed the hawk his gratitude.

"You'll have to stay here. I have a cabin deep in the

woods that I built for this purpose, for shifters to use as a safehouse whenever needed. But you aren't in the shape to travel up there. You'll heal a lot faster if you stay off your front leg. I just hope I don't have any visitors for the next few days." A smile twitched on his face. "My name's Asher Morestead. I'm a veterinarian here in Alder Ridge. This is Garrett Daly. He brought you here. And that's Nathan Marks."

Caiden looked at the surrounding shifters. He hoped one of them shifted soon so he could talk to them. He needed to let his brother know he was okay. Wyatt would be worried. Dakota would be too, but Wyatt would hide it from their sister. She'd be pissed, but it was what Wyatt did. Protected their baby sister.

"Get some sleep." When they all walked away, Caiden groaned. He needed one of them to make the call. Three sets of eyes glowed in the dark. He groaned again, moving his jaw up and down. Nathan started undressing and stepped off the deck. Through the railings, Caiden saw an auburn wind encircle the other shifter. He stepped back onto the deck as a bear.

I'm sorry. This couldn't wait until morning, Caiden explained, the sound of his echoed voice rough.

That's okay. What is it? Nathan tilted his head downward.

I need you to call my brother. To tell him what happened and to be careful for a while until we can track down the hunter that shot me. Caiden kept his head lifted, but his strength was slipping away.

Of course.

His name is Wyatt Greer. I'm from Firebrook. He gave Nathan his brother's phone number.

Does he know you're a shifter? One fury brow lifted.

He's a shifter, too.

I'll call him right away. Anything else you want me to tell him other than you're okay?

No. I'll be home in a few days. I'm Caiden. He'd talk to his brother when he got home. Right now, he needed to focus on pushing away the pain and healing.

Nathan nodded. Caiden repeated his brother's phone number and ensured Nathan that he wouldn't be asleep.

Nathan stepped off the deck to shift. He repeated the phone number aloud to the others, and Asher stepped inside to retrieve a phone. He passed it to Nathan after he finished buttoning his pants.

Caiden listened to the call, hearing his brother's voice through the line.

"Your brother is safe and in Alder Ridge. A friend of mine found him shot and brought him here to get him help."

"Shot? By who?" Caiden pictured his brother storming through a room, growing with his anger to take down any threat.

"He didn't say, or he doesn't know."

Caiden shook his head.

"He doesn't know," Nathan confirmed for Wyatt. "He's safe here and welcome to stay to heal. Our resident shifter docs say he needs a few days to heal before he can shift."

"Shifter docs?"

"Just a doctor and a vet who happen to be shifters themselves." Nathan looked between Asher and Garrett.

"Are you sure he's okay?" Caiden heard Wyatt's skepticism in his slow, emphasized speech.

"I'm sure." Nathan mimicked Wyatt's tone.

"Thanks for calling." It wasn't often his brother sounded lost. He'd ask Nathan or one of the others to call him again in the morning.

Nathan hung up.

Caiden thumped his head against the wood, and his eyes closed with the impact. It would be a long few days. But he considered himself lucky that shifters and not humans surrounded him. He may not be alive if not for the hawk.

WHERE WAS IT? Maggie searched behind the couch cushions, in the kitchen, her bedroom, and even the bathroom. She didn't carry a big wallet or purse. Just a hard case card holder in her pocket. But right now, it wasn't in any pockets of her clothes from last night. She was sure she took it to Asher's barbecue.

Maggie didn't keep much. A single bank account and a bit of cash. But necessary to get to work, buy herself lunch and groceries. Checking the time on the wall clock, Maggie was early. Always was. This was her chance at a new start. She'd do nothing to screw it up. And that meant taking her job, despite only being a maid at one of the bed and breakfasts, seriously. She had one other job in her life. A general store clerk. The few years when her step-brother lived away from home had provided her some freedoms.

Going all the way to Asher's on the other side of town might make her late. But she needed her wallet. There was no choice. She called for a cab and then called her boss.

"That's fine, dear. Don't you worry about rushing at all." Ruth was the sweetest woman Maggie had ever met. The last thing she wanted to do was take advantage of Ruth's kindness.

Maggie watched for the cab from the porch. A red hatchback pulled into the driveway. Jogging toward it, she hopped in the backseat and gave the driver directions to Asher's. She didn't know the address off the top of her head, only how to get there. Halfway through the drive, she realized she hadn't told them she was stopping by, not that they hadn't told her multiple times she was always welcome and to come by if she ever needed anything. In fact, they all seemed to go out of their way to make sure she knew that. Maggie sent a text to Gwen saying she lost her wallet and was stopping by to see if it had fallen out of her pocket last night. The driver pulled up to Asher's only minutes later.

He parked behind three vehicles, Asher's, Gwen's, and the truck the doctor had driven in last night with the injured bear in the back. Not waiting for a reply from Gwen, Maggie jumped out of the cab and jogged across the yard toward the setup of picnic tables. She didn't want to be any later than she already was.

"Maggie."

Maggie stumbled, startled by a male voice calling her name. She looked up at the deck, and the doctor stood at the top of the stairs.

"Is there anything I can help you with, Maggie?"

"Dr. Daly. I just came looking for my wallet. I thought I must have lost it here last night."

"You need to call me Garrett," he reminded her with a gentle smile. Last winter, she'd woken up in the hospital with him standing over her. Tyrone had come to Alder Ridge to take her, Ezaray, and Holly back. A fight in the woods led to Maggie getting shot. She was told Garrett showed up after she'd passed out and took her to the hospital. She hadn't seen him since.

"I'm just going to look around out here. I'm late for work." She wasn't late yet, but she would be by the time they drove back across town. Maggie searched the bench she'd sat on and the surrounding grass. She hadn't moved around much. It likely hadn't fallen out anywhere else. About to give up, the green stripe along the edge of the case caught her eye. Relief pulsed. She picked it up and held it up to Garrett before putting it in her pocket. An awkward grasp pinched her smile. She didn't have more to say to him and he came with so many negative memories. She trusted her friends here, and even Garrett fell into the same category, but that logic didn't always work for her.

Maggie started back for the cab, but a deep, rumbling growl sent a tremor up her body. She turned back to the deck. Garrett's mouth moved, and he stared to the side. The same spot they'd put the bear the night before. What the hell were these people thinking? They still had an injured bear recovering on the deck. And the doctor was stupid enough to stand there with his back to it.

She didn't have time to educate the doctor on bear safety. Taking slow steps back, her eyes on the brown visible through the railings and not on Garrett talking to the dangerous lump, she moved toward the cab. But she couldn't keep her tongue still.

"You shouldn't still have him here. None of you strike me as the type that wouldn't have bear smarts."

"I'll be fine." Garrett's lips moved to the beginnings of a grin, but the rumble from the bear grew louder and took his attention off Maggie. The sound instilled ice in her feet, but she needed to get out of there. She continued her steps toward the cab—small, slow, consistent.

Paws thumped against the wood, and his rumble buried into his stomach.

"What do you think you're doing? Stay still." Garrett turned to face the bear. His body relaxed, as if talking to a patient. The same way he'd talked to Maggie and the others when treating them after a fight. The image, the words, the tone—her stomach hardened as if it crystallized—the tiny rocks building on top of each other, growing. Her vision blurred. The bear's rumble turned to an angry growl, the sound ripping away the flashes of memory that played in her mind.

Maggie inwardly shook and focused on the doctor moving toward the bear. Words stuck in her throat. The bear's head popped up over the railing. His nose twitched frantically.

The commotion drew the attention of the others inside the house. Asher stepped out his front door, but the bear blocked his way. Gwen's head poked around him. The doctor seemed to gain some sense and moved out of the way. Asher didn't jump in, either. The bear wanted to go home and lick his own wounds rather than have humans do it for him. Maggie could understand that.

But she stood in the bear's path.

Maggie continued toward the cab, the same slow and steady steps, while looking back over her shoulder to gauge the distance to the cab. A single groan left the bear, who was now staring at her. She wasn't just in his way—she was his target. His stark eyes saw past her skin. She couldn't tell what colour they were from this distance, but they weren't brown as they should be. They calmed her for a moment until she remembered the animal they belonged to.

Her steps didn't stop, and the bear grew more agitated.

"Maggie, please stop. He shouldn't be moving the way he is. He's going to hurt himself." Asher's request was as ridiculous as the doctor treating the bear like a patient.

"It's okay, Maggie." Gwen stepped out from behind Asher.

She shook her head and took another step back. The bear growled and tried to take the steps down off the deck, but he stumbled. Asher and Garrett jumped toward him to catch him. They couldn't be that stupid, but they chose to offer themselves as snacks. Maggie took the opportunity. She turned and ran back to the cab parked behind all the vehicles. The driver's bored eyes stared at his scrolling thumb. She slammed the back door after jumping in, startling him.

"Go, now. Please." Her breath caught as her volume increased.

The driver shrugged and put the car in reverse.

The bear had been looking directly at her. She turned around and looked out the back window. They still had their arms around the grizzly and were trying to pull him back onto the deck with little luck.

He hadn't been trying to get away from them. He'd been trying to get to her.

2

———————

Caiden held back his roar as he landed on his injured leg. Garrett and Asher kept him from falling to the ground, but they weren't quick enough to stop his fumble.

The woman. Her spicy scent with red hair that flared to life diminished the ache in his body, leaving behind a fuzziness that hissed through his veins. He had no control of himself when he stood and limped toward her. She ran and the roar he held back let loose, rocketing forth as its own wild animal. He'd wanted to touch her, breathe her in, hold her.

Her scent lingered on the breeze. Asher and Garrett hefted him back up the steps, but he fought them until he saw the red and white car pull away with her in the back seat. They helped him back to his spot on the deck to lie down.

"It was her. It was Maggie that made you get up. You were chasing a scent." Asher cocked his head. The two of them towered over him with wide eyes. Caiden didn't understand what the hell came over him. He didn't know that woman. Had never seen her before and had never smelled her before. But the need to go to her still ran strong through his body.

Caiden nodded once. Her scent had kicked him into motion.

"Do you know what that means? Have you or any other shifters you know come across this before?"

He'd never heard of it. But the vet and doctor were about to explain it to him.

"She's your mate."

Mate. He closed his eyes. It explained the urge to touch her and claim her. But there wouldn't be a mate for him. He had all the fun he could ever want with women, as long as they didn't become attached. Caiden never allowed attachment on his end, and made it clear before their bodies ever hit the bed. A mate would be a responsibility, a living person he would take care of.

He needed to get the fuck back home before... What was her name? Caiden searched through the adrenaline cloud in his mind—Maggie. He needed to get home before *Maggie* showed up again.

Laura's screams filtered through his ears. He winced, tightening himself to push away the memory, the sounds. No. No mate. He growled—a deep throb moved through his muscles.

"He doesn't like the sound of that." Asher spoke low to Garrett.

"Maggie doesn't deserve to be hurt again." A protective roll prowled through Garrett's voice—a warning for the universe to take it easy on the girl.

Not his problem. It was simple. Don't acknowledge her, don't start anything. Heal and go home. She didn't have to be hurt by this. She was human. The way she ran from him, terrified of the animal moving toward her, she didn't feel the same pull as he did.

The sensation had been odd and something he needed to tell his brother and cousins about.

Caiden kept his eyes closed, ignoring the effects Maggie's scent still had on his system. Asher, Gwen, and Garrett moved away, going inside the house. Caiden didn't want to hear more about mates right now, anyway.

He had nothing more to do than lie here and heal. Wyatt would look after his restaurant, but it bothered Caiden that he wasn't there. The longest he'd ever left it had been a day or two. Being early summer, it was his busiest season at the restaurant and the lodge, not only with the locals, but with the tourists. After a long winter, people hit the road at the first opportunity and they always landed in a place like Firebrook.

The sun heated Caiden's fur. On a day like today, the patio at the restaurant would fill up fast. He'd be experimenting with new summer recipes and adding them to the menu last minute, earning groans from his staff.

What would await him after several days?

They'd have to go find who was hunting bears. His leg throbbed at the thought of getting shot. That fucking hurt. And he didn't intend to experience it again. The hunter had been nowhere near Caiden, and it hadn't been a shotgun. There was no self defense in this act.

He sighed and stretched in the sun. Caiden had nothing to do but wait and heal. And hope he didn't have to face Maggie again.

Vivid, deep eyes stared at her in her dream, while the rest was a hazy vision. The stark clarity of the bear's eyes tried to bite at her secrets, luring her to go to him. Maggie woke with a start, sitting up in bed. The bear's gaze haunted her dreams all night.

Her alarm chimed seconds after she'd already woken. She'd forgotten to turn it off the night before. Maggie liked to sleep in on her days off. It'd taken a long time, but she could rest peacefully at night. The last time she'd felt safe sleeping was when her step-brother first moved away from home.

That hadn't lasted long. Her freedom from him had been fleeting. When he saw the small fire of contentment she knew shone from her face, his anger lashed out and crushed her back to ashes. Frail, brittle, burnt bark that with the wrong touch or breath she'd crumble. That's what he did to her. So that he could use her own blood to moisten the ashes and mold her into what he wanted.

But the strength of the eyes in her dream didn't leave her crumbling to the ground as the wind picked up the dust. Power with an unknown depth beckoned her, forcing her to stand tall. In her dream, locked in that gaze, she became the woman of a different reality—the one where her mother had never married her step-father. It was the woman she wanted to be now. But why did that realization have to come from the eyes of a predatory animal?

Maggie kicked her feet until the blankets tangled at the bottom of the bed. Her heels bounced when she flopped them onto the mattress. Days off were long and lonely, but that was the last thing Maggie would complain about—a small price to pay to live independently, have a job, a life, a home. It may not be her house, but it was her home for now.

The only one that had ever felt like such since before her mother remarried.

Memories of her mother and step-father came in faint wisps, more like wishes than a reality that once was. The dread that followed with Tyrone smothered anything good she might have had with them, any normal childhood or teenage life.

This was her life. This was her happy. She owed Shaye a great deal for allowing her to live here rent free. Maggie squared away every cent, building a stockpile of finances to grow on. Now that she worked full time, she'd soon have enough to start paying rent.

She kept her routine even on her days off, except for sleeping in. Putting her hair under the shower, Maggie closed her eyes and breathed in the humidity filling the bathroom. She let the heat seep into her skin before she washed.

Stepping from the shower, she wrapped the towel over her shoulders and froze when someone knocked on the door. Maggie pulled in a breath, using the weight of the air to smooth out the rippling adrenaline under her skin, the same way she used to use her thumb nail to smooth out crumpled tin foil from school lunches. She hated even the few times she reacted when someone came to her door. It had been months since they killed Tyrone. Her past would never come back to haunt her again. But her mind wouldn't listen to reason and sometimes warred with itself over fight or flight, especially when she hadn't had much sleep.

"Just a minute!" She may still have a few internal panic attacks, but most of the time she controlled her outward reaction. After a quick dry, she threw on the closest pair of pajama pants and a t-shirt. She pulled the towel from her hair as she opened the door.

"Good. You're up. I have perfect timing." Shaye's smile filled her view. Maggie opened the door wider to let her in. "I want to take everyone out to breakfast. You haven't eaten yet, have you?"

"No. I just got up." Maggie squeezed the ends of her hair with the towel.

"Perfect." Shaye stretched the 'r' and her eyes widened. "Go finish getting ready. Woods' has opened up a new patio."

Maggie could never quite say no to anyone. Not that she didn't want to spend time with Shaye or the others. She'd built friendships she'd never had before, but embracing them was difficult, especially with Shaye being her landlord.

Shaye sat on the couch while Maggie left to dry her hair and get dressed. That was all she needed, all she knew how to do, anyway. Her last experience with makeup or hair accessories was in her early teens. Young teenagers never used the stuff properly, anyway. Maggie didn't bother trying.

When Maggie reached the bottom of the stairs, Shaye was already standing.

"Let's go." Her bright eyes widened and her excitement swooshed across the room, lifting Maggie's lips. Maggie smiled more in the months she'd been in Alder Ridge than in the last ten years. She knew she could be happy again if she let herself. She locked the door and got into the passenger side of Shaye's truck. "We're going to go pick up the others and all go together. I hope you don't mind."

"I don't mind."

They drove past Woods Bistro and across town to first pick up Ezaray and Holly, then to Asher's to pick up Gwen. Turning her truck around, Shaye backed in. Maggie's gaze went straight to the deck where the bear still laid, although his head was up and his eyes alert, pinning Shaye's truck through the gaps in the railing. When Gwen didn't come out immediately, Shaye, Ezaray, and Holly got out, but Maggie remained in the truck. All three stopped at the bottom of the steps and looked at the bear. Maggie's breath lodged, and her hand rested on the door handle. They were too close to the animal, yet none of them showed fear. They continued up the steps and past him to knock on the door before opening it to go inside. She wished she understood why they all treated that bear as if he wasn't a threat. Any injured wild animal was a threat, but especially a grizzly.

After several minutes, there was still no movement at the door. Her hand still rested on the door handle. Maybe she kept it there to escape, but to escape what she wasn't sure. Until she saw two small flashes from the deck. His eyes intensified, as they had in her dream. She needed to force the air from her lungs, and the pain of holding it there created pressure on her chest.

He closed his eyes and moved. The motion blurred through the white posts. His pronounced limp didn't hinder his sure and steady progress as he lumbered to the top of the stairs. Maggie's hand squeezed as her muscles tensed, popping open the door. His head jerked up with the sound. Staying in the truck would be the smart thing to do, but something about him pulled her. His awareness, his focus— they were clear in his eyes and all on her. Besides, who would warn the others that the bear was up and in their way when they came out of the house. She would think they all had enough sense not to keep the animal on the deck. But that was Asher's decision.

She opened the truck door and stepped out. She kept her hand on the open door, ready to jump back in if the bear got too close. At least his injury would slow him down.

CAIDEN HAD SMELLED Maggie on the women that went inside the house. They'd be waiting a little while. He'd heard what Asher and Gwen had been doing before jumping into the shower together. A knock on the door didn't make the mated couple pause.

The sweet and spicy scent that traveled past teased his senses and woke an instinct he wanted to ignore. He had to see her. Now he stood at the top of the stairs and watched her grip the open truck door, preparing herself to escape. She needed to get back in that truck. Caiden didn't want to go anywhere near her, but the breeze picked up and changed colour to the emerald he was familiar with. It twirled around her, lifting her hair over her shoulder and danced her scent over to him. He breathed deep and his exhale came out a low growl.

Gritting his teeth, he took the first step down. Maggie's grip tightened and her body flinched, but her feet stayed grounded. Caiden took the next step, keeping the weight on his injured side as brief as possible. He watched her as he struggled, hating his slow pace. He had already healed some in the two days he'd been here, but not enough to shift or go home. The days had been spent getting to know the shifters here—evenings spent in animal form swapping stories.

Once Caiden reached the grass, Maggie took a step back, so she stood closer to the door she still held open. He paused and tilted his head, then kept limping forward. He needed more of her scent, despite the fact he didn't want it. To touch her and breathe her in—the driving force moving his body forward. He wouldn't have her, so moving toward her now was a waste of time and pure torture. But he couldn't deny his need.

Fuck. What could it hurt? She didn't know what he was. Caiden wouldn't claim he wasn't selfish.

The back of her legs hit the truck. When he reached three feet from her, the door to the house flew open and the women barrelled outside, laughing. The sound echoed off the silence between Maggie and himself when they came to a stop. Slower footsteps hit the stairs.

"Caiden." Asher called after him. Caiden turned and saw him standing in the door. Looking back at Maggie, she held a frown, an adorable frown that he wanted to smooth from her skin. Of course she'd be wondering why Asher had called him by a name. "Caiden, you shouldn't be up."

He knew that. His leg and shoulder burned after the walk across the yard, but he didn't want to move away from Maggie now that he could breathe her in.

The women came closer and stood next to Maggie, waiting to get back in the truck. He couldn't let her go without touching her. Then she needed to leave and stay away from him. He didn't want a mate of any kind.

Caiden took the last few steps and pressed his nose to her hand. Her body tensed. He watched the goosebumps form along her arm. He scared her, yet she still hadn't gotten back in the truck. Running his nose over her hand, he pushed it to the side to slide his head beneath it, forcing her to touch him unless she pulled away. She wasn't breathing as her hand lay still on his fur. But it was more than enough to awaken a base instinct within him.

Maggie wasn't going anywhere.

"You need to come back and rest." Asher stood behind him now.

If he had to go back, Maggie was coming with him. He turned his head and gripped her shirt in the front of his teeth. A squeak escaped, and she pulled back, but she didn't tug herself from his hold. That would only make him grab her harder, and she knew it. While the rest of the people around them knew what he was and that he wouldn't hurt her, Maggie didn't. To her, he was just a grizzly bear. And she was cautious, scared, all the things she should be.

He kept his grip and turned back to the deck, forcing her to stumble along beside his head while he limped. The pace worked to keep her from tripping.

"What's going on? What's he doing?" Maggie looked back at Asher. Caiden hoped he didn't tell her. They'd said Maggie didn't deserve to be hurt anymore. Caiden didn't want to cause any more pain. He'd keep her with him for company, then he'd go home and leave her behind and none the wiser.

"He's not going to hurt you, Maggie."

A long gasp came from one of the women.

"Shaye? What is it?" Maggie kept walking beside him, her head whipping back and forth.

"Asher's right. He won't hurt you."

"That didn't answer my question." She held her hands up at her shoulders and looked to everyone around them, pleading for help. But they all exchanged the same knowing look.

Caiden reached the steps and paused, wondering how he'd make his way up without letting go of Maggie. He pulled her in front of him so she'd take the first step, then he limped up behind her. Back in his corner on the deck, he pulled downward to get her to sit.

"I'll stay standing thanks."

But Caiden couldn't stay standing for much longer. He pulled again, harder. She leaned forward and lost her balance. He waited until she caught herself before he let go of her shirt. Nudging her chest, he got her to sit.

"Can someone help me?"

"Not really." The women muttered together. Caiden frowned. He wasn't keeping her. He selfishly wanted her specific company while he lay here healing.

Caiden laid back down on the deck and set his head in her lap. His heart slowed, and his head swarmed with a euphoric haze. But Asher's next words interrupted his calm.

"Maggie, I think I need to tell you something."

Caiden turned his head toward Asher and growled.

You said she didn't deserve to be hurt. Keep your mouth shut. It didn't matter that they didn't understand each other in separate forms. Caiden hoped his point was clear. He wasn't so selfish that he'd have her know she was his mate, but that he didn't want her. His choices were his own.

3

———

A whimper strained to be freed from the bottom of Maggie's throat. They all stood there with jaws slack while the bear dragged her back to the deck to use her as a pillow. And now Asher has something he needs to tell her.

"Can you get him off me?" She mouthed the words in a manner bigger than her whisper.

"Not anytime soon. I need to tell you something about him."

"You think?" Her dormant snark escaped. Not a single person had treated this bear as the animal he was, and no one seemed worried when he grabbed her shirt.

"He isn't just a bear." Asher paused, as if he expected Maggie to respond. "He's a man. His name is Caiden. He's a shifter."

Maggie only stared at Asher. He wasn't making sense. There had to be more to what he was saying. She narrowed her eyes, turning them on the others around her. They all looked at her instead of Asher spouting the crazy things.

"Shifters are people who can change into a specific

animal. I'm a wolf shifter, as is Zachary. Nathan is also a bear."

She had to admit, if it was all true, it explained a lot of things. What happened in the woods this past winter with Tyrone. Wild animals, both wolves and bears, had emerged to circle Tyrone and the guard he'd brought with him. It was only a few minutes later that chaos ensued and one of them fired their gun, hitting Maggie and she'd lost consciousness.

"I'm an owl." Holly stepped up beside Asher.

"You? But how could I not know something was different about you?" Her step-brother had captured both Holly and Ezaray. They'd fought alongside and against each other for over two years. They were the only two who'd ever been capable of beating her, or coming close.

Shifters. She considered the definition Asher gave. People that changed into animals. And the grizzly bear on her lap wasn't a bear after all. So many questions hoarded her brain. Why? How? Can they control it? Is it true? Why should she believe him? What reason would they have to lie to her?

This was an important secret, otherwise they would have tried to tell this tale a long time ago.

But the bear was a man? Caiden.

Green eyes looked up at her over his snout. She wondered if the man's were the same colour. She tried to imagine that deep of a colour set into a strong face. He was a big bear. He must be a large man.

"Can he understand what we're saying?"

"Yes. He's one mind. Not a separate human and animal." Asher had relaxed against the door frame.

"Oh." It hadn't only been a bear that dragged her back here to use, but the man. Why? Why didn't he ask for a pillow or something more comfortable? Or why didn't he grab someone else?

All of her questions started with an ache that curved around her temples.

"Well, maybe you could get him a pillow so I can leave."

The bear—Caiden—pinched her shirt between his teeth again, holding it while he settled his head back down.

"It isn't a pillow he wants." Shaye's brows lifted high and her lips twisted to the side, as if pulling back a grin that wanted to be free.

"He was shot and is still healing. He's quite a ways from home. My guess is he's looking for some comfort right now."

Maggie wanted to glare at Asher's guilt trip, but turned away instead. If she insisted on leaving, it made her look heartless. But why her?

"Why don't we make breakfast here?" Gwen stepped back up on the deck. "We can eat out here with Maggie and Caiden."

"No. You guys go to Woods' and enjoy the new patio. I'll go next time. You guys don't need to miss out because of me." Because of the bear.

"We can't leave you behind." Ezaray climbed up the front of the deck, holding onto the railing.

"You can. It's fine." Maggie nodded in a way to get them moving.

"I'll stay with you." Ezaray started to sit beside her. Maggie didn't want to be the reason they missed out.

"No. Go, please." Maggie tried to smile. "I'm okay." She wasn't, but her friends didn't need to know that.

"Okay." Shaye looked around at the other women. "Can we bring you something back?"

"No, thank you." She hoped to have herself out of here by the time they finished.

A rumble vibrated low from Caiden. He nudged her belly, then turned his head to Shaye with a definitive nod. He didn't plan on her going anywhere for a while.

"Sure. We'll bring something back for both of you." They all filed off the deck, leaving only Asher behind.

"And I'm sorry, but I have to go to work."

"You're going to leave me alone with him?" She may not have wanted her friends to stay, but panic flared now that she knew no one would be inside the house to come to her rescue if the bear turned on her.

"I promise he won't hurt you."

Maggie couldn't control the shaking that started at the base of her neck and spread along her spine. Being alone with him brought more than concerns about him being a bear. She hadn't been alone with a man since they'd escaped the fighting ring.

"Maggie, I understand you're scared."

"I..." Her own denial crushed her thumping veins.

"You are. You have every right to be."

"But I need to get over it." Maggie's eyes landed on the bear's fur and she spoke through her teeth.

"No, you don't. You need to learn how to cope with it."

And apparently Asher believed sitting with a man disguised as a bear would be a good learning experience. Because of course that made sense. Maggie inwardly rolled her eyes and nodded to Asher. After a look at the bear on her lap, Asher left.

The bear's eyes had closed, and the tightness showed at the edges.

"You must be in a lot of pain." Her voice was a familiar whisper, cautious to speak to someone that had more power than her. And a grizzly bear definitely had more power.

He grunted.

"That was s…" What was she thinking? She cut herself off. Scold him, call him stupid for walking across the lawn, and he'd lash out.

He lifted his head and tilted it back. His eyes turned to emerald shards. He ran his nose up her centre, tracing the exact line of her anxiety. She stayed silent, but he did it again. Then a third time.

"I was going to say it was stupid of you to walk across the lawn in your condition."

Caiden nodded, letting loose his groan when he settled his head back down. Maggie let out the breath she'd been holding and hoped to make it sound normal.

"I'm sorry I called you stupid." That same apology never worked on Tyrone.

His eyes lifted, and he huffed out his nose. She didn't know what he meant.

After a moment, his eyes closed, and she felt the weight of his head settling over her thighs. The air seemed still and quiet with everyone gone. The sound of the birds echoed as they flew around the trees.

Maggie looked down at Caiden. Everything they told her about shifters shouldn't make sense, but they forced her to accept the crazy with it laying on top of her. She lifted her hand, wanting to touch him, wanting to soothe his pain. But her hand hovered in the air above his head. Why her? Why was he drawn to her and insisted she sit with him? And why couldn't Asher have told him to let her go?

Her hand floated down and her fingers stretched through his fur. It was a once in a lifetime opportunity, petting a grizzly like this. As she moved her fingers, he groaned. She tried to imagine the man beneath the animal. She wondered what he was like, where his home was, how he got shot.

Maggie moved her hand to run along his snout. His rhythmic moans resembled a feline purr and entranced her.

Trapped, pinned beneath him, she couldn't move. He didn't want her to. She blinked and snatched her hand back. The surrounding tranquility turned vicious. The birds' chirps rang as screeches in her ears. The unmoving trees swayed back and forth. Maggie turned her focus back on Caiden and saw the predator he was meant to be. Knowing he was a man beneath the fur didn't help. That was just another type of predator.

She squirmed, trying to move her legs.

"You have to let me go. Please." She hated that she begged. She stopped begging a long time ago.

Caiden lifted his head, but put his uninjured paw over her legs to keep her still. His eyes bore into her the same way they had in her dream, except now she saw their colour. The green changed to a warm shade, and she stared, her breathing evened out. But it wasn't enough. She wasn't ready for something like this. She wasn't ready for anything more than living alone and surviving each day.

CAIDEN SMELLED HER RISING PANIC, her sweet and spicy scent dispersing, growing thinner. Her heart pounded, and her skin turned clammy. But when he trapped her gaze with his, she breathed, and he found his lungs matching hers. Heat inflamed under his skin, spreading to create a warm contentment emanating from contact with her. His blood took up a chant of *Mate.*

No. He couldn't. It had been foolish of him to keep her here and now look at her. Terrified of him. He didn't know why, but he wouldn't question it, not when that was what would keep her away. He'd never hurt her on purpose. It bothered him she was afraid, but he wouldn't be responsible for her, so he wouldn't dig deeper for the answer.

She'd called him stupid. He was stupid. He never should have touched her. Now, a pleasurable hum sparked more than contentment within him. Arousal grew. Her eyes were a green to rival his own, and he wanted to see what fire they created when he had her under him and buried himself in her heat.

Fuck. Stupid.

With a groan, he pushed up, the pain returning as he pulled away from her. Caiden kept his eyes from hers and swung his head behind him, telling her to leave. Maggie didn't move. His lips quivered with a low growl, and he swung his head harder. She flinched, making Caiden angry with himself.

Walk away now, nymph. It's what's best for both of us.

She moved slow when getting up, each movement like a small step until she stood. Anyone else with shoulders as stiff as hers would have plastered themselves against the house when moving around him. But she walked steady and calm, despite her fear making sporadic appearances. It was a learned behaviour. She didn't put her back to him even when going down the steps. Taking them at a sideways angle, she kept her eyes on him. Caiden felt their touch and the distance increasing with each of her steps.

When she reached the ground, she turned away, checking over her shoulder every few steps.

"He couldn't have let me go when I had a ride."

Caiden could hear her eye-roll through her sarcasm. And now he wanted her back. Sass and spirit lay dormant inside her.

His chest vibrated, and he realized he was growling, low

and steady. *Mate, mate, mate* sang in his head, growing louder. His mate was walking away, and he wanted her back. Not him. Some instinct, a calling. The animalistic side of him. The growling grew louder, uncontrollable. Her footsteps hit the grass harder. As he saw her running, reaching the gravel, his growl turned to a roar. Maggie looked back. He turned on the deck, but stopped at the stairs, his roar still lingering in his throat.

He closed his eyes and tried to pull in deeper breaths. What the hell was wrong with him? When he touched her, his pain had receded and his frustration for being here and not home vanished. Maybe his roar scared her enough to stay away. The up-down mountainous path of sensation and emotions pissed him off. He needed to go home. He had a restaurant to run, a hunter to find. A mate, a female responsibility wasn't in the cards for him. Not since Laura.

When Caiden opened his eyes, Maggie was no longer in sight. He turned back and thumped back down on the deck. Long, solitary hours of waiting had filled the past couple of days, until evening hit and the place was full of people. He hoped there weren't many more.

Asher had been helping him off the deck when he needed to, but also said soon that Caiden could take short walks. He wanted to see how his leg was healing. When his leg mostly healed, Caiden could shift and let the magic of the change finish the process.

He started counting down the hours. As soon as he could get home, the sooner he'd forget about his mate —Maggie.

MAGGIE STRUGGLED THE NEXT DAY. Now late afternoon, she let the cab drop her off at the end of the road leading to Asher's instead of taking her home after work. Turn left and go see Caiden. Turn right and go see Holly. She had no reason to see either of them. Except for the emerald shards of Caiden's eyes that occupied her dreams again the night before. They called to her, soothed her, scared her. All she did right now in life was survive each day. She had nothing else to do, nothing she wanted. His eyes and roar were like a challenge. Do something, anything, that isn't part of your normal life.

She'd never made the initiative to visit friends herself. Maggie waited for them to show up at her door or call her in the evening. Visiting Holly would be regaining control over some part of her life. So would checking in on the bear—on Caiden. She couldn't deny she was curious about shifters. Sure, that was why her feet started walking up the gravel lane on her left. Curiosity over shifters, Caiden, and why he'd been so drawn to only her.

She had thought no one noticed her approaching when Asher's house came into view. But Caiden noticed. He stood, his head peering over the railing as she kept walking closer. Asher, Gwen, Nathan, Shaye, and Garrett were standing around the deck, focused on each other. It wasn't until she was twenty feet from them and Caiden moved to the top of the stairs that they realized someone else was there. They first looked at Caiden, then followed his gaze to find her.

"Maggie." Shaye stepped toward her and squeezed her shoulder. "What are you doing here?"

"I wish I knew. I guess I just wanted to see how Caiden was doing."

"That's what we're debating right now." Asher glared at Garrett.

"Asher thinks Caiden needs to wait another day or two and Garrett wants him to shift now." Shaye turned to stand beside Maggie.

"What does Caiden want to do?" Why wouldn't they ask him?

"He's kept his opinion to himself." Shaye leaned her head closer to Maggie's while the others continued arguing.

Maggie looked at Caiden, remembering his roar. Fear had leapt through her, making her feet pound harder against the ground. She didn't understand him. Her dreams hadn't helped, but only confused her more. Had he been trying to scare her away, or had he changed his mind about letting her go? With the way his eyes glowed at her now, Maggie didn't think he knew either.

As the others carried on, Maggie tilted her head, asking Caiden the silent question of what he thought. But his reaction wasn't an answer.

Caiden shook his head, and when his eyes focused on her again, they no longer glowed. His lips curled and a consistent low growl came from his chest. He was directing it at her. Maggie took a step back, and Shaye wrapped an arm around her shoulders. The others didn't notice the change in him, except for Gwen. Gwen hit Asher's arm to get his attention, then joined Maggie and Shaye on the ground.

Caiden continued to growl and pointed at the lane with his nose. His eyes didn't shift to any others, only Maggie. He didn't want her here. He took a step down and repeated the motion. His gait was steadier, putting more weight on his injured leg than before. He moved with more of a lumber than a limp.

With his next step down, he growled louder. A shiver started in Maggie's core, but she held it in. Her steps back were smaller than his forward, and Shaye's and Gwen's arms around her back kept her from falling backward as her steps became clumsy.

Caiden swung his head toward the road when he stood only inches from her. He kept swinging and growling as if saying, "Go on! Get out of here! I don't want you here." She understood him now.

"No." Her voice didn't put her foot down. The sound had trembled, but she lifted her chin. "I'm not leaving." She stood her ground against her own fear. Her timid statement made him pause. But then his lips took on a vicious curl, and he shoved her stomach with his nose. Maggie stumbled back, a small screech getting caught in her throat. Shaye and Gwen caught her before she hit the ground. He nudged her again.

"Caiden, stop. You're scaring her." Shaye tried to stand in front of Maggie, but Maggie stepped to the side. She didn't want to hide. Terror infused her, but she didn't want to hide. They'd all assured her that Caiden wouldn't hurt her, and none of the men standing there were coming to her aid. They only watched this play out.

"I'm not," she pulled in a breath, "I'm not leaving."

His jaw clamped shut and his nostrils flared. Turning away from her, she stared at his back as something happened. His shoulders hunched upward, matching the height of the bump that defined him as a grizzly.

"Caiden, stop. You're not ready." Asher moved away from the others. Caiden was shifting. Bones popped with an unnatural sound. He groaned as his front legs changed. Maggie winced, her mind telling her to look away, but she didn't. The surrounding air turned green, the same shade as his eyes. It emanated from his chest and swirled around him. The air sparked with beautiful magic, even after the gruesome sounds of his body changing. The green faded away and standing there was a man larger than she'd imagined. His hair was short and black and he hung his head and heaved in air. His back expanded, exposing well defined muscles with each breath. Maggie's eyes continued to rove over him until she reached his butt. She let out an unintentional squeak and lifted her head straight into his line of sight as he looked over his shoulder. A full beard covered his face and his eyes were set into his features. They glowed now, not only with the pain from shifting but with an intensity that was all for her. A bear suited him.

"How do you feel?" Garrett stepped forward.

Caiden lifted his left arm and rolled his shoulder. "A little stiff."

"I wish you would have waited another day." Asher's tone sounded regretful.

He turned his head back to Maggie. "Couldn't control it."

"I understand that." Nathan huffed and he smirked.

No one else spoke while Caiden stared at Maggie. He turned toward her. The muscles on his back were a mild reflection of the ones on his front, narrowing down to a growing erection. Maggie tried to look over his shoulder, but he closed the distance. With only a few steps, his shoulders blocked her view, and it forced her to meet his eyes.

"I'm sorry I pushed you." His voice hummed with sincerity. "But you should leave."

"You should make up your mind." Maggie slapped her hand over her mouth. Her tone still sounded timid, but that had been the kind of backtalk that drew Tyrone's attention, the kind that always put her in the ring. And Tyrone wasn't even comparable to Caiden.

Maggie's mouth dried, and she flattened every muscle in her face, smoothing her expression. Caiden frowned, and turned away.

"Thank you for your help. I wouldn't have survived."

"You're welcome. I'd like to invite you to stay for a few more days. Meeting more shifters doesn't happen often around here." Asher stepped around him and pulled Gwen to his side.

"Thanks for the offer and that would be nice sometime." His head tilted down. "But I need to get home. I'll stay another night and head out in the morning."

"You can return the truck I stole when rescuing you." Garrett crossed his arms, but his face lit with amusement.

"Sure. I know whose it is, anyway."

"We'll give Maggie a ride home." Nathan flanked Maggie's other side, taking up the same protective position as Shaye. She'd only just got here, and they were trying to manage her. Maggie understood they meant well. They'd all been more than kind since the day she arrived with Ezaray and Zachary. She didn't know how she could change how they treated her. They found her at her worst and couldn't seem to look past that broken girl.

"Thank you, but I don't need a ride."

Nathan and Shaye startled for a moment. It was the first time Maggie had ever said no to any of them when they were only trying to help. But she came here for a reason, to see Caiden, not to be ushered away.

Caiden trapped her gaze. She'd always thought a full beard hid too much of someone's features, making it difficult to read their expressions, but not so with Caiden. Everything tightened when he clenched his jaw, and his brow was as expressive as a set of lips. His eyes never seemed to stay the same shade of green for more than a few minutes, but maybe that had something to do with her.

He turned on his heel and stalked toward her—tall, powerful, naked male. He towered over her. Maggie didn't know where to set her eyes. His dark hair on his chest didn't hide the curves of his muscles. What sat below that was close enough that Maggie almost felt it touching her. Heat reflected from him like rocks placed around a fire. She warmed in places she didn't recognize. For a man who didn't want her here, he seemed to have trouble keeping his distance.

"Still can't make up your mind?" Maggie closed her eyes and turned her head away, waiting for his censure. She didn't understand why she spoke so freely to him. His whole being encompassed a challenge for her.

"Oh, I've made up my mind, little nymph."

Maggie shot her gaze back up to his in time to see his narrow. He turned and walked to the house. She watched his retreating back and definitely didn't allow her eyes to lower to his naked ass.

CHAPTER 4

The woman had crawled under his skin. So scared of what came out of her mouth. But he wouldn't be as attracted to her if she cowered. Damn, he wished she would cower. It would be so much easier to leave her behind.

The shifters here, and their mates, were protective of Maggie. Since they'd discovered she was his mate, he'd been warned more than once of her fragility. He saw it. She stood with hunched shoulders most of the time, except for the small moments she spoke to him. Fire lit her skin for only seconds as her snark escaped her.

Caiden looked at the deck as he walked over it to go inside. Days spent there healing. At least there had been the company of other shifters and even their pairs. They'd built a family or pack of their own. Caiden already had his brother and cousins. He didn't regret the time getting to know the other shifters. Hearing their stories piqued an interest. Learning of other groups in neighboring towns was a good resource to have. Especially since the wolf shifter pack outside of Firebrook only tolerated Caiden, Wyatt, and their cousins.

Of course, Asher and Zachary had found some of Caiden's stories of the wolves funny. The teenage pranks they'd played on each other. Asher vowed to visit Firebrook as soon as he had time for a vacation.

Others started filing inside behind him, but Maggie's scent filled the house. He growled low. He'd thought Nathan and Shaye were taking her home. Caiden turned on her. She flinched and turned her head, but as she pulled in a breath, she tilted her head to meet his eyes. They were full of so much of her soul. This time, she trapped him. Fuck, he couldn't turn away from her.

Gwen broke from the group. "I'll find you some clothes."

Caiden blinked. "Thanks."

"If everyone is hungry, I'll throw something in the oven. I think I have a lasagne in the freezer." No one objected.

Asher left for the kitchen, and the others stared between Caiden and Maggie. He'd heard how each of them had met their mates. He'd wanted to ask so many questions, but he hadn't confirmed that Maggie was his mate, despite how many times they asked. Caiden wouldn't claim her. Laura hadn't been his responsibility, yet he'd caused her death. He'd upset her, and she'd run off. Some logical part of him knew it hadn't been his fault. Wyatt, his parents, her parents —they all had told him over and over for a year it wasn't his fault. But he couldn't let her go. He wouldn't be directly responsible for anyone again.

Gwen hopped down the stairs with a pile of clothes held against her chest. She smiled as she passed them over, and Caiden dressed. Standing naked in front of everyone hadn't bothered him, neither would dressing in front of them.

One by one, they all floated to the furniture and took

their attention off Caiden and Maggie. What they expected to happen, he wasn't sure, but he felt like a sideshow. And the way Maggie's skin fluctuated in shade told him she felt their eyes too. Maggie took a seat on a footstool, and Caiden found the empty chair across the room. Asher walked in and started the conversation.

"I've been thinking of adding more to the cabin near the pack." He took a seat on the arm of the couch next to his mate.

"What would you add? We finished it months ago." Nathan pulled Shaye onto his lap.

"It only has basic furniture."

"It's not used often enough to have more. That's its purpose—safety. It doesn't need aesthetics."

"That doesn't mean it shouldn't be comfortable." Shaye poked her mate in the chest.

"Are you talking about the cabin you told me about?" Caiden leaned forward, resting his elbows on his knees. With his shoulder bunched and then putting the weight on it, he winced. Trying to hide it, he readjusted himself and sat back.

"It's time you let me look at that." Garrett pushed off the wall.

"It's fine."

"Don't care. Sit up straight and take the shirt off." Garrett waited until Caiden held the balled up t-shirt in his lap. He ran his fingers over the muscles in his back and over his chest. When he reached the muscle running from his neck over his shoulder, Caiden hissed through his teeth. Maggie's gasp echoed in his ears. Caiden snapped his eyes to her. Her lips pinched, and she panted through her nose while she followed the doctor's movements. The nymph was just as drawn to him as he was to her.

Garrett increased the pressure and Caiden groaned. Maggie jumped to her feet, her eyes searching Caiden's face rather than watching Garrett. Her hands fisted in front of her stomach. Garrett stopped to look over his shoulder.

"Everything okay, Maggie?"

Maggie blinked and shook her head. "I'm fine."

Caiden's skin chilled without her attention on him anymore. She turned from the room and he focused on each of her soft steps up the stairs. He itched to follow her. Rolling his shoulder, he pushed the doctor off him. "Thank you. I'll be fine."

"I'm the one that should determine that. But you're right. I think you'll be fine. You're sore though. I'm not sure how long that will last."

"He wouldn't be if he'd waited another day or two." Asher piped in. "The shift would have had enough magic to finish healing him."

Caiden pulled the shirt back over his head. "Excuse me." He mumbled, unsure and uncaring if anyone heard him. His eyes hadn't left the stairs since Maggie took off, and now he had the need to follow her. He inhaled deeply to find which room she was in. Listening outside one, he heard water running. Caiden didn't knock.

Maggie slapped wet hands over her mouth to smother her silent scream. She lowered them to turn off the water and dry her hands and face.

"What are you doing up here?" Her voice didn't gain any volume. She held onto the sink counter as she faced him.

"I don't know." Caiden shut the door behind him. Her gasp wasn't audible, even for him, but her lips parted and her chest rose half an inch.

"What did the doctor say about your shoulder?" Her eyes found where the wound used to be below his shirt.

"I'm fine." Caiden should stay where he was, against the door where the wood would keep him grounded, but he took a step toward the nymph instead.

"It's amazing how fast you healed."

"Shifters."

"Right."

"Garrett examining me bothered you." The second he'd groaned, she stood. The concern in her eyes hadn't lasted long, but it was there and ready to lash out at both him and Garrett.

"Why would that bother me?" She blinked a few times and her neck flushed. She wasn't a good liar.

"You tell me?" Another step toward her and he lifted his chin.

"I don't know."

"Why did you come here tonight?" He wanted to know. If he was the only one with an attraction, he wouldn't hurt her when he left her behind. He hadn't realized she was drawn to him.

"To see how you were doing."

"Is that the only reason?" Maybe she could still walk away from him. If he could give her something to walk away from.

"Yes." Maggie started retreating as he moved closer. His ears buzzed, and his muscles tightened. His hands twitched to touch her.

"You shouldn't have come." His voice sounded like a disgusting threat. Maggie shivered. Caiden inwardly cursed. Pushing her away didn't mean he had to scare her.

"I'm already here."

Caiden huffed and the side of his lips lifted. "Why do they all coddle you?" He tilted his head toward the bathroom door.

"You don't want to know." Her lips tightened, and she tore her eyes from his, looking directly ahead at his chest. The top of her head barely reached the top of his ribs.

"I wouldn't have asked." He shouldn't have asked.

Maggie shook her head.

Caiden didn't have control of the situation anymore. He shouldn't have followed her. He shouldn't have stepped into the room. And he shouldn't be standing this close. A hint of fear tinged her scent, but it wasn't strong enough to push him away, not when he smelled her interest. His mind clouded, and it surprised him he was still standing straight. His left hand lifted, the ache subsiding with her so close. He ran a single finger from her chin and along her jaw. Her entire body froze. Heat singed his finger.

A shrill ring broke through the haze of the moment. Maggie jumped back and breathed again as she reached for her phone from her pocket.

"Fuck." Caiden cursed, catching her eye. "No."

Hurt sliced through her green irises and she snapped her mouth shut. Caiden stormed from the room. He didn't want to see what he'd done to her. He was getting out of Alder Ridge first thing in the morning and he wouldn't be taking his mate with him.

Scene 5

Maggie tried to pull in air with little success. It had already been too much with Caiden standing so close, but when he touched her, she'd been paralyzed. He'd followed her upstairs and closed himself in the bathroom with her. She hadn't known his intention. With everyone downstairs, she hadn't needed to worry. It didn't stop the old fears from rising. Pushing them away, she'd tried to look at Caiden as someone she wanted to understand.

Her phone still rang in her hand. Exhaling, she swiped the screen and answered. "Hello?"

"Is this Margaret Scott?" The male voice on the line was stiff and professional. Maggie's entire body turned cold—a hollow chasm bore from her throat down her centre. She had no reason for any professional person or business to contact her. She had nothing but his tone to guide her instincts that told her to drop her phone and run. "Hello?"

Maggie swallowed. She searched the room, the unadorned walls, the corners, the single door, for a way to escape. She couldn't run from a voice.

"Miss Scott?"

"Yes."

"I'm glad I tracked you down. My name is Brian White-hall, a lawyer. I have an urgent matter I need to discuss with you."

"What type of matter?"

"It involves your late mother."

"My mother?" Her mother had been gone for almost ten years.

"Yes. We've been unable to reach Mr. Belenger for months. Is he with you?"

"No, I'm on my own." She didn't understand what Tyrone would have to do with anything from her mother.

"Okay." The lawyer paused. "Are you able to come to Firebrook to confirm your identity and settle this matter?"

"Can we handle this all over the phone? Do I need to be there in person?" A full pain in her chest expanded with the thought of going back there.

"Unfortunately no. Not under the circumstances. I'll be able to explain more when you arrive. You can call me back at this number with your arrival date and I'll have every-thing ready for you."

"I don't drive. And I can't go back there. Is there another option?"

"I wish there were. Please come as soon as you can. I'll be in touch."

Maggie's phone slipped from her hand as soon as the lawyer hung up. The thump on the bathroom mat pulled her from her shock enough to bend down to pick it up.

Ice filled her blood and she was surprised to find herself leaving the bathroom and already walking down the stairs. Caiden was standing at the bottom.

"What's wrong, Maggie?" Shaye crawled off Nathan's lap. Pushing Caiden out of the way, she set her hands on Maggie's shoulder to get her attention.

"I have to go home." Her blood slowed through her veins.

"Okay. We'll take you home now." Shaye pulled her along. No questions about why, just there to usher her away to protection.

"No. Not that home. I have to go back to where I grew up."

"Where's that, Maggie?" Garrett, the man she'd only known as the doctor, stood beside Caiden. Years of seeing him as the enemy was difficult to let go. But he'd proven himself over and over since then.

"Firebrook." It was the one place she vowed to never go.

The air changed as Caiden bristled. Heat cascaded off his shoulders onto hers, melting the icy fear formed by the lawyer's call. When she looked at him, his eyes had narrowed. He stalked away. She thought he was going to leave the house, but he turned back to his seat in the living room.

"When do you have to go back?" Shaye guided her away from the stairs.

"I don't want to go back." She sighed. "He said as soon as possible."

"I'm sure someone here will take you in the next few days." Shaye nudged Nathan out of the way and sat Maggie on the couch—too close to Caiden, who's disgust hadn't disappeared since he left her upstairs.

"Caiden's from Firebrook." Asher still lounged on the arm of the couch.

The air trying to escape Maggie's lungs stuttered as if she were caught in an ice storm with cold air whipping her breath away. She turned her head, knowing the redness that filled her face. The sensation wasn't new. Humiliation was supposed to be an emotion, not the sensation of sharp spider legs crawling up her face and into her hair. He'd recognized her. That was the only explanation for his hot-cold behaviour. The reason he looked on her with such disgust now.

"No. No, no, no," she whispered to herself, not allowing her personal denial to fully form on her lips. "I can't go back. There has to be another way. I can't go back with Caiden. With anyone." The others would have only heard distressed mumbling.

"It's okay, Maggie. Who was on the phone? Why do you have to go back?" Shaye's hands moved up and down her arms. The doctor moved the footstool closer and sat. Gwen had pulled away from Asher and went to Maggie's other side. She was surrounded by people who wanted to help, but the whole situation smothered her.

These people had helped her when she had no one. They knew what she'd been through, but only the last two years of it. They had no idea of the humiliation and abuse she'd suffered before that. Already looking at her with so much pity, caution, and gentleness, she didn't want them to know the rest of her past.

"I'll find another way." Maggie wouldn't give them any other answers.

"You could go back with Caiden."

"I'm sorry, but I have to leave first thing tomorrow." Caiden's eyes landed on Maggie, their weight heavy against her. If he'd recognized her, then of course he wouldn't want to saddle himself with a burden.

"I think it's best if one of us takes her, anyway." Gwen set a hand on her shoulder, but looked over her head. "She'll need someone she's comfortable with."

"I'm sure she'll be fine with Caiden."

"Oh yes, fine. I know exactly how *that* turns out. Maggie isn't ready." Shaye glared at her husband.

They talked as if she wasn't in the room, as if she was their responsibility to care for. Her jaw clenched, and the first surge of anger in a long time rose inside her. Being managed like a responsibility. They meant well. They'd helped her in ways she could never repay. Rescuing her, giving her a place to live, helping her find a job. And the most important, being friends. Being treated that way by friends hurt a little more than she'd like to admit.

She wanted to speak up, wanted to tell them she would do this alone, but the words never formed. Without a car or even a license, Maggie had to rely on someone. That someone wouldn't be Caiden.

"One of us could go with her and Caiden. I'm sure Woods' will give me some time off work last minute." Gwen looked around the room.

"No. Thank you all for offering, but I don't want to go back." Maggie straightened her shoulders.

"Is it something you can handle from here?" Garrett leaned forward on the stool.

"I don't think so." The lawyer had been adamant that nothing could be done until she arrived.

"What was the call about?" Garrett tried to pin her with a look she was too familiar with—his doctor's-orders look. It wouldn't affect Maggie anymore.

She shook her head. "I'm going to go now. Thank you." She didn't know what she was thanking them for. Coddling her, helping her, or accepting her own invitation for dinner.

"Do you want a ride?" Nathan spoke from the side of the room.

"No, thank you."

Maggie walked from the house and tried not to look back at the others, but her head tilted to the side and the only set of eyes she saw were Caiden's.

CHAPTER 5

F uck. He was trying to run home as soon as his bear legs could carry him to get away from her, and the little nymph was going to follow him, anyway. Firebrook wasn't big enough that he wouldn't see her, wouldn't smell her. Caiden pulled in a breath of her scent now and fought against the shutter of his eyes as they tried to roll back into his head with the pleasure of it. Pulling her onto the deck the day before had been a mistake. One he was trying to fix by pushing her away. Physically pushing her hadn't worked, and now nothing would.

His insides curled with a sugary sweet desire and his damn cock jumped. These sensations were too strong and their outcome scared him. Mates hadn't been something he and the other shifters they knew even considered. He didn't like where this was going.

Caiden had the urge to run out the door and leave for home tonight.

He hadn't torn his gaze from her since he'd stalked away. Now she was leaving. She turned her head and caught him staring, but he wouldn't look away now. Her lips pinched for only a moment before stretching out again with her fear. The smell of it, strong and sour, trying to take over her natural scent. Caiden's nose curled and the way she flinched, she saw it as something other than a reaction to her emotions.

Her aversion to Firebrook had to go deep. Firebrook was small, full of tourists, surrounded by mountains. Nothing could tear him away, not even his own ghosts.

They all waited until her footsteps on the gravel faded.

"Do you recognize Maggie?"

He shook his head. The people changed there often enough that there could be someone he didn't recognize. Maggie looked young, and it seemed like it'd been a long time since she'd been back.

"You could take her." Garrett sat down on the arm of a chair.

"She doesn't want to go back and I'm not waiting. I'm leaving in the morning."

Garrett and Asher exchanged a look that pissed Caiden off. Gwen took the seat Maggie had left and turned herself toward Caiden.

"Maggie's sweet. Please don't hurt her." Gwen rested her hand on his arm, tilting her head back to meet his eyes. He knew exactly how sweet she was from her scent. Being reminded of it only made his mouth water.

"I won't hurt her. I'm going home. I have no connection to her." Except he did. She wasn't here, and her pain still lingered inside him.

"You wouldn't have to wait for her. Her boss would let her go right away."

"Maybe someone should go with her, too." Gwen turned toward her mate. "I don't know if she's ready to go alone."

Caiden bit his tongue to keep from asking questions. It wasn't his business, and Maggie wasn't his responsibility.

"I'm sorry. I can't help her."

They let it go, reluctantly. After an awkward silence, they continued their conversations from before Maggie came down the stairs. When the oven beeped, Caiden followed the others to the kitchen to eat.

Once they'd all finished, Nathan, Shaye, and Garrett left, leaving him with Asher and Gwen in their living room.

"Caiden." The wolf started, and Caiden anticipated a lecture coming. He hadn't known Asher long, but it didn't take a lifetime to learn the personality of the wolf. Leader, mentor, guide. "Maggie's your mate. How can you leave her behind?"

"I'm sorry. She doesn't know about being my mate. This won't hurt her."

"Maggie's already hurting." Asher stated the obvious. But it wasn't his problem.

"She has a great support system here with you. I can't help her."

"She's your mate. One of us could take her or even come with you and her, but I'd feel better if she had someone that knew the town, knew the people." Gwen rested her hand on Caiden's arm. Wide eyes pleaded with him to share her sympathy.

"She said she doesn't want to go. I can't force her to come back with me."

"I think she needs to go. Not just because of that phone call." Asher's voice trailed off in thought.

"One of you can take her when she's ready."

"I don't think she's going to let anyone take her." Gwen looked toward her husband, but kept contact with Caiden's arm.

"Then why would she let me?"

"You don't know her. And I think she'll plan the same thing you are. To drop her off and leave her alone." Gwen tilted her head as if asking a question, but it was more like a confirmation of his plan.

But it would be one hell of a painful drive.

"Please. We all want to make sure she's safe." Gwen was a difficult woman to say no to.

"Once I drop her off, she's on her own." He wouldn't be the one to make sure she stays safe. Not his mate, not his woman, not his responsibility.

"Okay." Gwen stood straighter and grinned, but pinched her lips between her teeth and leaned back, letting him go, attempting to cover her excitement. "Thank you."

Caiden scowled. He'd fallen into a trap and couldn't recognize what it was. "I'm still leaving first thing in the morning, so if she's coming with me she needs to be ready on time." And he was banking on her being late.

"Let's go convince her. Come on." Before he could tell her no, Gwen bounced out of the room. Fuck. He'd been manipulated, and now he was on his way to see Maggie.

MAGGIE PULLED the collar of her sweatshirt over her mouth when her front door shook. The tea in her hand jostled over the cup, burning her skin, but she didn't register the heat right away. The phone call would just be the start. Her past was coming back to haunt her. Whoever was at her door was next. She bit the edge of her sweatshirt to hold in her cry. She hated it had only taken a single phone call to unsettle months of gaining independence.

"Maggie. It's Gwen. And Caiden."

Her panic didn't dissipate like it usually did after someone announced themselves. She felt as broken as the day Zachary and Ezaray brought her to Alder Ridge. Caiden unsettled her. Against her better judgment, she let her curiosity win and went to see him. But he didn't seem to know what he thought of her. Pushing her away one minute and the next, towering over her with concern. Whatever reason he had for coming to see her, she didn't have the energy for.

Maggie held the door open only a crack. Even for Gwen. She didn't want to see anyone tonight.

"Can we come in?" Gwen stood in front of Caiden.

"I was just going to bed." She gripped the door, wanting to close it. But she couldn't be that rude to Gwen. Caiden, on the other hand, she had nothing against being rude to him.

"Please, Maggie." Gwen pleaded.

She looked past Gwen at Caiden. The night outside set him in darkness, but his eyes flashed in the dimness. His sheer size and the eerie glow terrified her. Or maybe it only added it to her current fear. Her past was coming for her. No, that wasn't right. Something was forcing her back into her past.

Maggie opened the door wider. She hunched her shoulders and crossed her arms. The energy or desire to hold her chin high wasn't in her.

Caiden closed the door behind them. She didn't invite them in or move to the living room.

"I'm sorry to come so late, but I wanted to talk to you. Are you okay?" Gwen lifted her hand to touch Maggie, but lowered it when she met her eyes.

"I'm fine." That was the only answer that would make this conversation go faster.

"You're not." Caiden's dark voice lashed at her, exposing

her lie. Maggie swallowed. An angry green pinned her between his narrowed eyes. She didn't ask for him to come, yet he seemed upset to be here.

"We want to help."

Maggie didn't need to answer her. Any explanation she had sounded weak or ungrateful. They'd all done so much to help her. All she wanted to do was live. Life had been giving her a chance—until now.

"Have you decided to go?" Gwen shifted on her feet, glancing back toward the living room. Maggie didn't move. Whatever conversation they would have would be close to the door.

"No. There has to be another way. I tried calling again, but he insisted on me coming there."

"Since you won't let any of us take you, Caiden has offered."

"I've offered, have I?" He glowered at Gwen.

"Yes, you have." Gwen pinned him with a quick upward brow, then turned her gentle smile back on Maggie.

"Caiden?" Maggie didn't want forced help or pity. She didn't want anyone going out of their way for her.

"He can take you back with him tomorrow."

"Thank you, but no." She reached for the door to swing it open, intending to kick them out, but a large hand wrapped around her wrist. She froze. Caiden slowly moved between her and the door.

"What was your phone call about, Maggie?" His voice smoothed, as if coaxing a spooked deer. She supposed she wasn't very different from that.

She shook her head and refused to look at him.

"You're terrified of Firebrook. I can't understand that."

"You're not me." Firebrook is beautiful. She wished she missed it as much as it deserved to be missed. "It was a lawyer." Simple, vague answers. He didn't need to know anything.

"There are only a couple of those. What did they want?"

"I have to..." Telling him anything about her mother, the house, or her family could trigger who she was. What choice did she have? Mr. Whitehall insisted her presence was necessary. Staying here wasn't an option. She refused to allow any of her current friends to know the Maggie she was ten years ago.

"Maggie?" Caiden gave a small tug on her wrist, but forceful enough she had to take a step closer to him. She looked up. He was a stranger. She only needed a drive. After that, she didn't have to see him again.

"Okay." She caved. "I'll go. I should talk to my boss tomorrow first." And delay the trip as long as possible.

"I'm leaving early. If you're coming with me, we leave at five." Only a matter of hours.

"Don't worry, Maggie. Asher and I will call Ruth." Gwen stood back by the door, her hands clasped in front of her.

"I'll pick you up in the morning. Get some sleep, Maggie."

Maggie grabbed her wrist as soon as Caiden let go. His odd tenderness vanished. A shiver ran over her from the sudden change. She had no idea the colour green could have so many temperatures.

Gwen wrapped her arms around Maggie while Caiden left, stomping down the front steps.

"Everything will be fine. I know you don't want us involved, but please call us if you need anything." Gwen's face pinched. Their care was genuine. Any other time, any other issue, and Maggie would accept all the help they were willing to give. But not when it came to her past.

Maggie only nodded and shut the door behind Gwen.

The last time her world tilted, it had stayed at that angle for years. Now, she'd be back in that hell in a few hours.

CAIDEN ROLLED his shoulder as he walked up to Maggie's door. After smelling her fear the night before, he didn't pound as hard against the wood, but he also didn't announce himself. The sky was lightening from black to a lighter blue, with only a few stars left. She better be ready, or he'd leave her behind.

Her spike of sickly sour fear seeped under the door. Slow steps brought her closer. When she opened it, she already had a jacket on and carried a small suitcase.

"You're ready." He'd imagined himself sitting on her couch waiting for her while she looked for excuses to stay or only packed this morning.

"I'm ready." She didn't sound ready. She could have said "I'm scared" and it would have sounded the same. Her voice was so small each time she spoke to him.

"Let's go then." He stepped off the deck and waited for her to lock up behind her.

"Isn't that the truck Garrett used when bringing you here?"

"Yes. I know who it belongs to." His brother would be happy to have the lodge's spare truck back.

"I suppose you know everyone in town."

"Most." Caiden took her suitcase from her and put it in the back. She stood with her hand on the handle and pulled in deep breaths. Caiden waited until she opened her door before he went around to his.

Leaving her safety terrified the poor girl. Caiden didn't want to force her to go through with this. But not his responsibility and not his business. The attraction he felt toward her messed with his mind. He'd need to remind himself of that often.

Caiden rolled his shoulder again before backing out of her driveway. He felt the improvement in the muscle, and the ache and stiffness had subsided. They had at least a four-hour drive ahead of them. He wanted to be back at his restaurant by noon. Drop Maggie off wherever she needed to go, say goodbye and ignore her by staying inside his kitchen. He had his plan. But hiding would have to come after he talked to his brother.

Wyatt would worry until he saw Caiden for himself, despite any phone calls he'd received to say he was fine. And Caiden would be the same. He and his brother were closer than most. Having both shifted for the first time gave them something to bond over. A shared secret—one they shared with their sister, too. Even though the wind had pushed her away that day, Caiden and Wyatt told her everything, and even showed her their shift once they gained control of it. For years, Dakota walked the woods alone, hoping to see the wind again and become a shifter too. But it never happened.

Maggie didn't question shifters much, although he supposed she had more on her mind to deal with. Not that she was sharing. He didn't want to know, anyway.

After the first hour, the sun peeked over the horizon. Maggie lifted her arm to shield her eyes. Caiden watched her squint and try to position her arm to cover the glow. Wyatt always had a couple pairs of sunglasses in every vehicle he owned. After years of losing them, he started stock piling them everywhere. Caiden reached up and pushed on the small storage hatch in the ceiling. The little sunglasses compartment opened.

"Here. Try these." He passed her a pair that would probably fall off her face, but they would do the job. Then he pulled up the middle console between them and stuck his hand in there to search for another pair while still looking at the road. They were tight against his temples. They must be his sister's. "Trade." He passed them over and waited for her to take them and place the others in his hand. Better, but the plastic had already warmed from her skin.

Being this close to her was just as painful as he'd imagined it would be. Every time he inhaled, his chest ached and his erection grew. The fucking thing wouldn't stop. He didn't understand why he couldn't control this. He didn't want a mate, yet that's all that crossed his mind since his eyes first heated at the sight of her fiery hair and green orbs that matched his own.

"So, you grew up in Firebrook?" He hoped talking would distract him.

"Yes."

"How long has it been since you've been there?"

"Almost ten years." Maggie kept her eyes out the window, avoiding him the only way possible in the cab of a truck and giving vague answers.

Caiden gave up. She didn't want to tell him her past. He shouldn't have asked either.

"You don't like me, do you?" Maggie turned her head toward him, but her eyes never lifted.

"I don't know you."

"Are you sure?"

"Yes."

"Then why did you try to get rid of me even after you pulled me along to use as your pillow? You didn't want to bring me any more than I wanted to go."

"I don't have an answer for you." Not one he could give. Caiden would get rid of her and keep his distance until all this passed. Out of sight, out of mind. His cock had other ideas. Take her, enjoy her, show her pleasure beyond her imagination. Get her out of his system that way. But with what stirred inside him when she was near, he wouldn't be able to let go of the responsibility.

He'd been responsible for Laura's death. He wouldn't allow anyone to be hurt by him like that again.

"You're right. I didn't want to bring you." He might as well set boundaries with Maggie before he lost control of himself.

"I'm sorry Gwen made you. I'm sorry I agreed."

"It's fine."

Maggie sighed and leaned her head against the window.

"Maggie." He wanted to ask her where he needed to take her, hoping it was a place to stay. The last thing he wanted was her sitting on the streets or staying in one of their cabins. His instincts told him she wouldn't be able to afford one of the hotels in town. Being a massive tourist attraction, hotels were expensive. Their cabins were too, but they made them available when needed for emergencies and for locals who needed a temporary place. If Maggie was from Firebrook, whoever she was going to meet would direct her toward him and Wyatt.

When she didn't answer him, he leaned forward. Her eyes were closed and her lips parted. She was asleep. Dark shadows circled her eyes. With how prepared she was when he arrived, he doubted she slept at all the night before.

So much for using conversation to distract him and for setting boundaries.

Drop her off and drive away. He could do it. A buzz started behind his ears. He was lying to himself. He wasn't sure if he could abandon her and not at least check in. But maybe he wouldn't have to. The arrival of someone like her would start a frenzy through all the gossip-loving locals. It concerned her that Caiden had recognized her. He didn't, but someone would. Knowing would satisfy his curiosity, and he'd never have to go near her.

Caiden listened to her breathing—surprised the rhythm calmed his raging turmoil over the redheaded nymph. Her whole being could fit between his hands. His palms itched. He wanted to try.

He shook his head. What the hell was he thinking? He wouldn't lay a hand on her. Caiden reached over to the centre and adjusted the controls to blast himself with cold air and left her side warm. The shock on his skin would calm him down. And listening to whatever radio station had a signal here. Static would fill the speaker for a while when driving between the mountains, but any noise would be better than his own thoughts.

The shifters in Alder Ridge knew more about mates. They all had mates of their own. In hindsight, he should have asked questions. They would know what to do to pull away from it. Because each time he saw her, smelled her, the chant in his head grew.

Mate. Mark.

If he didn't figure this out on his own, then he'd have to deliver Maggie back to Alder Ridge and ask Asher and the others how to get rid of this urge.

CHAPTER 6

The slowing of the car woke Maggie. She rubbed her eyes and lifted her head. They were driving down the main street into town. The buildings and signs hadn't changed. Some faded, some repainted and vibrant. It made her heart ache. She wished she could look at this place with joy. But all she felt was the humiliation caused by Tyrone. As if the town itself looked upon her with censure and judgment.

Her skin heated, and she squeezed her eyes shut.

"Where am I taking you?"

She gasped, remembering Caiden was driving. "I don't know. I mean, I don't know the address right off. It's in my phone." She pulled out her phone and found the e-mail from the lawyer. "Brian Whitehall's office." She started to say the address, but Caiden cut her off.

"I know where he is."

Maggie sank against the seat. Eyes from the street gravitated toward the large vehicle. Maybe they all recognized it as the one stolen by Garrett. A stolen vehicle would be widespread news around here.

It took not even five minutes to drop her off at the lawyer's office on that same main street.

"Here you are." Caiden got out and walked to the back. Maggie couldn't move. Right now, the truck sheltered her. As soon as she stepped out, she would set foot in the place she vowed never to return to. The people here thought so many things about her. She was crazy, unstable, mentally ill, physically ill. Her red hair was as bright as it always had been. Her defining feature. She'd only have to count down the seconds until someone called her by name. The word would spread even from the lawyer's office.

Margaret Scott was back. And alone.

The truck door opened and Maggie jerked back toward the centre. Her hand covered her mouth, smothering her cry. Caiden held the door in one hand and her suitcase in the other. The scowl knitting his brows together kept her in place.

"You're not okay."

Maggie shook her head. She wasn't. She almost regretted not allowing someone to come with her. But she'd never be able to start anew if they found out what her life had been like here. They were delicate enough with her as it was, thinking she'd only experienced the same captivity in the fighting ring and nothing more.

"Come on, nymph. I'll walk you in."

"Why? You don't like me." Her eyes darted around, searching the sidewalk until Caiden tilted his body to get her attention.

Caiden's lips twitched. "I never said I didn't like you. Come on."

"I can't."

"Maybe if you tell me why, I can help." For a moment, he looked like it was a true offer. His head leaned to his left, and his eyes challenged her to open up to him. Despite the way he'd treated her up to this point, she saw a loyal soul in his eyes. Until they narrowed at her with suspicion with her continued silence.

"No. You don't want to help me."

"Then I'll wait." Caiden set her suitcase on the ground and crossed his arms. Maggie straightened in her seat and closed her eyes, trying to bring up some sort of calming image. But the only one she could think of was Caiden's scowling face. Deep green shards in his eyes and his thick beard that did nothing to hide the strength in his jaw.

"There's no way to avoid any of this." Maggie said it to herself, but she knew Caiden heard her. At least he didn't comment. She moved her legs out of the truck, and Caiden stepped back. She reached for her suitcase. "Thank you for driving me."

He nodded and shut her door, turning toward the office behind him.

"No. Please don't walk me in." Someone stronger beside her would only colour the opinions of the locals. Caiden was definitely stronger, not only in the physical sense.

"Okay." He moved back toward the vehicle. Leaning against it, he stuck his hands in his front pockets and watched her.

"Please don't do that either. I don't want the attention."

"You're going to get it whether you like it or not." His eyes travelled down her body before he pushed off the truck. When she looked up and down the sidewalk, she realized he hadn't been the only one staring at her. Most people went about their business, but there were a few pairs of wide eyes directed at her. Stunned like seeing a ghost. With her head down to the ground, Maggie walked into the building that held the lawyer's office.

The stale air carried a chemical hint, as if a janitor had just walked past. A long desk blocked the back offices. An older woman sat to the left and a younger one, about Maggie's age, sat on the right. The older woman flashed a bright smile then went back to frowning at her keyboard. Her name was on the tip of Maggie's tongue. Hassle. Mrs. Hassle. She always sat in the second pew at church.

But when the younger woman looked up, Maggie froze. With her darker hair, Maggie hadn't recognized her. But Kristine Lavoie's features hadn't changed over the years.

"Can I... Oh. Yes. Mr. Whitehall is waiting for you, Maggie." Kristine slowed her speech. Wide eyes and a gentle smile directed her toward Mr. Whitehall's office. She remembered Maggie. Remembered her as weak, slow, incompetent. One of the more popular theories. The easiest one for Tyrone to feed, especially when Maggie turned into a quiet mouse. The stories that had stemmed from that had been what hurt the most. Everyone always being nice, too nice.

Maggie didn't respond. She only followed the direction of Kristine while she spoke into an intercom. The office door opened just as she reached it.

"Miss Scott. Thank you for coming so soon." He let her in and shut the door, cutting off the curious eyes of her old classmate.

Maggie took a seat in the wooden chair in front of his desk.

"Do you have anyone with you?" His lips straightened in his round face and his eyebrows disappeared under grey hair.

"No. You didn't say I needed someone else."

"No, of course you don't."

Maggie was disappointed that even a lawyer would fall

for the rumours and lies. She'd never freely give anyone that power over her.

"Mr. Belenger provided us with all the documentation stating him as your guardian at the time of your mother's death."

"I was sixteen, and that was a long time ago." She quelled the urge to ask how he became her guardian.

"Yes." Mr. Whitehall gave a solid nod and squared his shoulders.

"I have a couple pieces of identification with my current address. What else do you need?"

"As long as they're government issue that's enough."

Maggie passed over her I.D. and her social insurance number she had to get in order to work in Alder Ridge. It had been an annoying process to get all of that back with nothing left, but Shaye had helped her with all of it. "What is this about?"

"Your mother's house. There was more after her death, but with Mr. Belenger as your guardian and when you couldn't be found over the years, the estate stayed with him. I'm afraid it's only the house left." His statement echoed, unfinished. Tyrone must have spent or sold anything else of her mother's.

"My mother owned a house?"

"Yes. The current tenants have been there for a few years and have expressed interest in buying the property. They've been inquiring since before Mr. Belenger's disappearance. He said he would consider it. The tenants have been quite insistent since losing contact with their landlord."

Maggie tried to stay calm. Tried to project herself as a functioning adult. But she had zero experience with anything like this. She wasn't even sure what house her mother had owned. They'd moved in with Tyrone and his father when they married. She didn't want to decide on a house she hadn't known about. Logical, small steps. What would be the first thing to do?

"I'd like to see the property."

"Of course. We must give the tenants at least twenty-four hours' notice. What time of day do you prefer?" Mr. White-hall picked up a pen, ready to take down times.

"As soon as you can." Maggie lifted her chin.

"I'll arrange it and contact you with the time." He made a note on his blotter.

"Did my mother have a will?" What else hadn't Maggie known about?

"She did." Older eyes met hers with sympathy.

"May I see it?"

"Of course." He nodded and stood from his desk.

Maggie held back her tears and prepared herself to look at the last words of her mother.

CAIDEN CURSED. He was doing a fucking terrible job at putting distance between himself and Maggie. Offering to help her with whatever kept her frozen in place. Then giving in to his attraction and eyeing her like he'd have her for dinner. He hadn't lied when he said she'd get attention. His and the attention of others in town. She was new and others would be curious, but it would blow over soon enough. And she'd go back to Alder Ridge. Caiden needed her to go back to Alder Ridge.

His blood fizzed as he parked his brother's truck outside the main office of the lodge. The door burst open, and Wyatt filled the entrance.

"It's about time you're back." Wyatt scolded him the only

way an older brother could. Standing an inch taller than Caiden, many had believed they were true twins growing up rather than Irish twins. Many still had trouble seeing the difference as they aged and both kept full beards.

"Yeah. If the vet had his way, I'd still be there."

"I'm glad they outvoted him."

There'd been no vote. It hadn't even been Caiden's decision. Maggie. Her presence and his need to feel her skin with his own prompted the shift.

"How's my restaurant?" Both brothers owned the entire lodge and resort, but they each had their specialties. The restaurant belonged to Caiden. The cabins that had still been standing had been worthless. They'd bought the land and built it all from scratch.

"It's fine, and you know it." Wyatt snapped with impatience.

Caiden had an excellent staff, trained them all from nothing. It was necessary when he lived half his life as an animal.

"Are you okay?"

"Yeah." Caiden rolled his shoulder for his brother's inspection. "Like new."

"Bullshit. It hurts." Wyatt followed him inside after Caiden tossed him the truck keys through the air.

"Only a little ache. It's already a lot better than yesterday." Caiden moved behind the front desk and took the stairs to their apartment.

"What happened?" Wyatt was desperate for more answers.

"I'd like to go get to work." To hide.

"No. Not until you tell me what happened. How the hell did you get shot?" It shouldn't have been easy for the hunter to get the drop on Caiden.

He turned around in the middle of the open room and faced his brother. He spoke as he pulled his shirt over his head to get ready for a shower. "I went out after the lunch rush at the restaurant. I needed a break and went to search for Theo. The wind was steady and in the wrong direction, and he was far enough away. He'd used a rifle. When I stopped at the river, he shot. I turned to fight, but no one was there and I could feel consciousness fading. I ran. The hawk found me before I could reach the public roads."

"Why the hell didn't the hawk just bring you here? He could have scented the other shifters in town."

"He knew the shifters in Alder Ridge and one of them is a veterinarian and he a doctor. They had to operate to get the bullet out and repair the bone for it to heal. As much as I agree and I would have preferred they brought me back here, he made the right decision." Even though that decision led him to a mate he couldn't claim.

"We need to find out who it was. But I don't understand why someone would do this." Wyatt leaned forward and slapped his hands on the kitchen table.

"I'm worried about asking around for people who've decided to hunt bears. My gut tells me that isn't what this was." Caiden wished he had a better explanation.

"You think it was a specific attack on you?" He swung his head up. Caiden met the worry in his eyes before moving to the bathroom door.

"I don't see how or why, but there's more to it." A specific attack could mean someone knows what they are. Caiden hoped that wasn't the case. "We should warn our cousins. They could be after all bears. All large bears. Or," he didn't want to say it, "shifters." Their cousins were also bear shifters. They needed to know what was going on.

"Then, we wait." A pained sigh escaped Wyatt.

"And be vigilant."

MR. WHITEHALL PASSED MAGGIE A TISSUE, and she passed back her mother's will. Jewelry and family trinkets, all meant to be hers—gone. She remembered her mother wearing some of what she'd described her in the will. Some Maggie had worn to school dances in the early years of high school. Even the one date she'd been on, her mom wrapped a simple gold chain around her neck. Her step-brother had sold it all. They were only material things, but after so many years, it would have been nice to hold something from her mother or step-father. He'd been a wonderful dad for the years he'd been around. There were times that Maggie had been happy.

But that didn't last. Especially since her mother revised her will only a year prior to her death stating Tyrone as her guardian and that the house would become Maggie's on her eighteenth birthday. So as long as Maggie never showed up, it stayed with Tyrone for him to control.

"I've contacted the tenants and will await their response. As soon as I hear from them, I will let you know. We'll be able to get into the house sometime tomorrow."

"Thank you." Maggie knew it was time for her to leave, but many things kept her rooted in the wooden chair. She didn't want to face Kristine or any others, she didn't have a way around town other than her own feet, and she didn't have anywhere to go.

"Is there something else I can do for you?"

"Where's the nearest place to stay?"

"The Riverdown Inn. It's about a block away. There's a few other hotels and cabins as well."

She remembered that hotel and some of the others. Designed with tourists in mind and priced to match. "Where would be most affordable? I have a small budget and this trip was a bit out of the blue."

The lawyer eyed her and thought for a moment. "The best place would be Bearbrook Cabins. They often allow discounted rates for locals in need."

"I'm not a local."

"You count." He reached into a desk drawer and pulled out a set of keys. Opening his office door, he gestured for Maggie to precede him. "Kristine, call my next appointment, please, and tell them I'll be a few minutes late."

"Of course." Her wide eyes landed on Maggie and looked onto her boss with a soft smile. Maggie could imagine her thoughts. She'd heard those thoughts spoken aloud anytime someone helped her. *So kind of him to help the poor thing.*

Mr. Whitehall led her to his car and drove toward the end of town. The businesses through the town centre still held their rustic charm, but with bright coloured siding and shingles. The overall look and feel hadn't changed.

They reached the lodge and cabins. Most of the buildings hadn't been here before, and what cabins still stood had been empty and crumbling. She couldn't remember who owned them, if anyone even had. But now, they looked new, the lawn mowed, flower gardens with large rocks littered the open space between the cabins. The main lodge stood only twice the size of one cabin. And each one had a prime view of the lake they surrounded. A wooden sign with Bearbrook Cabins carved into it hung from two chains over the steps. It didn't look like a place with discounted rates. It looked like it would be the most coveted place for tourists.

"It's beautiful." The words slipped from her mouth.

She found that happening sometimes. When she'd normally keep thoughts to herself, they made their way out.

"The owners did a lot of work to this about seven years ago. The whole town is very proud of it."

He parked and waited for her at the front of the car. She got her bag from the back seat and followed him up the steps. Her head spun as she tried to take in all the details. The grass had never been shorter than her knees. No flowers, gardens, or paths leading to each building.

A low wave of cold air blew her hair from her face. A man at least the size of Caiden stood behind the desk. He looked up and greeted Mr. Whitehall with a lopsided smile that tilted his beard.

"Brian, how are you today?"

"I'm just fine, Wyatt."

Wyatt leaned and looked around the lawyer. "What can I do for you?"

"I have a client visiting town who needs a place to stay while here. This is Margaret Scott. Miss Scott, this is Wyatt Greer. He's one owner of Bearbrook Cabins."

"Nice to meet you, Miss Scott. Do you know how long you'll be staying in town?" He leaned forward on the counter rather than flipping through a book or typing something on the computer.

The lawyer looked at her to answer. Maggie was used to others answering for her. "No. I'm not sure how long."

"Okay. Not a problem." He reached under the desk and pulled out a key. Walking around the front, he opened the door for both of them.

"Thank you, Wyatt. I have more appointments this afternoon. I'll be in touch, Miss Scott."

He didn't leave time for Maggie to respond, and he left

her following a large stranger. Her feet stuck to the wood of the last step.

"Mr. Greer?"

Wyatt turned.

"You didn't say how much for the cabin."

"Oh. I thought Brian explained it to you."

"He said you often have discounted rates for locals."

Wyatt's brow lifted, and his grin was just soft enough to show. He retraced his steps back toward Maggie. "Discounted means free, or we settle at the end of your stay. It changes with different circumstances."

"Free?"

"Yeah. If that's what you need. If you'd rather not accept it for free, we'll settle an appropriate amount when you checkout." The skin around his eyes crinkled, and that's when she noticed their colour. A bright green, the same as Caiden's.

"That's very generous."

"Shit happens. Sometimes people need a roof and money shouldn't hinder that." He started his hike along the gravel path and she followed. A thin path of grass grew along the centre. He took her to the farthest cabin. It sat partially into the trees, but the front had the largest view of the lake. To her, it looked like the best cabin. Why would this be the one they saved for local discounts? This one should never be vacant.

Wyatt unlocked the door and held it open for her. She walked past him and stepped inside. It was clean and bright. A bed sat above her in a loft and the main level had a kitchenette, sitting area, and bathroom at the back.

"It's the smallest cabin. I'm sorry there isn't a lot of space, but someone the size of you shouldn't need much."

"I don't. This is lovely. Thank you."

"You're welcome. If you keep following the path, you'll find the restaurant around the other side of the lake. There are also many smaller ones in town. And if there's anything else you need, don't hesitate to call the main building or even just walk over." He gave her a side nod and a wink before shutting her in.

Maggie set her bag down at the bottom of the ladder that led up to the bed. She took her time looking around the cabin and in all the cupboards. Not that she expected to find anything. Moving to the front, she stared at the lake. The water rippled with the breeze. It was the largest lake in Firebrook. She'd spent many hours trying to hide on the other side of it. She'd even eyed these cabins a time or two—thinking she could turn one into a hideout, a home away from Tyrone when he was around. He'd always found her long before she could ever reach a cabin.

Maggie was finally hiding in one. But not from Tyrone himself—just from his image.

CHAPTER 7

What the fucking hell? Why could he smell Maggie? Oh, he knew why. She was inside the cabin. The last and smallest cabin, the one she would end up staying in if she didn't have a place of her own when she came to town. But knowing that didn't stop the curses squeezing past his lips as he breathed in her scent lingering in the air. He'd never get away from the nymph walking past her every morning and every night.

Her scent did more than infuse into him through his nose—it melted into his skin until it tingled, an itch to go to her. His hands would fit the whole way around her waist, easily cradling her against his chest while he ravaged her mouth. Before he realized what he was doing, he'd taken several steps toward her door.

Fuck.

Turning on his heel, he stomped toward the main lodge. The wood of the stairs to their apartment creaked under Caiden's weight. Wyatt sat on the couch, eating leftovers he'd picked up from the restaurant, when Caiden slammed the door.

"I met your road trip companion today," Wyatt called over his shoulder. Caiden hadn't told him about Maggie. "I recognized her scent from my truck. She's cute."

An unwanted growl started low in Caiden's stomach. Wyatt lifted a brow, and his fork paused in the air.

"Something wrong?"

"Why is she staying here?" Caiden made a conscious effort to move his jaw when he spoke so he didn't grind his teeth when he asked.

"Brian brought her. She didn't have anywhere else." Just as Caiden suspected would happen. That didn't change how he felt about having her near. "Is there a reason we shouldn't let her stay? You're the one who brought her to town."

Yes, but not a reason he wanted to discuss with his brother.

"It's fine."

Wyatt set his plate down on the coffee table and stood. "What is it?" His big brother tone didn't work on Caiden anymore, not since they were teenagers. Being born the same year took away his authority when Caiden reached the same height and size. "Anything I should know about her?"

"No. There's nothing wrong with her." Absolutely nothing. Quiet, but snarky little nymph who'd called a grizzly bear stupid. No, there was nothing wrong with the woman he couldn't get out of his mind. He hadn't left his kitchen all day, hoping to experiment with enough recipes to get the scent of her from his nose. None of it worked. It was still there. At one point, he'd even created a dessert that smelled just like her. A twist on an apple pie. The spice and sweetness filled the whole restaurant. Customers had asked for the new dessert, but Caiden ate the whole damn thing. It had been fucking delicious, just as he knew Maggie would be.

Nothing wrong with Maggie, but there was something wrong with him.

These emotions were more than mere arousal or attraction. Their strength rivaled that of a bear, or two. It would be dangerous to get close to her. It already felt like it was too late. Ever since Laura, Caiden wouldn't allow himself to get close to anyone. Her death still hurt, and he hadn't even been dating her, but he'd been responsible. If he hadn't given her reason to believe he liked her, she wouldn't have run off. He didn't want to be directly responsible for anyone.

"Caiden." Wyatt stepped around to the back of the couch. "You okay? Is it your shoulder?"

"I'm fine." He'd lost his growl in his voice. Thinking about Laura did that.

"She's from Alder Ridge?"

"Yeah. Now. I guess she grew up here." Caiden pulled out more leftovers from the fridge.

"Odd. I don't recognize her."

"I think she's quite a bit younger." He didn't know and shouldn't want to know.

"What's she doing here?"

"Not sure. She wouldn't say. Just asked me to drop her off at Brian's office. Did she say how long she's staying?" Caiden kept his eyes on the microwave that spun his food. If he met his brother's eyes, he'd see more to why he was asking than just curiosity.

"She doesn't know."

"Great." Caiden abandoned his food and stalked to the bathroom for a shower. He only had one way to ease himself. It wouldn't work, but that didn't stop him from trying. Because knocking on her door wasn't an option.

MR. WHITEHALL PICKED her up before lunch the next day. The tenants were more than cooperative with the hopes they'd soon be able to buy the home. They had asked Mr. Whitehall to express their gratitude and to ask if there was anything they could do to help Maggie decide. Maggie only smiled, not knowing what she wanted to do.

She stopped outside of Mr. Whitehall's car. The small house had freshly painted shutters and a flower garden in the front yard. Her mom had a garden. Flowers. But not those ones.

"Miss Scott?" Mr. Whitehall was waiting at the door. Maggie had been young when she'd lived here alone with her mom, the memories resurfacing now that she saw the house. She stepped inside, unsure of what she'd remember. Not much looked familiar. The floor was laminate made to look like wood. Bright white counters were a stark contrast to the dark stain on the cupboards. These renovations weren't new, but they weren't something she'd seen before.

"When was all this done?" Maggie pointed around the room.

"They did this before Mr. Belenger took possession. I believe your mother and step-father made the renovations before your step-father died. They'd rented this out for years before then as well."

Maggie walked past the kitchen and into the living room. She didn't notice the floors or walls, but looked at the pictures hanging on the wall. The same young couple filled most of them. A trip to the beach in the south. A wedding with the whitest of dresses and long curling train. Pictures with kids, but no sign of kids showed in the house.

Mr. Whitehall didn't interrupt her while she walked up

the stairs. The first room on her right hit her harder than she'd imagined when the rest of the house hadn't jarred her. They'd set the room up the same way hers had been. A half dresser with a large vanity mirror and a single bed on the opposite wall with a floral quilt. It wasn't her furniture, but it resembled it in a way it took her breath away as a memory hit her.

A little girl, Maggie, running from the room to the bedroom at the end of the hall. Maggie walked down the hall as if following the memory. The last bedroom resembled nothing like she remembered, but the memory of the little girl filled in the blanks. Her mother sat at a desk writing a letter.

"Mama, I demand you listen to me." The girl's fists slammed down on her hips.

"You demand?" Her mother glanced over her shoulder, but kept writing.

"Yes. I have a story you must listen to."

"And I'm busy." She smiled and set down her pen. Turning in her seat, she pulled Maggie into her lap. "I'm listening. Tell me your story."

Smart little girl, knowing even then she deserved to be heard. Maggie wiped a tear from her cheek, wiping away the memory with it. That little girl must still be inside her. Even now, she was showing Maggie that she needed to speak up. She didn't deserve to be kept quiet. And she was the only one keeping herself quiet now. Tyrone wouldn't show up and silence her, pull her away to fight and train, or spread seeds of doubt through her community and among her friends.

Lifting her chin, she went back downstairs and faced Mr. Whitehall.

"Is there anything I should know about the house?"

"The tenants haven't mentioned any problems to me, but I'm sure we will do an inspection before the sale agreement."

Maggie wanted to know more. She wanted all the information about the house and the entire process before she decided. But that was just her lack of knowledge driving that. What she had to ask herself was what she would do with the house if she didn't sell. She sure as hell didn't intend to live in it. As much as she wanted the connection to her mother, it wasn't here. The house wasn't the same anymore. It'd had a whole other life since Maggie and her mother.

"Is there still a mortgage on it?" She didn't know if that was a silly question, but Mr. Whitehall had been kind to her. He wouldn't judge her questions.

"No."

The money from the sale of the house would be a blessing. She'd have a strong sense of security and an ability to live without worry or concern. Her only other option would be to continue to rent it and use the income from that as a source of income of her own for many years to come. But what would her responsibilities be as a landlord?

"I'd like to take some time to consider my options."

Mr. Whitehall's eyes widened, and he gave her an approving nod. "That's a smart thing to do, Miss Scott. I can get you in touch with a real estate agent later this afternoon. They'll be able to answer all your questions about selling the house."

"Thank you." Maggie considered calling Shaye and she still might, but it would be the people in this town that she had to deal with.

Mr. Whitehall drove her back to the cabin. She'd considered asking him to stop for her to grab something to eat, even some groceries. All she had was a muffin from the main lodge. Her stomach rumbled like a truck over hard rocks. But she couldn't ask him to go out of his way when he had other appointments to get to.

Back at the cabin, she considered what to do. Although she'd convinced herself it was time to be heard, to stop silencing herself, she wasn't sure if she was brave enough to leap into the den right away. The restaurant wasn't a far walk. She hoped there would be a seat that would help her blend in.

The sounds outside echoed off each other. There was a peacefulness to this place that she'd forgotten. Probably because it never held peace for her. Crunching on the gravel sent a nervous flutter through her belly. She walked to the window and moved the curtain.

Caiden.

He walked toward the cabin from the direction of the main lodge. She wondered if she'd see him again. Without him staring back at her, Maggie didn't feel like shrinking. Tall and broad and wearing a black long sleeve shirt that must be way too warm for this weather. She still dreamed about him. His eyes had been taken over by his body. Now that she wasn't sitting in fear, the sight of him naked sunk in.

His contradictory attitude confused her. If she hadn't been so concerned with stepping foot in Firebrook, she might have noticed more about him. He hadn't wanted to bring her, yet he still did, and he still helped coax her from the truck when he dropped her off.

Caiden stopped suddenly on the gravel and his head whipped up toward her cabin, to the window she stood in. Maggie let the curtain fall back into place and jumped back. She hadn't made a sound. How had he known she was there? She stayed back from the door and window, hoping he continued on his way. When she gathered the courage to check, she couldn't see him. But then someone pounded on her door. She screamed, but cut it off short.

"Calm down, nymph." Caiden snapped from the other side, irritation lowering his tone.

Maggie closed her eyes and calmed herself before opening the door.

"Have you left this place yet?"

Maggie frowned, unsure what he meant or why he would ask. "Yes."

He frowned at her stomach as if he heard it begging for food. "But you haven't eaten."

"I had a muffin this morning." It was now almost three in the afternoon.

"Not enough. Let's go." He stomped away from the cabin and paused when she didn't follow.

"Where?"

"To get you something to eat. You're not bound to stay inside the cabin."

Maggie was hungry and she couldn't live off the muffins from the lodge each morning. She picked up her wallet, tucking it in her back pocket, and locked the cabin door behind her to follow a man who kept pushing her away, but still helped as long as he got to look grumpy doing it.

CAIDEN WATCHED Maggie from the corner of his eye. She searched up and down the path and around every corner and hiding place like a rabbit looking for predators before venturing from the hole in the tree's bottom to search for food.

When he'd gone to work that morning, he'd noticed

there had been no movement from her cabin. Back at the lodge for his own break, he'd asked his brother if she'd been out. Had she been to the lodge to look for food or had anyone seen her around? Wyatt had only shrugged. The cabins weren't stocked. That was the responsibility of whoever stayed in them, unless they couldn't leave themselves.

Maggie may have a purpose for being here and have reasons to leave, but he'd seen enough of her and how she acted around others. She wouldn't. Even if that meant forgoing food.

"You're taking me to the restaurant?"

"Yes."

"Really, I'm okay. I can get something on my own."

"Then that's what you should have done."

"How did you know where I was?"

"Besides catching you staring at me from the window?" Her stare had felt like a fishing line hooked him around his neck. "I own the lodge with my brother. And I smelled you." He hadn't been able to rid himself of her scent.

"Smell? Oh."

"Yeah." He tapped his nose. "There are perks to being a shifter." Not much of a perk when he needed to forget her.

"What is the restaurant like?"

"Moody, kind of like the cabins. We spread the theme across the whole place."

A small sigh of relief left her lungs, and her shoulders seemed to relax. She'd been worried about what she'd find at the restaurant. "You don't like being in public."

"You could say that." They chose this place for its proximity to the woods.

The wind shifted, and Caiden caught the scent of a deer. He threw his arm out to stop Maggie, but she hadn't been paying attention and ran into him. The contact sent a jolt of heat up his limb that spread throughout his body like a flash of light. He ground his teeth against the dizziness that plunged in his head.

Focusing on why he stopped, he pointed to the side of the path. The deer stood just past the next few trees.

"What…"

"Shh."

A mule deer poked its head out and sauntered onto the path. Its ears twitched and his head turned, acknowledging them. Maggie's small gasp of awe was worth the interruption to his walk back to work, where he would sit Maggie down on her own and go back to his kitchen.

The deer moved on, and Caiden lowered his arm.

"I remember seeing deer all the time walking through town. Alder Ridge is similar with their wildlife."

"It is." Although bigger, it had a more city-like centre that the wildlife's main habitat had moved further away. "How old were you when you left?"

Her mouth opened and her head turned back to the path. "Are there more?" She ignored his question.

"Not close, but they're moving this way." Caiden kept walking. "You didn't answer my question."

"No, I didn't. I'm sorry."

That was fine. Not his business and he shouldn't try to learn more about her, anyway. The more he knew, the more attached he'd become. He led the rest of the way to the restaurant without asking any more questions.

"This wasn't here before." That almost answered his question. They'd built the restaurant the same year they'd bought the cabins and started renovating—seven years ago.

"Come on." Against his better judgment, he gripped her elbow and guided her inside. One by one, the people seated near the entrance stopped talking, like a choreographed wave of silence and stares. But then whispers followed. Whispers that Caiden heard perfectly.

"It is her!"

"Where has she been all these years?"

"Was she working with her brother?"

"No, there's no way she'd have the capability."

"Then what did he do with her?"

"He must have had someone looking after her all these years."

"But I heard she's here alone."

Caiden looked at Maggie, and her pale skin no longer looked so pale. A bright flush filled her neck and face. He doubted she heard them, but she saw the stares, saw their mouths move and their bodies leaning toward each other.

He'd intended to deposit her at a table of her own and leave her, but not now. The judgment coming from the locals hurt her. He felt his chest constrict and knew it wasn't his own reaction.

Bracing himself against the heat he expected, he placed his hand on the small of her back and turned her around. They left out the front, and he took her in through the back entrance to the kitchen. Her eyes never looked up from her feet as he nudged her into a seat in his office.

"Maggie?"

Nothing. She didn't react.

"Maggie? What were they talking about?"

Her throat moved as she swallowed, but she didn't look up. The flush in her cheeks toned down to a pink, but she wasn't with him. She couldn't hear him. He stood back and waited, hoping she would come to on her own.

He'd have to touch her again to get her attention.

Crouching on the floor in front of her, he put his face in her line of sight.

"Maggie." His firm command of her name had her eyes widening. They took a minute to focus, but when they did, they found him. Now that her attention was back and on him, Caiden realized how close they were. He couldn't stop his hands from rising and resting on the outside of her thighs.

"Caiden?"

"Yeah, little nymph." His voice changed, an intimate vibration to help pull her from her waking coma. "What were they talking about?" This tiny woman shook. And Caiden enjoyed touching her, calming her.

"Talking?"

Caiden tapped his ears. "You might not have heard them, but you know why they were talking and staring."

"You heard them, didn't you?"

"Yes, but I don't understand it."

"I should go." She tried to stand, but Caiden firmed his hands, his fingertips squeezing to keep her still. She gasped and all her anxiety was flooded out by something even more potent for the animal grasping for control. Arousal swam through him—her arousal. He didn't want her to go anywhere.

"You still need to eat." He circled his thumbs over her knees and stood. Her pulse jumped. "Stay put."

Caiden left her in the office and put together one of the lunch specials for the day and a piece of the dessert he'd made again first thing this morning. He'd only eaten half this time.

"Here."

"Thank you."

He sat on his desk with his arms crossed and watched

her eat. Slow nibbles at first, but as her stomach continued to protest, she ate more steadily.

His redheaded nymph—*his? The—the* redheaded nymph had secrets that linked to Firebrook and if he believed any of what the locals said, those secrets had something to do with her brother.

Caiden reminded himself to stay out of it, not to get involved, but the thought of her receiving that treatment everywhere she went pissed him off. When she was afraid, she hid her snark, and that was what Caiden would rather hear from her. Just so he could kiss it off her lips.

Fuck, he was in so much trouble.

CHAPTER 8

Maggie finished the food. She'd never tasted anything quite like it. Setting the plate on his desk, she looked up at Caiden, who hadn't stopped staring at her. It had been a little disconcerting for him to watch her eat, but she had no reason to complain.

"I'm sorry." She looked straight ahead.

"For what?"

"For causing a scene out front and for zoning out. It was kind of you to bring me back here." Her formal tone crooned like a practiced one. Not one of her own. She tried to meet his eyes.

"Apology not accepted." Disgust dripped from his curled lips.

"What?" Who the hell declined an apology?

"You didn't cause a scene. You walked into a room. They were the ones that created the scene."

"I suppose that's true." He had a point, but they directed it at her—because of her.

"What happened to your brother?"

Her breathing stopped and her heart thumped one final

hard beat. Maggie tore her gaze from him, humiliation heating her skin again. Intimacy charged the air—being alone with someone and cornered with the truth.

"Look at me, nymph." Using his nickname for her didn't lessen the sharp demand.

"It was only a matter of time before you made the connection." Dismay broke through her voice.

"What connection?"

"Who I am."

"I don't know who you are." Caiden pushed off the desk and moved toward her.

"Then why did you ask about my brother?"

"Someone out there mentioned him." His head tilted to the main restaurant.

"Oh." He may not know now, but he soon would. And she didn't want to see how his eyes change when he did.

"What happened to him?"

"I don't want to talk about it." Every muscle in her body stilled. No moving, no talking.

"Then what's your plan, Maggie?" He towered over her —an intimidating figure, despite his handsomeness. But the taunt he threw down when he said her name stirred something in her core. The little girl from her memory earlier slapped her in the face.

"What are you talking about?" Now she met his eyes.

"You're not really going to sulk inside the cabin for the rest of your time here, are you? Barely even leaving for food?"

Maggie's jaw dropped, but with it, so did her humiliation. She hadn't felt real anger like this in a long time and boy, its toxicity purred. If people didn't treat her with kid gloves, then they ignored her. Not Caiden. He didn't know her and the stories that went with her name. Or what she'd been through since then. He didn't see the damage beyond repair on the inside, how she'd been conditioned by Tyrone. The splash of cold water from being treated like any other person doused her mountainous self doubt.

"Well?" He crossed his arms, pulling his shirt tight over his shoulders. His lips twitched the longer she didn't answer. He was too used to getting his own way, and no one would ever control her again.

Maggie stood. "Thank you for the food. And thank you for escorting me from the restaurant. But what I do from here is no concern of yours, grizzly. I have enough people judging me. I don't need it from you, too."

Her legs steadier than she'd imagined, she turned and left his office. Heat encased her back when she stopped in the busy kitchen to search for the exit.

His hand snaked around her middle as he turned her toward the back door. His fingers splayed, planting a seed of desire. Hot breath blew against her ear and his body curled around hers. "I'm making you my business, nymph."

With his hand sliding from her, Maggie bolted for the door, almost knocking over the teenager washing the dishes. Her feet wanted to run, but she refused to let them. She refused to allow Caiden to be right. But he was. She'd cowered every moment she'd been out in the open.

Maggie didn't deserve this. Her past couldn't haunt her. It wasn't a living, breathing thing. Tyrone wasn't even living and breathing. He wouldn't show up the next day now that she'd left her home.

She wouldn't stay in Firebrook, but she would be here until she'd dealt with her mother's house. There had been a time when she loved this place. Maybe she needed to find her own peace.

But it wouldn't be with Caiden, or anyone else,

breathing down her neck. Her attraction to him was because she'd experienced nothing like it before.

If he would only make up his mind about her, she could let it go. He acted as if he despised her, but his touch scalded.

No. Not Caiden. Not someone so domineering. But if she ever wanted a relationship at all, she should start by making sure she was heard. It was time to change the minds of the past.

Caiden didn't have to go far to find out information on Maggie or her brother. As soon as he stepped into the main restaurant, his bartender approached.

"Was that Maggie Scott?"

"I don't know her last name, but that was Maggie." He'd rather not encourage the gossip, but this time the gossip held information he wanted.

His bartender looked at him and waited, as if Caiden would offer every little detail.

"What's she doing in town? Does it have something to do with her brother?"

"Who's her brother?"

"You don't know?" The shock only pissed him off, as did the curious looks from people at the nearby tables listening to their conversation. "Her brother is Tyrone Belenger."

Caiden kept his reaction to himself, refusing to feed the judgment. He remembered little of Tyrone himself, but he knew who he was. He'd been a few years younger than Caiden and Wyatt, so they'd seen him in school. And they blasted his name across the news not even a year ago. Running an illegal fighting ring for women in the city. That explained some of the whispers, but others concerned him. The ones about Maggie herself.

"Back to work, Matt." Caiden went back to the kitchen and talked to his sous chef. Once Jay ensured he could handle another day without Caiden around, he left. Maybe Wyatt would remember more about Tyrone and Maggie before they'd left town.

Wyatt's truck wasn't at the main building. Caiden hopped in his own to search for him. He could wait. He should wait. But trying to deny his attraction to Maggie for so long only made touching her that much more of an obsession. And he preferred to gather information before he saw her again.

He found Wyatt coming out of the hardware store. "You wouldn't believe the questions I've had about our new cabin guest."

"Yeah, I would." Caiden hardened his jaw.

"You've had the same."

"Not exactly." Caiden told him he found out the name of Maggie's brother. "How much do you remember about Tyrone?"

"Not much. He was cocky, but friendly enough I suppose. I remember he had a step-sister, but I don't recall ever seeing her. I don't understand everyone's shock."

"There's more to it."

"Wyatt. Caiden." Brian Whitehall stopped beside them. "I'd hoped I'd run into either of you before going all the way out to the lodge. I've been trying to call Miss Scott, but she hasn't answered her phone or my messages."

Caiden's blood chilled, drifting through his body. She'd run off, away from him. Something was wrong, and it was his fault. Again. Caiden shook his head. He might have pissed her off, and she walked away, but that didn't mean she ran to the woods. He would have found her on the path back. Maggie had made it back to the cabin. Caiden inwardly cursed at his premature panic.

"I'll go check on her and relay your message. I'm heading back there, anyway."

"Thank you. Tell her the real estate agent would like to meet with her first thing tomorrow morning. I left all the details in a voicemail."

"I'll tell her."

"Brian." Wyatt stopped him before he walked off. "Why does she need to talk to a real estate agent?"

Brian hesitated. He was a damn good lawyer who respected the privacy of his clients, but he also understood privacy didn't go far in a town like this. "Her late mother's house."

"Do you know why it's surprising to people that she's here?"

"Not the exact reason. Her step-brother, Tyrone Belenger, became her guardian after her mother died when she was sixteen, but Maggie hadn't been seen since the day she died." Brian's eyes wouldn't stay still. He knew more than he was letting on. There was more than just her connection to Belenger.

"Thanks, Brian." Caiden tapped the lawyer on the shoulder and abandoned his brother on the street.

People had stopped him several more times with questions about Maggie and about his time in Alder Ridge. Gossip lovers searching for any angle on a story. His sudden disappearance hadn't gone unnoticed.

"Caiden!" The one person he always made time for, but this particular moment elicited a groan. He turned, and Dakota jogged toward him.

"Hi, Dakota." His sister wasn't someone to avoid, even if he didn't want to discuss Maggie.

"Since when don't we invite the guests of the last cabin to dinner? She's been there a few days and I'm only hearing of her now. From everyone else I might add." His sister wasn't wrong. They always extended a more than warm welcome when they had someone staying in that cabin. They often treated other guests the same, but they reserved that cabin for locals most of the time. "Well?"

"She likes her privacy, so I didn't intrude."

"Nonsense. She can say no."

"No one can say no to you, Dakota. You don't let them." His sister was a beloved force in Firebrook. She turned her innocent smile with mischievous eyes up at him.

"Then I guess I should go introduce myself."

"No." All lightheartedness left Caiden's voice. He grabbed Dakota's arm. When she turned her eyes from his hand to his face, he let go. "I'll extend the invite, but we shouldn't make her feel pressured. She's from here, but hasn't been back in a long time. Give her space, Dakota."

"I know the rumours. I remember her. You better not believe a word people say about her." Dakota's chin lifted to narrow her eyes. His sister had her own way to threaten her brothers.

"I don't, but I haven't heard anything specific."

"Good. And you don't need to hear the specifics. Go invite her to the lodge. If you don't, I will." She jabbed a finger at his chest, then leaned up on her toes to kiss his cheek. Dakota left the way she came.

He was distracted with trying to decipher what little he'd heard of her as he reached his truck. He pulled out onto the street in the direction that would lead to his restaurant. And also to Maggie's cabin.

Caiden couldn't deny the urge to see her. And now it wouldn't matter. If he didn't invite her to the lodge, his sister would—and she wouldn't allow Caiden to make himself scarce. Caiden didn't want a mate, but as long as she was staying in Firebrook, his mate was unavoidable.

MAGGIE PACED THE TINY CABIN. She stood on an edge with two choices, jump over or jump back. Backward provided a place to hide, take small steps, live in Alder Ridge, work a minor job, and live her life with the occasional outing with friends. Friends, that although they meant well, still coddled her. She wouldn't deny that she'd needed that time, but she was over it. Not over what happened to her—never that— but she didn't want to just exist. In some aspects of her life, she wasn't more than a sixteen-year-old girl. Experiencing attraction to Caiden showed her that. Butterflies had filled her stomach, and her palms had begun to sweat. Excitement and the sensation of being lost had spiked inside her.

One date. Only one was all she had. Tyrone came home that night, and that guy never talked to her again, but he talked about her. Maggie remembered the next day. So hurt by being ignored and finding Tyrone standing outside the school to pick her up with his smug grin. He hadn't driven her home that afternoon. He'd taken her to fight.

Not a week later, she'd overheard the news of her mother's death. Tyrone had walked away with the officer at the door and wouldn't let her hear anything else, explaining to the officer she wasn't home. She'd begged Tyrone to tell her what happened, but he wouldn't. He hadn't even let her attend the funeral.

Controlled. She'd been nothing but controlled and not

even by the people who had the right. Her mother and step-father had been the only bit of hope in between Tyrone's visits. But they hadn't believed her about Tyrone. She stopped trying when she saw it would damage her relationship with them. Maybe if she'd pushed more she could have made them understand, but at the time, she needed them more for her.

Maggie had turned into her own worst enemy. She was the one that controlled what she did, limiting her life. Caiden might be an asshole, but he had a point.

With a nod to herself, Maggie pulled out her phone and called Shaye.

"Hello? Maggie?" Other voices in the background stopped when Shaye said her name.

"Hi. I need some advice."

"Of course. What is it?" A chair scraped across the floor.

"I'm here to deal with my mother's house."

"Oh." That apparently hadn't been what they imagined her trip was about.

"I don't know what to do or what the process is. Are there things I should consider before making any sort of decision?" Her friends had always helped her, but she'd never been the one to ask for help.

"There are a lot of things, but the first thing to decide is if you want to sell. After that, the process and the decisions that go with all of that will follow. Would you like me to come up there?"

"No, thank you." She tried not shout. Maggie didn't want anyone by her side for others to see as someone looking after her. A guardian, of sorts.

"Okay. Have you met with a real estate agent yet?"

"I have a meeting with one tomorrow morning." She'd listened to her lawyer's three messages. She knew the name and location. Kayla Wade was only a year older than Maggie. Not knowing what to expect from the other woman rattled her nerves. Which rumour about Maggie would she follow?

"Good. You're going to want to have an appraisal done on the property and an inspection."

"Okay." Maggie let out a breath. It gave her something to start with.

"What are your options other than selling? Would you plan on living in the home?"

Live in Firebrook? Coming back for only a few days was bad enough, but to spend her life here would be miserable. She'd already had a miserable life here. "No, I don't think so. It's sell or continue to rent. The current tenants want to buy it."

"That's good, Maggie. You already have buyers. That will speed everything up."

"Can I call you tomorrow after I meet with the real estate agent?" Being on her own didn't mean she couldn't reach out for help. As long as that help didn't come running to take over.

"Absolutely. You don't have to decide right away. Take the time you want to think it over."

"Thank you. One more thing. I haven't had a chance to call Ruth. Was she able to find someone to fill in for me on such short notice?"

"She did. She said to take all the time you need."

"Thank you." Maggie ended the call and flopped herself onto the small couch. She'd felt guilty for leaving Ruth hanging, but she was glad someone could fill in for her. Maggie would have to call her as soon as she knew when she was returning.

Things were changing for her. She'd lived in a protective bubble in Alder Ridge. That was what she'd needed, but she'd been feeling the strain, that she would soon outgrow that bubble. Maggie hadn't wanted to admit that, but now that she was here, she recognized how her friends had been managing her. Not maliciously, and she adored them all for that. And she couldn't deny that had helped her after first arriving in Alder Ridge. Maggie had slowly gained independence as an adult for the first time.

Now she was here on her own. It was terrifying, but this was right, even if it was too soon.

The knock on her door still startled her, but she took a deep, slow breath rather than reacting. Caiden stood on the other side of the door—broad, imposing, yet there was a sense of comfort that came from the bear-like man.

"Brian was trying to get a hold of you."

"I got his messages. I hadn't called him back yet."

He nodded once, but didn't leave. Instead, he walked into the cabin uninvited and took the door from her grip. Shutting it, he stepped closer to her. Maggie tried not to back up.

"What are you doing?" Maggie lifted her chin to meet his eyes.

"I want answers."

"Well, you won't get them. Not from me."

"You'd rather I got information from them." He pointed to the door. "The public full of gossip and theories and even accusations."

Maggie couldn't pretend that didn't hurt. Their theories probably hadn't changed over the years, only evolved. But now Tyrone's true self had been exposed, what he'd been capable of, what he'd done. She'd known some would rope her into his plans.

"I don't want information from them. I want the truth from you."

"Why? You don't want me here, remember."

"I've never said that."

"You didn't want to bring me."

"Not the same thing."

Maggie took a step back, resting her neck from the awful angle of looking up. His eyes swirled like fire—green flames spitting heat toward her, burning for something. If he didn't say the things he did or push her away, she'd think they were all for her. But what did she know of that?

"Maggie. What did he do to you?"

That was the first time anyone ever asked that. The question froze her breath, and tears built in her eyes. But someone who couldn't make up his mind about her didn't deserve those answers, as much as she wanted to tell the truth. "None of your business." Her voice cracked, and she turned away from him, cutting off his heat that warmed her.

"It is my damn business." His hand reached out and grabbed her waist, pulling her against him. She crashed against his chest.

Throwing her hands up, she tried to push him away. This time when she spoke, there was no sadness. "It isn't. You don't need to know anything about me. I'm here for one thing, then I'm leaving. The rumours and stories will die again. And I will never come back here. Let me go." Maggie struggled against his hold.

Caiden's hand rose and gripped her chin, trapping her. "That's all they are, rumours and stories. You aren't anything they say you are."

Maggie shook her head against his hold and the rest of her body stilled. Her past was full of so many lies and this man saw through them all without even knowing her. His mouth was an inch from hers. Even though his beard had yet to touch her skin, she could almost feel it. As she stopped struggling, relaxing against him, his hold changed.

There was no way to escape his firmness, but the heat from his eyes moved to his hands. The only warning was the flex in each of his fingers.

Caiden tilted his head and kissed her. There was no gentleness, only sheer want and need. She didn't understand her body's reaction to him. Heat hummed and need filled her core.

He moved over her mouth until she opened for him. He slid his tongue along hers. His growl in his chest below her palms vibrated. It coiled inside him until it released with power. His hand moved from her face and stroked her hip. He thrust his body against hers as he held it in place. His erection jumped against her stomach.

Maggie didn't know what to do. She'd never been kissed like this before. Hell, no one had ever kissed her. But anything she might have experienced as a teenager wouldn't have held the raw power pulsing between them. It all came from Caiden, but it encompassed both of them. Desire licked down her spine.

Caiden's hands moved to her butt to pull her against him. Her feet left the floor, and she pointed her toes downward. But then everything chilled.

Air filled the space between them, and he caught her waist as he dropped her. Blinking, she met his eyes, worried about what she'd see. His lips tightened and his eyes filled with a dark green. With a disgusted huff, he let her go and moved away.

Maggie tried to hide the hurt. She was good at hiding that, but maybe not with him. He was the first person since her parents to be this close to her, to know some of the truth.

"You can come to dinner at the lodge tonight." It didn't sound like much of an invitation.

"No, thank you."

"Why?"

"I don't need any more from someone who can't make up his mind."

"If you don't, my sister will be here and she isn't easy to say no to." He lowered his tone as if his sister was a threat.

"Good. I need practice." Maggie didn't want the confrontation, but she'd do it if she had to.

"And then she'll drag my brother in here with her too."

"Caiden, you don't have to do anything to help me." Maybe if he didn't feel obligated since he brought her, he'd leave her alone.

"I'm not."

An inner, immature part of her wanted to stick out her tongue and say fuck you. But the woman she was now wanted to thank him. He wasn't coddling her, keeping his distance, smiling fake politeness and patting her on the head.

"Nymph." Her nickname this time sounded more like a curse.

"Fine." She sighed. Pushing back against Caiden was one thing, but pushing back against Wyatt and their sister would be another.

"I'll come pick you up."

"No. What time?"

Caiden eyed her. Maggie didn't back down. It was hard not to look away under his stare, but she didn't want to be managed. If she was going places, she'd get there herself.

"An hour."

"Okay."

Caiden didn't move to leave. She watched his muscles bunch. His erection still stood proud despite the distance between them now. Oh, she was curious. He'd opened that up for her. A kiss like that created images she wasn't sure were possible.

She hoped Caiden didn't see the thoughts floating through her mind. Maggie pointed to the door. "You can leave now."

His lips twitched, but he turned away and left. Maggie needed to prepare herself better if she were to see Caiden again.

CHAPTER 9

What the fuck had he done? He'd lost control. The more she denied giving him an answer, the more he wanted to shake her. She just stood by and let people think and say horrible things. And by the sounds of it, they've been doing it since she was a child.

She'd tasted exactly as the dessert he'd created. He'd been spot on with the spices. Her flavour swelled on his tongue. With the reminder that she planned to leave, he caved. It didn't matter how close he got, these feelings carried strength too much for him. But she'd be leaving. He wouldn't need to keep her as his mate.

He'd known the rumours lacked truth. What did she experience at the hands of her step-brother? He'd headed an underground fighting ring for women. Kidnapping, buying, acquiring women in any way possible, and forcing them to fight. They'd never caught him, but several of those he had working for him and his patrons had been. They'd given the whole story. Where had Maggie been during that time?

Caiden froze on the path to the lodge. Maggie had been

one of his fighters. He wanted to find the bastard—to kill him. Take him to the woods where no one would see four grizzlies tear him apart. He, Wyatt, and their pairs wouldn't hold any remorse over a man like Tyrone.

How did she end up in Alder Ridge? There was a story there. And he bet the shifters in Alder Ridge had firsthand knowledge.

Caiden sighed. He had to let it go. Just as he'd let Maggie go. Mate or not. She could not be his responsibility. With his family around this evening, he'd keep his hands off her. He was sure an emergency would arise at the restaurant that would call him away in the middle of dinner. Sooner if luck favoured him.

Stomping into the lodge, his sister was already waiting.

"What did she say?"

"She's coming. She'll be here in an hour."

"Good. Now get cooking genius." She backhanded his stomach and sent him to the kitchen. He loved his sister, but there were days he wished he could throw her.

In the kitchen, he started pulling things out of the fridge. The front door swung open, and Caiden heard his brother's distinct stomp of his boots, followed by their cousins'.

"It's raining!"

Fuck. Maggie was walking. It wasn't far, but far enough she'd be drenched when she got here. Not his problem. She wasn't his. If she didn't want to walk in the rain, she could call and cancel. That's what she should do.

Wyatt walked into the kitchen. "Dakota says there's a guest coming tonight. And that you invited her."

"Not my choice. Our persistent sister made me."

"But I want to know why you wouldn't want to invite her." Wyatt leaned against the counter beside Caiden.

"What makes you think that?"

"I know you, Caiden. Too well. You've been on edge since you got back. I assumed because of the hunter, but it's her." Wyatt's face didn't hold the grin Caiden would have expected.

"Drop it, Wyatt. I mean it."

"For now." His brother left, and Caiden finished cooking, even taking the time to make something for dessert. Before he realized it, he was making his new creation from the restaurant. Not only did her taste still linger on his tongue from the kiss, but her smell filled the lodge.

"Hi, Maggie." His sister's voice echoed into the kitchen. "Did you walk here? You're soaked. You should have called for a ride. I bet Caiden knew you were walking. That asshole. Come on. I'm sure I have some dry clothes upstairs." Dakota never gave Maggie a chance to respond.

Two sets of lighter feet sounded on the stairs above him, and his brother appeared in the kitchen's doorway. Wyatt leaned against the frame and crossed his arms.

"Don't look at me like that. You knew she was coming, and you knew she doesn't have a car with her."

"But you were the one who invited her."

Caiden tilted his head back to look at the ceiling. He didn't want her here. The animal inside of him had perked up, ready to sidle up next to his mate. But not Caiden. Wyatt left and it wasn't long when Dakota and Maggie came downstairs.

Caiden stayed in the kitchen as long as possible, not emerging until he had food to carry to the table. Maggie sat by the fire with Dakota, Wyatt, Noah, and Tavis. The clunk of the plates on the table turned all their heads.

He didn't want to look at Maggie, but there was no stopping him. She turned her shoulders to face him, and her tongue licked her bottom lip. His cock hardened and he groaned. Wyatt cleared his throat, breaking the instant spell of his mate. His brother understood what was going on now. He'd be able to scent the arousal in the air from both of them, and he would have heard Caiden. The ever changing eyes of their cousins told him to expect questions later.

Caiden left to get the rest of the food, and Wyatt followed.

"That's why?"

"It's more than that." Caiden sighed.

"Better explain quick."

"The shifters in Alder Ridge said she's my mate. They've all mated. I didn't ask anymore questions because it doesn't matter. But apparently Fate sticks her head in and gives us mates. I won't take on that kind of responsibility."

"Why not?"

"You know why." Caiden ground through his teeth. "But the pull toward her is strong. I didn't want to bring her."

"I think you should have gotten more information from those people."

No kidding.

Wyatt grabbed a bowl and left. Caiden took the rest and followed him out.

"How are you liking the cabin, Maggie?" Although all of the Greer men looked similar, Maggie noticed more similarities between Noah and Wyatt. The same thoughtful eyes and easy disposition.

"It's nice."

"Nice?" Dakota snorted. "I won't argue that, except it's tiny. It has the best view, but that doesn't make up for it's size."

"Has the town changed much?" Tavis carried the same reserved persona as Caiden. She found the mirrored personalities between the cousins amusing—not that she would point that out to them.

"Not really. Like a picture in a book." Even with it's growth over the years, the town still carried the same theme, look, colours. Like old west charm meets coastal waterfront.

"Was the lodge or the restaurant here before you left?" Tavis leaned back and took a pull from the beer he held. That was the closest they'd come to asking about her past.

"No." Dakota answered for her as Maggie was shaking her head.

"Only half of the cabins were standing and mostly falling down." Now the area shone like it had always belonged. The landscaping flowed naturally and the cabins weren't crowded together.

"Are your parents coming up for your birthday, Dakota?" Noah nudged Dakota with his elbow, making her sway.

"No, I don't think so." Dakota didn't look upset. A smile played on her lips. "Besides, I'd rather they come during holidays. My birthday isn't anything special."

"Of course it is." Tavis threw his arm around Dakota's shoulders. "At least make your brothers treat you to dinner. I'm sure Caiden can make something decent." Tavis chuckled.

"How old will you be? Twenty-eight?"

Dakota frowned at Noah. "Twenty-nine." Dakota was only five years older than Maggie. Close enough in age that she may have remembered Maggie. But she didn't push for information. She must remember—she knew the lodge hadn't been here when she left. Yet, she was still kind to her without hesitation, lending her clothes and never letting the conversation settle. Much like the women in Alder Ridge, except for one thing.

They worried about her. Holly and Ezaray fought alongside Maggie for two years. An unerasable history that made finding a different relationship with them difficult. They've healed and found their life and independence, but they seemed to hold Maggie back thinking she must not be ready for anything more.

Wyatt emerged from the kitchen, followed by Caiden. They all stood and approached the table. Maggie kept her eyes averted from Caiden, not wanting to be drawn into him. She tried to sit on the other side of Dakota, ensuring distance between them, but Wyatt smoothly inserted himself to hold out the chair for her. By the time Caiden finished setting the rest of the food on the table, Wyatt, Noah, and Tavis had taken the other seats.

She couldn't avoid him.

Caiden's elbow brushed hers, but he snatched it back, covering it up by reaching across the table. Maggie wanted to scoff. Did he think she wouldn't notice? Every move he made with his body heat so close to hers shot a thin flame up her arm.

"So why did you send Caiden out of town instead of sending one of the lodge hands?" Dakota looked at Wyatt. All four men froze. Maggie realized the brothers hadn't been truthful with their sister. Stupid men.

"He was free."

"No, he wasn't. He never leaves town at the beginning of the tourist season."

"You should tell her." It wasn't Maggie's place to say anything, but she didn't feel right keeping her mouth shut. Dakota didn't deserve the lie.

"Nymph." Caiden mumbled next to her. A warning snapped at her skin.

"Stupid." She shook her head and forked a bite of food.

"Arrogant, overbearing assholes. What's going on?" Dakota slammed her silverware down on the table.

"Someone shot Caiden in the woods. Another…" Wyatt paused and looked at Maggie. "Someone found him and took him to Alder Ridge. He's been healing there since then." Wyatt's even and steady voice annoyed Maggie, as if getting shot was a common occurrence.

Dakota's chair scraped against the floor and it fell backward as she stood. She stepped around Maggie and shoved at her brother.

"What the hell, Caiden? Where were you shot?" She searched Caiden's upper body while he swatted her hands away.

"Across the shoulder. I'm fine. Would you get off me?"

"Where were you?" Dakota eyed Maggie as she asked slowly.

"Maggie knows what I am. You can relax."

"I wondered." Wyatt nodded.

"What happened, Caiden?" Dakota retook her seat.

Caiden retold the tale, and it was also the first time Maggie had heard it. They hadn't given her the details in Alder Ridge, only that a hunter had shot him.

"That's not hunting. That's stalking." Maggie frowned at Caiden. Why would they make this sound like some accident?

"We know."

"Are you going to do anything about it?"

"Yes, little nymph. We are." Caiden reached up and moved a strand of her hair from her face. But his hand moved away from her.

"Good. And what is it you're going to do?" Maggie angled toward Caiden.

"That's for us to figure out." Caiden ignored her and her questions.

Maggie huffed. "Is that a polite way of saying none of my business?" She forgot they weren't alone. To talk to someone like this, to let out her true thoughts, was freeing. A potent drug slithering through her system. But only with Caiden. Only he pulled it out of her. She didn't want to stop. She felt more like herself. This was her chance to relearn everything about her. Maggie didn't know what kind of person she'd been. There hadn't been the time for her to explore that. Caiden was her chance to explore.

"That's right." Caiden turned and put one elbow on the table and the other on the back of the chair.

"In case you forgot, you're the one who pulled me along like your personal toy to lie on and keep you comfortable."

"That doesn't mean you can insert yourself into this."

"Inserting myself?" Maggie's voice rose and she fully faced him. "Asking a question isn't inserting myself. If I decided to join you on a hunt for the hunter, that would be inserting myself, grizzly." She put in as much attitude as she could muster into the last of her statement.

Caiden leaned down, his nose lined up with hers. "You answer my questions and I'll answer yours."

"Sorry to interrupt." The other voice shook Maggie. Wyatt leaned forward. "You did what to her?"

"I really want to know the answer to that, too." Noah tilted himself around Caiden and Tavis leaned forward from the other side of the table, his lips twitching.

Maggie pulled herself away and Caiden turned his head. "Now that is none of your business."

"I have a feeling the shifters in Alder Ridge are a chatty bunch." Wyatt's teeth showed through his wide grin. "I got to talk to Nathan a few times over the phone with updates on you."

"Maybe we could all take a little road trip." Tavis leaned back.

"Fuck off, all of you." No heat incited Caiden's voice, only a sigh, as he turned back to his dinner.

Maggie replayed everything she'd said in her head as the others started talking of the lodge. Her skin warmed. She'd been too forward with him. Maggie never dared to speak to anyone like that, not for a long time. She barely remembered how she acted toward others before Tyrone took over. Caiden hadn't gotten mad at her in front of his family, but what would he say or do to her later?

Maybe all the frustration would result in another kiss.

No, she didn't want that. He was too much, too intense. Especially after the way she spoke to him, it would be best if he stayed away.

"I'll get the dessert." Dakota hopped from the table. She left Maggie with four men staring at her.

"You're embarrassed by something." Wyatt pointed it out instead of Caiden.

"It's because of how bold she was when sparring with me." Caiden grinned down at her. He knew. He saw it all.

The heat in Maggie's cheeks increased.

"I'd rather your snark than to watch you change colour." There was nothing intimate in his words, but his tone rumbled and heated like that kiss in her cabin.

Dakota returned with the dessert before Maggie had time to respond. She couldn't be more thankful. Maggie didn't know what to say to that.

Caiden dished up six small plates. It smelled like an apple pie, but looked nothing like it. She recognized it from the restaurant. He set one plate in front of her and leaned closer than he needed to. His breath brushed her ear while his beard reached her neck.

"It tastes just like you."

Maggie forgot how to breathe.

Wyatt coughed on the first bite and pounded on his chest. "Sorry. That went down the wrong way." He pushed the plate away while his eyes jumped from her to Caiden. He'd heard him. Tavis was suddenly devouring his plate and the table shook from Noah's silent laughter.

Maggie twisted her head down and ate the dessert. Dakota rambled on, oblivious to what just happened. Maggie saw many of the same traits in Wyatt she recognized in Caiden, and assumed he was also a shifter. The cousins also seemed to have exceptional hearing. But she wasn't sure about Dakota. She wanted to ask. But she'd said enough for one night.

After everyone finished and Dakota slowed down, Caiden stood. "Come on, nymph. I'll walk you back to the cabin."

"Thank you, but I'll walk myself back." No more taste tests for him.

CAIDEN HAD BEEN MORE than wrong. Having his family around hadn't made him safe from getting closer to Maggie. She sparked to life next to him, and he couldn't help but feed the flames. He hadn't meant to offer to walk her home. Her you've-done-enough refusal had been a blessing—the break he needed.

He started clearing the table after she left. When no one helped, he frowned at each of them. "What?"

"You're not an asshole. Why are you acting like one?"

"What are you talking about?" He set the dishes down and turned on his sister.

"I'm not blind. There's something going on between you two and yet you wouldn't walk her back to the cabin."

"She didn't want me to walk her back. You heard her."

"She's right. You are stupid." Dakota shook her head and grabbed a dish. After she disappeared in the kitchen, Caiden looked at his brother and cousins. Wyatt shrugged, but his lips split into a grin behind his beard. Noah and Tavis only raised their brows.

The rain had stopped. Maggie would be fine. The sun was still on the horizon, and the daylight would linger long enough for her to make it back to the cabin. She wouldn't wander off anywhere else on her own. His mate didn't need an escort, nor did she want one.

Mate. Fuck. That's what she was to him. How many times since she sat next to him in the passenger side of his brother's truck had he called her his mate? Sarcastic or not—the words were true. She was his mate. As long as she didn't stay that way. It didn't seem he had a choice in this matter. Not when he realized his feet had already carried him out of the lodge and up the path, following her.

"Maggie." He called after her when he rounded a corner. She turned and let him catch up.

"I don't need you to walk me back."

"I know that."

"Then why did you follow me?"

"They pointed out that I'm not an asshole."

"You're not?" Sarcasm peaked, then Maggie shut her eyes. "I'm sorry."

Caiden tilted her chin up. When she opened her eyes, he let her see him grin. He enjoyed her backtalk.

Maggie took a single step back. "The cabin is just over there. Thank you, but I'm fine."

Caiden nodded, but once she took a few steps, he followed. Maggie whirled around and glared at him. Caiden only shrugged.

He tried to follow her inside. Just one more taste of her. Another kiss. He could trust himself with that much. It was a lie, but his mouth watered.

Maggie rushed inside and quicker than he gave her credit for, she turned and slammed the cabin door. He leaned against the wall beside it.

"You seem mad." He spoke loud enough for her to hear him through the door.

"Go away, Caiden."

"I like the way you say my name. Say it again." He tilted his body toward the door.

"Go. Away. Grizzly."

He laughed. "I like that one, too."

She swung the door open, creating a breeze to make her hair fly over her shoulder. He straightened and inched into the doorway. She wouldn't be able to shut it again without hitting the toes of his boots. "What do you want?"

"This." He cupped both sides of her neck and claimed her mouth as quick as she'd slammed the door. She melted. Maybe not against him like he wanted, but she didn't serve up any resistance. He smelled her arousal growing. She was right there with him, but it seemed neither of them would admit it. That was fine with him. They could have some secret fun, and she could hightail it back to Alder Ridge. As long as she understood this wouldn't go anywhere. It may take him a decade to get over her, but he would do it.

He slid his hands down her shoulders and back. He'd

told himself no more than a taste. His cock tried to lead, to urge them inside. It almost had his arm twisted.

For a moment, Maggie didn't just stand there and take what he gave her. Her hands clutched his arms, and her tongue moved tentatively along his. A minor exploration, unsure if she was taking the right steps. He deepened the kiss and slid his hand to her hip, where he moved his thumb under her shirt.

At the first touch of his skin against hers, she gasped and pushed on his chest. He didn't go easy. With another shove, Maggie lifted her knee. Caiden barely avoided her, taking the hit on the inside of his thigh. He winced as the pain tried to dig deep into the muscle. Her next push got him out of her way to slam the door. The deadbolt clunked and the chain of the upper lock rattled.

At least one of them had the strength to fight the urge. An urge to which even Maggie wasn't immune.

CHAPTER 10

Maggie tossed and turned the entire night. The loft that held the bed creaked each time she flopped. Nothing worked to disperse the butterflies down her chest or the branding heat from Caiden's touch. It had only been his thumb on her skin, but it had been enough to sear. Instead of sleeping, she'd imagined what would have happened had she pulled instead of pushed. But that was her problem—only imagining. She was no match for a man like Caiden.

Checking her phone, she still had three hours before her meeting with the realtor and Mr. Whitehall. They were hoping she'd decided, but she was far from it. Memories of that house were few and far between. The smart thing to do would be to sell. The couple living in it had made a beautiful home. She didn't want to be the cause of taking that away. But having not lived an adult life, Maggie needed to learn about the process of both decisions first.

Deciding sleep wouldn't happen since even now her mind raced with images of Caiden and his hands, Maggie kicked the blankets and got up to shower. She made it quick, no need to linger. But it still left her with too much time.

Looking at the front door, Maggie wondered what she'd encounter if she went into town on her own. Would the stares be as bad as she imagined?

Grabbing her wallet, she placed her hand on the door-knob. This would take more courage than she thought she had. Venturing out on her own in Alder Ridge was easy. No one knew her past, her history, the rumours that followed most of her childhood. Firebrook was a world she hadn't enjoyed.

But Caiden's words from the restaurant scratched at her insides. She didn't need to accept the rumours, and hiding would only give them validity. It didn't matter she didn't plan to stay in Firebrook—Maggie deserved to have the truth revealed.

She opened the cabin door and stepped out. Locking it behind her, she started her walk into town. This had always been her favourite time of year here. The warm days in between the rainy ones held the scent of spring and the mountains that held the aura of hope. The hope had never lasted long for her, but this time something more filled the air. No one was coming for her. No one was sitting in the shadows, waiting to control her life, force her to conform.

Maggie made a conscious effort to keep her eyes averted from everyone she passed. Their eyes hit her like sharp arrows, but they didn't matter. Their opinion didn't matter. She knew the truth, and all she had to do was live it.

The walk to the coffee shop had been like riding a bike. She didn't have to think about the path she took, which streets made the walk shorter, which shops she'd pass on the way. Not much had changed in the main part of town. A new shop or two, but most places had outside improvements to keep up with the demand the tourism industry created. A new jewelry shop caught her attention—all handmade with rocks and gemstones. And an ice-cream and candy shop.

Passing Bella's Bakery, Maggie breathed in. The scent pulled many memories of times with her mother. A bi-weekly date they never missed since before Maggie could remember. The scones there were the best in the province. That time with her mother had been one thing Tyrone could never take away from her—not without outing his treatment of her to her mother or his father.

She paused outside of the bakery and closed her eyes, taking the moment to remember her mother. She hadn't grieved enough over her loss. A smile crept over her lips, sad and nostalgic. Her mother had been her best friend. Her only friend. And yet she still hadn't made her mother believe how Tyrone treated her.

Letting the past go, Maggie continued on. The coffee shop sat just around the corner from the bakery. The smell of strong coffee blasted her as she reached the front of the shop. With her lack of sleep, she needed something strong.

Slowly, just as at Caiden's restaurant, some of the people inside turned silent one by one. The wave of it followed behind her with every step. Any who hadn't been concerned by her entrance were silent now due to the environment. The people waiting in line even stopped mid-order and stepped to the side. They stilled as if she were a dangerous mob boss—the sight of her putting fear in the locals. But that wasn't the truth. Some sat in awe, some leered, and others just searched the room.

"Go ahead, Maggie." The woman at the counter wasn't much older, but Maggie didn't recognize her.

"No, thank you. You were ordering. I'll wait in line." Like every other person.

"I don't mind waiting." She smiled at her like she would when indulging a child who came in with a loonie to buy herself a treat.

"I'll wait in line, thank you." Maggie kept her chin up and met the woman's eyes, giving her the chance to see the clarity in hers.

"Oh." The woman's indulgence disappeared. She took a moment to meet Maggie's gaze, the she continued with her order. Some conversation picked up around her until it was her turn.

"I'll have a large latte, please." The cashier winced before making Maggie's drink. While she waited, Maggie braved a glance around the shop. In the back corner, a large smile caught her attention. Dakota stood in the corner, looking smug as she watched the entire scene. Maggie allowed herself to smile back. Dakota gave a solid nod. Maggie wasn't alone.

She paid, and the cashier passed her the latte, but kept her hand around the cup. "Careful, it's hot."

No shit. But Maggie kept her sarcasm to herself. Being rude wouldn't get her anywhere with these people.

"What else would it be, Jackie?" Dakota sidled up next to Maggie and gave the cashier her own *no shit* look. Dakota turned that same look on everyone else in the restaurant. Some laughed enjoying the sarcasm and others frowned. They went back to their own coffees and treats.

"You didn't have to do that." Maggie whispered to Dakota.

"Yeah, I did. Besides, it was fun." She followed Maggie out of the shop, leaving Maggie to get the door. A small thing, but something she was thankful for.

"Thank you."

"I don't know what went on with you and within your family growing up, but it was obvious you were on the shit end of the stick. It was easier for people to believe rumours and gossip rather than something terrible happening in their own town. Don't worry. You'll show them." Dakota gave Maggie a quick hug and left.

Maggie wasn't sure if she'd be here long enough to show them anything, but she decided not to back down if she could help it.

Taking a sip of her coffee, she walked to Mr. Whitehall's office, prepared to ask the realtor all her questions and ready to learn what she needed to know to sell a house.

CAIDEN STOMPED past Maggie's cabin, Wyatt beside him. He'd kept his distance, and it was tearing him apart. The animal inside controlled most of his thoughts and actions. He found his canines dropping anytime he thought of her. His vision changed with the sharpness of the bear's. He had to shake his head being so close to her now. Her scent flashed through him, and his shoulders popped with a premature shift.

"What the hell? We aren't even in the woods yet." Wyatt walked faster beside Caiden. They were on their way for a run with their pairs, Theo and Huck. Caiden had gone out the night he'd returned to see Theo, missing the connection they had, but he'd been too busy since then to get out for a run. Noticing his mood, Wyatt insisted they take the day off together.

"I'm fine." Caiden popped his shoulders back into place.

They were still too close to the public to allow himself to shift.

As soon as they broke through the trees, Caiden ran, tearing his clothes off on the way. Wyatt would gather them and hide them. Over the next rise, Caiden inhaled deep and allowed his eyes to shift. Ensuring no one was around, he shifted. The change tore through him with the same ferocity with which he craved to claim Maggie. Pain ripped at his muscles even after the wind took over the magic. His bones settled into their new positions. His claws dug into the ground as he heaved in air. Maggie's scent permanently stamped itself in his core, despite the distance between him and her cabin.

Wyatt appeared in front of him, naked after having stashed their clothes. He did the same check of the area before shifting.

What's wrong with you? Wyatt blocked Caiden's path when he would have started their trek through the woods.

Nothing. Caiden tried to step around him.

Bullshit. We don't hide things from each other. Wyatt shoved his head against Caiden's.

Caiden's lips lifted in a snarl.

It's Maggie, isn't it?

Caiden's snarl turned into a full growl when his mate's name echoed with his brother's voice. *I don't want to talk about it.*

You need to do something about it.

Wyatt was right. Ignoring her and keeping his distance hadn't been working. She'd taken his advice and left her cabin. But he seemed to follow her trail wherever he went. Her scent milled about town, faint and dispersing. Images of her interrupted his thoughts day and night, but the worst sensation was feeling her skin under his fingers, her lips molding to his. He could feel it now, as if they were locked together at this moment.

His bear had been on the surface for days. He had to hide in his office several times to calm the beast. Sharp vision heralded the onset of shifting each time and the animal in him took over his voice.

I'll figure something out.

Wyatt stepped out of his way, but threw out his opinion, anyway. *What you're going to do is go see Maggie.*

No. He would take it too far if he saw her.

Caiden ran, leaving the conversation behind as much as his brother. Not that Wyatt stayed behind for long. The two bears needed the freedom, and it quickly turned into a competition. By the time they reached their pairs, they'd stopped to wrestle several times in the middle of their race, trying to slow the other down.

Theo and Huck stood on a large boulder, but once Caiden and Wyatt were in sight, they'd jumped off and loped toward them.

Caiden enjoyed this wild side of himself. He and Wyatt had embraced this life with ease. Being out here and having an animal living inside him was natural. Buying the old cabins on this side of town hadn't just been about a business decision. It kept them grounded with these roots. They knew this area and these mountains—an intimate relationship. They knew the animals, families, packs that all lived here. Including the pack of wolf shifters on the outskirts of Firebrook. The bear shifters didn't bother them, and the wolf shifters kept to themselves. A tolerable relationship.

The bears rolled with each other for a while before they all sauntered to the brook for a drink and hopefully a fish or two.

But after a quick drink, the pairs stood on the bank. *We have something we need to show you two.*

Caiden and Wyatt exchanged a look. They followed them upstream. Caiden paused.

This is where I was shot.

We know. Theo nodded. *I found the blood and followed the trail, but I was too late. The trail came to a dead end.*

I'm sorry you had to worry.

I'm only glad you were safe.

They kept following, and about the point that Caiden was sure would be too far for someone to get an accurate shot, they stopped. Wyatt cursed, and Caiden stared as anger built steadily inside. Someone had camped here, and long enough and often enough that wind and rain hadn't wiped away all the evidence. Too bad there was no scent left for them to track.

He planned this. Wyatt didn't need to say it, but they all needed to hear it.

Did you two notice anyone up here the past several weeks? Caiden looked between the two pairs.

I wish we had. We've been mostly downstream from the spring thaw. Huck's eyes held regret.

It's not your fault. Wyatt nudged his pair.

But now we have to ask, were they hunting any bear, or me?

They haven't been back since. There's nothing fresh here. Caiden's pair circled the area.

We need to be more cautious of who comes up here. Since you're back and uninjured, whoever it is might try again. He hated how right his brother was.

If they're after just a big bear, we all need to be careful. Caiden looked at Theo. *We're identical. If he's after me, you're in danger too.*

They spread out and searched for more signs, more

tracks, or anything that could tell them who it was. Finding nothing only pissed all four of them off.

The search had been a good distraction from Maggie. But now that they were on their way back, Caiden could taste her. Shifting hadn't helped like he thought it would. It only made him more aware that he had a mate waiting for him to claim her.

MAGGIE ALLOWED Mr. Whitehall to drop her off at the cabin. The meeting with Kayla Wade left her feeling confident. Kayla simply shook her hand, welcomed her back to town and offered her services in any way possible.

Maggie made her decision regarding her mother's house, and both Kayla and Mr. Whitehall went out of their way to make the arrangements that would allow for Maggie to return to Alder Ridge while they finished with the sale. Maggie had given the appropriate smiles, but there was a small part of her that wasn't ready to leave. She'd spent the past few days exploring Firebrook with new eyes. The eyes of the adult she should have been. Her damaged soul receded enough to allow her some freedom. Knowing that no one would turn the corner and strike her with fear and settle fear in those around her gave her the strength to hold her chin high against the stares and whispers. Maggie saw the whispers, felt the heat of wide eyes. The sympathetic smiles no longer humiliated her—they angered her. They all lived off rumour. She wasn't a rumour.

Torn between two lives. One she'd built in Alder Ridge, and one she should have had here in Firebrook. Would she have loved this place if she hadn't suffered from Tyrone? Maggie thought so. Maybe she would have gone to school and come back. Or she would have started her own business or shop to contribute to tourism. Dreams hadn't been available for Maggie, not since she'd been too young for them to stick.

She wanted to see what Firebrook held for her, so she knew what she was letting go when she returned to Alder Ridge and her friends there. Alder Ridge didn't have Caiden.

The thought of his kiss wouldn't go away. Nothing she did pushed it away, or rid herself of the heat that flared at just the thought of him. She hadn't seen him since she slammed her door in his face. A few times, she'd considered going to his restaurant to see if he would emerge from his kitchen. He seemed to have a strong sense of when she was near. His hot and cold attitude toward her made her curious, which would he choose? Ignore her or come out and growl at her.

There was a problem with what she wanted. Maggie didn't have a reason to stay, and she couldn't stay on Caiden and Wyatt's charity simply because she wanted to. She needed to tell Caiden she was leaving and then plan to get home.

Maggie left the cabin, intending to find Caiden. But as she stepped outside, Caiden stepped from the woods with his brother behind him.

His eyes found her instantly, and she stopped. Wyatt smiled and lifted his hand, moving in front of Caiden to leave him behind. Caiden slowed, but he kept walking.

"Caiden." Maggie called out to him. She tried not to shrink from the stark green of his eyes. There was an animal at the surface. She looked to the woods and wondered what the brothers had been doing. She imagined a couple grizzlies out for a run. The bear still clung to him.

"What is it, nymph?"

"I wanted to thank you again for driving me here and to thank you and your brother for letting me stay here. But I can't accept this for free. I can talk to Wyatt to settle on that." Whatever she paid might not come close to what the cabin was worth, but she'd feel better if she paid them something.

Caiden took slow steps toward her while she talked. "What are you trying to tell me, Maggie?"

"I've finished what I need to do in town. We can do the rest remotely. I'm leaving."

Maggie didn't miss the tightening of Caiden's body, but his words displayed the same cold dislike he'd started with. "Okay. How are you getting home?"

She took a moment before answering. That had been too easy for him. What happened to making her his business? The kissing, the touching—what the hell had any of that meant to him? Licking her lips, she answered him. "I'll call someone from Alder Ridge to pick me up." She wouldn't ask him or anyone else in Firebrook for a ride.

"Good." He didn't move, but his nostrils flared and he lifted his chin. Remembering the animal he was, Maggie realized he was scenting her. Closing her eyes, she let Caiden go. He wouldn't give her what she craved, what he started. Her foolish immaturity rang strong.

Maggie turned back to the cabin.

"You're really leaving?" Caiden's voice changed. It wasn't his own. His syllables rumbled smoothly. She faced him again and his eyes not only changed colour, but changed shape.

"That's what you wanted. You never wanted me here, remember. It's what I want." It's what she had wanted.

"Is it?" Caiden closed the distance by taking the two steps up in one with ease. "Or do you want me?"

Maggie hoped for something from Caiden, but now that

it stared her in the face, she didn't know what to do. She'd never been in this situation, not even close. A high school crush with a first date didn't measure up against the desire between herself and Caiden.

Caiden moved the last few inches, and Maggie stepped back to keep them there.

"I don't understand what you want me to say."

"You shouldn't say what I want you to say. Tell me the truth."

The truth. What was her truth? It was so simple. Nothing held her down except herself. "I don't want to leave. Not yet."

"That's fucking right you aren't leaving yet."

Air left her lungs in a rush as he grabbed her to slam against his chest. She looked into eyes that weren't human, but filled with so much warmth. Spreading his fingers along the back of her head, he bent and kissed her. It had more power than any of the others. His intent reflected strong as he claimed her mouth and his erection nuzzled against her belly.

She'd hoped for a reaction from him, but she was getting far more than she thought she could handle. Not that he was giving her much room to handle anything.

Bending his knees, he wrapped an arm around both thighs and lifted her off her feet. He didn't break the kiss, and the hand at the back of her head only left long enough to open the door. The cabin shook as he slammed it shut and her feet touched the floor.

"I shouldn't be in here. I tried to stay away from you. But then you had to say you were leaving. Fuck, little nymph. Neither one of us are going anywhere now." His lips moved up her jaw and down her neck. If that had been all he did, the fire inside her would have a slow and steady rise. But no.

His hands clutched her shirt, fisting it so it stretched to its limits. As she thought he was about to rip it, he growled and lifted it over her head. Her shorts quickly followed, pooling around her ankles.

Maggie knew where this was going, but only from an educational standpoint, and she supposed an instinctual one with the way her body heated and responded to his. An uncontrollable sliver of fear and uncertainty sliced her core. It wove its way into the desire building there. Euphoric adrenaline pumped through her, urging the situation forward.

Caiden leaned back. Her skin chilled without his direct contact.

"All white never looked so good."

It had embarrassed Maggie to shop for anything more than basic needs. White cotton had been her choice. A matter of comfort had factored into her decision. Now she wished she had been brave enough to reach for the lace, or even some colour. But what colour wouldn't clash with her red hair?

CHAPTER 11

Caiden ignored Maggie's fear. It wasn't of him. It was only a healthy dose that added to the fire between them. Coming inside had been a mistake. Turning away from her would be near impossible after this. But no matter how many times he tried to let go, the animal in him gripped harder. His canines lengthened and retracted as he fought with himself. Maggie was his mate and no matter what he wanted, he couldn't deny that, as she fit so perfectly with his hands cupping her waist. She was his.

At least for now.

Mate. Mark.

Instincts called to him. They had him pulling her bra free and tearing the fabric of her panties away.

It felt wrong to touch her with such rough hands. Looking at her now, she was precious. His and precious. Her skin smooth and unmarred. Hard pink nipples protruded toward him, begging to be touched, licked, pinched. He shouldn't be rough with someone so perfect, but that's what he was going to do. Her unblemished canvas would hold proof of his claiming. And every bit he'd ensure she enjoyed.

"Caiden?" Her whispered uncertainty did nothing but spur him on. The sound of her voice was all he needed.

"Don't be backing out on me now, little nymph. Not when we're both right where we want to be." He slid his hand down her side and inward. She gasped, and every muscle tightened as he played with the oversensitive button. Running his fingers through her folds, he gathered more than enough moisture to reduce the friction over her clit. He didn't want her to come, not standing in the main room of her cabin. Caiden wanted her on her back, the two of them nose to nose, so he could watch the change in her green eyes and watch her hair flame as it spread out over the pillow.

Her cut-off breaths turned to uncontrollable moans and Caiden took that as his cue to push her further. He slid his fingers in to drive into her heat. And what a heat it was. Maggie cried out and clutched his arms.

"So fucking good." Caiden nipped the shell of her ear and nudged her backward. Releasing her, he lifted her so her breasts were level with his mouth. Her hair fell around her face as she looked down at him.

He ran his tongue around one nipple and sucked it into his mouth, letting it go with a small pop.

"These need a topping. I have lots at the restaurant. What's your favourite dessert, nymph?" Caiden wanted to know so he could turn her into it.

"Ice cream." She had no idea what she'd just agreed to.

He knew how sinful his grin looked. He didn't need her small gasp to tell him. Caiden planned to turn her into a deluxe sundae.

Caiden sucked and licked her nipples—tasting the same dessert he'd made, but this time topped with the frozen cream—while he walked her toward the ladder that led up to the bed.

"Are you ready?" He had to ask her before he set her down. As soon as she hit the floor and he rid himself of his clothes, he wouldn't be able to wait.

Maggie's hands rested on either side of his neck, tiny against him. Even up in his arms, the weight of her was less than a tray of plates at the restaurant. She nodded.

"Speak up." He suspected she'd spent too much of her time silent.

"I'm ready," she whispered.

He plunged his fingers into her core again. "You definitely are." He let her slide down his body, then turned her around to face the ladder. His clothes were sprawled across the floor before she made it up four rungs. Her ass, round and too perfect, gave him an amazing view and opportunity. His canines lengthened of their own accord, but Caiden still allowed himself to lean forward.

Maggie screamed as he bit her ass, leaving his mark behind but not puncturing the skin. "Hurry it up, nymph."

She doubled her efforts to get up the ladder. At the top, she turned to stand at the edge of the loft. Caiden braced his feet and tightened his grip with one hand. The other hand snaked between her legs to cup her ass. Pulling her forward, he latched his mouth onto her clit and sucked.

Maggie threw her arm across her mouth to muffle her cries, but Caiden wanted to hear her scream with pleasure. Silence didn't suit his snarky nymph.

He sucked harder, using his tongue against her, until her arm was no longer enough to contain her sounds. Her legs quaked. That was his cue to pull away.

She stumbled backward, but he gripped her hip to steady her while he finished his climb.

Mate. She was his mate. Caiden couldn't fight that any more. *Mark.* The chant was more like an instinct he didn't yet understand, but he knew as soon as he buried himself inside her, it would all make sense.

"On the bed." Caiden's playfulness had vanished, leaving a fierce need.

Maggie visibly swallowed, but she obeyed. Crawling backward, she settled herself in the centre. He lowered himself over top of her, grabbing the back of her knee to bring her leg over his hip. Claiming her mouth, he ground himself against her core.

Caiden lost himself in her, but was exactly where he was meant to be. He'd deal with that in the morning. For now, she was his. He deepened the kiss and angled himself so he lined up with her entrance. One forceful thrust and he buried himself in her cunt. He roared, and Maggie cried out, struggling beneath him. His instincts had him gripping her hips to keep her in place, but she continued to struggle. Then it all hit him. She'd been a virgin.

"Fuck, Maggie. You should have told me."

"Not your business." Wisps of words came out through her gasps. He should have put it all together or had some sort of consideration after figuring out who her brother was and what she'd been through with him. But that was just it. He didn't know what she'd been through. And she'd been with him every step of the way since he kissed her outside the cabin.

"It's my business now. And Maggie? I can't stop or slow down." He was going to hell for this. He held onto her hips and slid out only to fill her once again. Each time, her cries turned more into moans, and soon she was undulating beneath him, taking everything he gave.

Yeah, Caiden was going to hell—not for this, but for

letting her go and finding joy in being the only man between her legs. He hoped he'd be the only one.

MAGGIE HAD TRIED to pull away from Caiden with his first thrust. But she wasn't pulling away from him now. She craved everything he gave her. One hand still gripped her hip to keep her where he wanted her, and the other fondled her breast. She didn't know how parts of her body connected to others. Each suck, lick, kiss, tweak added to her core.

Caiden angled his hips, adjusting hers at the same time. Her back bowed. The spot he hit amplified all the sensations and directed them straight to her clit. She needed something. She knew what it was, but didn't know how to get there—what she needed to do to reach that point.

"Keep your eyes open. I can't wait to see what they look like when you come." He stared at her face as he continued to thrust and manipulate her body.

"When will that be?" Maggie hadn't expected herself to whine.

Caiden laughed. "When I let you."

She didn't understand how he could control such a thing, but she wasn't in control of her body right now, either.

"I'm not ready for this to end, but I can't hold back much longer. Just know, I'm not finished with you yet, nymph." His thumb moved inward to stroke her clit. She looked up at him, just as he'd asked. His eyes had changed, and she saw his canines sticking down from his open mouth.

Maggie gasped.

"You shouldn't forget I'm an animal."

"Wouldn't dream of it, grizzly."

Caiden chuckled. "Come, Maggie. I'm ready to feel how tight your cunt can really get."

Maggie's cheeks heated. He had no trouble saying what he wanted. His grin was a sexy one as his free hand moved up to stroke her cheek.

"Now," he whispered.

Something happened at his demand. Her body tightened, and sensations rushed. Maggie whimpered. "I don't know what to do."

"Let go."

Maggie didn't know how to do that either, but it all built at her centre until it could no longer be contained. With a deep moan, she exploded. Her hips rocked in time with the wave. Caiden roared and stole her mouth, sucking in every sound she made. His hips thrust faster and harder, making the loft creek. He tore his lips from hers and buried his face in her neck.

He bit her. She cried out, expecting pain to explode, but her orgasm gained new traction and blew through her. His cock pulsed inside her, spreading more heat.

He released her neck, licking at the wound. They both groaned as he pulled himself free of her. Maggie turned her head to look at him, but his face blurred. She fell asleep with a blissful sigh.

Her body still hummed when she woke with Caiden's hand cupping her jaw. She must have only slept for a few moments. Caiden panted above her, all sense of the sexy and playful bear gone.

"I'm so fucking sorry, Maggie. I meant to pull out and I sure as hell didn't mean to bite you."

She hadn't considered any protection, and making him pull out hadn't occurred to her either. The small chance of getting pregnant placed panic in her chest, but she hid it.

She didn't want Caiden to see her worry. Being a virgin and not understanding the basic sensations of all this was embarrassing enough.

Caiden gripped her chin and tilted her head. "Mark."

"Mark?"

"I've left a mark."

"Oh. I'm sure it will go away." She lifted her hand to cover it, but Caiden gripped her wrist and held it in the air.

Caiden's chest vibrated, and he leaned down. He ran his tongue over the bite and she shivered—a straight shot from the mark and down one side of her spine.

Someone knocked on her door. Maggie jumped and clung to Caiden's arms.

"What do you want?" Caiden turned his head and called down.

"The pairs found something." Maggie recognized Wyatt's voice.

Caiden gripped the back of her neck and kissed her. Quick and searing. "Take a shower. Get some sleep." He got off the bed and went down the ladder. Maggie sat up to watch him leave, holding the blanket to her chest. Caiden dressed and opened the door. Wyatt's eyes met hers, and Maggie squeaked, flopping back on the bed.

"What did they find?" The voices of the brothers faded away.

Maggie stared at the ceiling, reflecting on what she'd done. She could have a normal adult life. The thought of it sat in front of her in vivid colour. It didn't have to be with Caiden, or anyone. But when she'd thought she'd been happy in Alder Ridge, all she'd been was content, settled with existing.

It had been foolish not to have any protection with

Caiden, and she wouldn't make that mistake again. But Maggie made a promise to let her true self shine.

WHAT THE FUCK had he done? He seemed to ask himself that question a lot with Maggie. Careless, foolish, and out of control. He'd been about to tell her to go back to Alder Ridge, but his brother knocked. Even so, he would have fucked her again. Caiden couldn't get enough. Her taste filled his mouth, even now as a bear, and following Wyatt through the woods to meet up with their pairs again.

Theo and Huck lifted their noses in the air when the brothers approached. Their eyes landed on Caiden.

Where is it? Wyatt said they'd found a trail that hadn't been there before and looked like someone attempted to cover it up.

This way. They led the way to the south of town, the opposite of the cabins. An area of the woods they rarely travelled. They had more than enough space on the north side of town. That side reached toward the mountains and held more appeal for all of them. They didn't need to claim more territory than they needed from other wildlife.

The trail was barely visible, with no scent left after time and rain. But someone still flattened enough in an obvious path.

This could be anyone and for many reasons. Locals hiked often.

True, but this leads in the right direction.

The pairs had a point.

We should keep a closer eye on this side of the woods for the next while. Wyatt sauntered along the trail, pausing every so often to find the next track. *This is too faint to follow it all.*

We'll keep watch. The pairs nodded together.

Be careful. Caiden nudged Theo before heading back toward the cabins and the lodge.

They found their clothes again and shifted, but before the brothers broke through the trees, Wyatt stepped in front of Caiden.

"I thought you were keeping your distance from Maggie."

"I intended to."

"But?"

"She said she was leaving."

"So instead of letting her go, you took her to bed." Wyatt's lips twitched and struggled.

"This is amusing to you?"

"Oh, yes."

Caiden pushed past his brother and headed toward the lodge. His feet stopped him outside of Maggie's cabin.

"Go back to her bed, little brother." Wyatt clapped him on the shoulder and kept walking.

"No," he growled, low and painful. One and done. This was a good opportunity for a clean break. He'd talk to her in the morning with everyone fully dressed and showered, so he couldn't pull in the scent of her arousal that he still smelled from outside her cabin. Caiden had told her to get a shower. Was she still lying naked in her bed, or had she listened to him?

He hoped she hadn't listened. He liked the idea of her lying there with his scent all over her, with his mark on her neck, and his seed in her core. Fuck. That had been a mistake. If he refused to be directly responsible for a woman, no way could he do it for a child.

Caiden forced his feet to move and continued to the lodge, to his own bed. After spending himself with Maggie, he should sleep well, but just the thought of her name sent new thrills through his body. He wouldn't be getting any sleep tonight. Not while her taste coated his tongue and he still felt her wrapped around his cock.

Not when he knew he'd taken her virginity and claimed her in a way no one else ever would. He might not make her his responsibility, but Maggie would always be his.

Keeping her would never be possible with a hunter after him. She'd be in danger here. If she didn't call someone to come get her, he would. Tomorrow.

He'd kept himself distanced from women for twenty years. Caiden never let them believe anything could happen between them. He hadn't with Laura either, but being young, they'd both been emotional. Caiden had considered her a friend, a good friend, and that had been enough to lead her on. Her death had resulted from breaking her heart. He couldn't forgive himself for that. Maggie already had enough pain. Caiden wouldn't be the cause of any more. At least any more than he'd cause by shipping her out of Firebrook as soon as possible.

CHAPTER 12

Maggie moaned when she stretched. She hadn't known pain could be delicious. Once Caiden had left, Maggie fell asleep before getting up to shower. The bruises on her hips ached as she swung her legs off the bed. Her breasts tingled with extra weight and her core throbbed with a need for more. She'd fallen asleep with a surprising thought. Maggie decided to stay in Firebrook for a little while longer.

She wouldn't attach herself to Caiden, but neither would she deny herself an experience. And she had the opportunity to enjoy the town she should have growing up. But that meant she had to do one thing first. Talk to Wyatt about staying longer and paying for the cabin. A few days, maybe a week, would be all she could afford.

Grabbing her clothes, she climbed down the ladder and went to the bathroom to shower. Her neck throbbed as she washed over it. The rest of her body flared, wishing Caiden had come back to her cabin.

Clean and dressed, Maggie thought of containing her hair in braids, but she hated the look of herself that way.

That was the strict image Tyrone had forced on her. His prize fighter. Instead, she dried her hair and brushed it until it shone. The red waves framed her face. She felt ready to face this small corner of the world.

Her first stop was at the main office of the lodge to talk to Wyatt. She didn't find him behind the desk as she thought. He was out front, cutting a piece of wood that fell to the ground when he reached the end. The saw wound down. She wanted to get his attention, but didn't want to startle him while using power tools. Wyatt turned to her. Maggie hadn't made a sound. Caiden had mentioned increased hearing in shifters.

"Good morning, Miss Maggie. What can I do for you?" He set the saw down and leaned against the sawhorse.

"Good morning. I want to ask you about payment for the cabin. I know what you said when I arrived, but I don't need to stay anymore."

"Caiden said you were leaving."

That was the truth, but he also said he wasn't finished with her. Maggie tried to not let it bother her. She would leave, in her own time. "Yes, but not yet. I'd like to stay for a few more days. I can't accept free lodging when I'm staying of my own choice."

Wyatt narrowed his eyes and crossed his arms. Maggie kept still under his scrutiny. "I can appreciate that, but I can't charge you. It's only a few more days. I don't have anyone lining up to stay there. You have all the time you need."

"Thank you, but I don't want to take charity." She didn't want people to see what others gave her or provided for her. Maggie needed to stand independent.

Wyatt's head swung like a nod, and he grinned, pushing off the sawhorse and walking toward her. He grasped her shoulders and bent his head to look at her. "It's not charity, Miss Maggie. And no one needs to know." His hands squeezed before releasing her and going to work.

It was impossible to strike up an argument once he started the saw. She dropped her shoulders, deciding to deal with it later, and continued into town. Her first goal was gifts for Ezaray, Holly, Shaye, and Gwen, then she intended to go to the bakery to have her first scone in over eight years.

The jewelry shop she'd passed the other day was new. The smell of several candles filled her nose as she stepped inside. Everything from fruity to floral. They mixed to a sickly scent on the left side of the store, but as she moved further in, she distinguished the different candles. And deeper still, they displayed the jewelry on several shelves, as well as at a centre counter.

She chose gemstones that matched each of the women's eyes. They sat in small round cages and hung on an adjustable string. Taking the four necklaces to the front, she picked out a candle for herself. The label read *Apple Cheesecake*. It reminded her of the dessert Caiden had made, although that had been more like a brownie than cheesecake. Smiling to herself, she grabbed one for each of the others and set them next to the necklaces on the counter.

Her smile disappeared when she met the frown of the cashier. Maggie recognized her face, but couldn't remember her name. Not that it mattered. The girl seemed to have a firm opinion of Maggie.

She manually punched in the items on the cash register, her fingers hammering with force. With each glance at the next item, the girl's eyes rolled over Maggie.

Maggie had her wallet ready in front of her and when she opened it to take out the cash, the girl leaned up on her toes and peered inside. Snapping it shut, she placed the cash on the counter.

"I suppose being associated with Tyrone Belenger has some perks." The girl slowly slid the money toward her before picking it up and handing over the change.

"What's that supposed to mean?"

The girl raised a brow and bagged the items. "Here." She held the two paper bags out, and left Maggie's question unanswered. She hadn't really needed to ask. She could figure it out. The girl thought the cash in her wallet was a lot more than what it was and that came from the winnings of those fights. The same fights she fought in.

Maggie wanted to throw up and barely held back a gag. People either thought her a simpleton or Tyrone's partner in crime. A victim never occurred to any of them.

She wanted to go back to her cabin and hide. But that wouldn't do her any good either. With a deep breath, she pushed the exchange with the cashier away and tried to move on, not allowing the judgmental girl to ruin Maggie's trip to the bakery.

But receiving similar treatment there dissolved her power. The bakery only had a couple customers and two people working behind the counter.

Maggie placed her order, but no one moved. No one answered. Maggie didn't deserve this. She knew that to her core. She'd healed enough to know she didn't need to take it. But her feet took two small steps back. She landed against something solid.

"What the hell is going on in here?" Caiden's chest vibrated against her back. "The woman placed an order. Give it to her." The two people behind the counter weren't immune to the command in Caiden's voice. Their expressions blanked, looking at him, but they moved to get

Maggie's scone. They dragged the process out as much as possible.

"What is it? Why is everyone so quiet?" A young blonde, a familiar young blonde, stepped out from the back. She looked around the bakery, then to the two employees moving like slugs. But when her eyes landed on Maggie, those blue eyes turned to ice and she crossed her arms. Maggie had seen that stance on the woman's mother. Bella Boone owned the bakery and her daughter, Bonnie, stood glaring at Maggie.

But the icy shards were quickly turned onto the employees.

"Did the floor turn to mud? Give her her order along with an apology. Then you can take the rest of the day off." *Take the rest of the day off* didn't really sound like just a single day off. Even the few customers had returned to their own drinks and pastries as if Bonnie could force them to *take the rest of the day off*. Telling them all to sit in a corner and think about what they've done.

Maggie took out a five-dollar bill and a toonie, passing them over to the one holding out her scone, but Bonnie swatted Maggie's hand away.

"Nope. This on the house." Bonnie's boss-face softened and she sighed. "I'm really sorry about all this, hun. I promise, it will never happen again. You make sure you come back here."

Maggie could only nod. She had no words to combat the way they'd treated her and then the genuine kindness of Bonnie.

Caiden pulled her out of the bakery, but not before giving his own warning look to everyone there. On the sidewalk, Maggie caught her breath and passed the bag to

Caiden. "I'm not hungry." The hollow in her stomach protested, but it also churned, angry and sick.

"You are hungry." He passed it back to her. "Why did you just stand there and take that?"

"There was nothing for me to say in that situation." She walked down the sidewalk, back toward the cabins. "People with opinions will twist whatever I say into what they want to hear."

"Because they don't know the truth."

"No one knows the whole truth. And I'd like to keep it that way." Maggie tried to pick up her pace to get away from him, but he had more than one advantage to keep himself beside her. The road leading to the cabins was bare, no one walking or driving by. Caiden stepped in front of her. His green eyes flashed and roamed down her body. Shivers followed his path until his eyes landed on her neck. They widened, and heat pooled in her core.

"It's still there." He took a step toward her.

"What is?" Maggie lifted her hand, but Caiden grabbed it before she could cover her neck.

"The mark."

"It was only last night. Of course it's still there."

"The wound healed. It's a mark." His voice changed inflections from disgust to satisfaction. Blinking, he tore his eyes from her neck. They returned to their normal shade. "Next time, stand up for yourself, nymph. I know you have the right kind of sass in you."

Maggie's body quaked under her skin. Her choices were to accept what he said or haul off and hit him. The man commanded respect from everyone in town. It was easy for him to speak up and be heard, easy for others to accept what he said and did.

She stepped around him and slowly walked back to her cabin. Footsteps sounded behind her.

"Please, don't." She didn't turn to speak to him. He stopped. Maggie hurried as fast as she could without running. She'd go back to hiding. And rethink her decision to stay in Firebrook.

IT HAD BEEN her plea that made Caiden stop. He wanted to follow her and push. He wanted the truth, to be the first to know everything about her. How could anyone not see the rumours for lies? What had her life been like before leaving Firebrook? Caiden assumed it had been a piece of cake to what it was after.

She easily snapped back at him, but no one else. At least that was something.

When Caiden saw the mark on her shoulder, he'd wanted to grab her. Primal satisfaction filled his blood. Desire and need to mate and mark her again. There was no wound—only a distinctive crescent mark tinted her skin. It didn't look like something that would go away. Part of him didn't want it to. She was his, and that mark ensured everyone knew it. All shifters, anyway.

He spun on his heel and inwardly cursed, taking the longer way around the lake through town to get back to the restaurant. He didn't want to pass her cabin and tempt himself any more.

Caiden paused in front of the bakery, shaking his head. Maggie deserved to be left alone.

Not that Caiden had any intention of leaving her alone. Not after this. Not after seeing the mark and how it had changed. Her past might not be the business of anyone else in town, but it was Caiden's.

His mate.

This was getting out of hand. He'd planned to stay away from her, ship her back to Alder Ridge. Not make a deeper connection with her that would only hurt both of them when she left.

Caiden kept walking.

Once back at the restaurant, he worked in his office except during the lunch and dinner rushes. The entire day, he tried to talk himself out of his plan—telling himself to stay away from Maggie and to call the shifters in Alder Ridge to come get her, whether or not she was ready to leave. That's what he should do, but his mind didn't stop concocting plans to bury himself deep inside her again. To watch her own fire burn bright and bring out the beautiful, sassy woman she still tried to hide out of self-preservation. Her life had taken a complete turn. Self-preservation for her wasn't the same as it once was. Now she needed to shine to live.

And he seemed to be the one to bring it out in her. He'd regret not seeing it. He'll regret letting her go after. The same boundaries he always set with women, he needed to set with Maggie. Set the boundary and stick to it.

Caiden hovered in the kitchen after closing and after sending the last of his staff home. His phone in his hand, he saw his two choices. Call Alder Ridge or call Maggie. Send her back or take her himself and make her shine.

Putting his phone to his ear, he waited for her to answer. He couldn't push her away.

"Hello?"

"You haven't left since you got back this morning, have you?"

"That's not your business."

"I already told you, I'm making you my business." That wasn't the boundary he'd intended to set.

"What do you want, grizzly?" Despite sounding exhausted, she had enough in her to hand him the snippy pet name.

"Come to the restaurant. Now." Caiden hung up before she answered him. If she argued and refused to come, he would go to her. And she wouldn't like the mood he'd show up in.

Caiden started cooking. He'd asked Dakota to drop off lunch for Maggie, but he doubted she'd ventured out to get anything since then. Not since what she experienced earlier.

He had just flipped the fish for the last time when she walked in the back door of the kitchen. She paused.

"You're cooking?"

"Yes. That's what a chef does."

"You demanded me here to feed me?"

"Yes."

"I can take care of myself."

"I know you can, but you don't. Sit."

"I don't want to sit."

"Sit down and eat, nymph." He took the pots and pan off the heat and gripped her shoulders. Allowing his body to press along hers, he backed her to the chair and pushed her down. He grinned as she thumped onto the low stool. Caiden dished up two plates and put one on the small table beside her.

"Why?" She stared at the plate.

"Why what?"

"Why are you doing this?"

Caiden shrugged. He didn't want to tell her why. Didn't want to admit how attracted he was to her and how seeing his mark stirred things inside him he didn't understand. Caiden didn't want to tell her she was his mate. That fact would be irrelevant when she left town.

She forked her food into small bites and watched her plate.

"What were you doing in the woods yesterday?"

"We were out for a run." He wasn't about to tell her what they'd found regarding the hunter.

"A run. As bears?" Maggie only peeked up before bites when asking her questions.

"Yes."

"So Wyatt is a shifter, too. What about Dakota? Or Noah and Tavis?"

"Dakota isn't. Although, she'd wished she were for years. Noah and Tavis are both bear shifters." Not only blood family, but shifter family.

"Are there any more here?"

"There's a wolf pack of shifters nearby." Caiden doubted Maggie would meet any of them soon.

Her lips twisted in thought as she continued to eat. She looked up when she finished.

"Thank you. That was delicious. And I was hungry."

"You're welcome."

"I don't understand you."

"You and me both." He hated his own back and forth with her. "Are you still hungry?"

"I'm good now."

"I was hoping for dessert."

"Dessert?"

"Yeah. You." Caiden craved her taste, but this time, he intended to have a little fun with what he had available here. His other reason he wanted her at the restaurant. If he'd only wanted to feed her, he could have taken the food to her and then followed her inside to her bed. But no, he wanted the ice cream sundae he'd promised himself.

"Caiden?" Her breathing picked up. She wanted him too, but her question chilled a bit of his desire.

"What do you want to do, Maggie? Do you want to go back to your cabin?"

"I'm not sure."

"You are sure. You're just scared to tell me what you want."

"I want to stay."

"That's my nymph."

Caiden pulled her from the stool and settled her on his lap. Pulling her down for a kiss, he claimed her mouth with no mercy—trying to fight against his gut telling him to push her away.

MAGGIE'S CORE still ached from the night before. Her morning had been a splash of her personal reality—momentarily freezing anything she'd felt toward Caiden. Until he'd shown up. He'd demanded answers. He hadn't coddled her on the walk back to the cabin. Maggie should thank him for that, but she didn't want to tell him he was right.

Dakota had brought her lunch, and she knew that hadn't been her idea. Caiden had sent her. Maggie spent her day hiding. She'd even called the girls back in Alder Ridge. Her intent had been to ask for them to come get her, but something stopped her every time. She didn't deserve this, and she needed to stand up for herself.

She might be upset with Caiden, but it relieved her when he'd told her to come here.

Now, with his mouth over hers, she felt like she had the night before. There wasn't any reason she couldn't have a normal life if she only got out of her own way.

Caiden's hand skated under her shirt. A tingling heat spread under her skin. He lifted her shirt, forcing her arms up. He smirked as he looked at her breasts.

"Is everything you own white?" His lips still lifted as he kissed along the top of her bra.

"Is that a problem?" She lifted her chin, but her insides curled with insecurity.

"No. But for someone with so much sass, I'd expect vibrant colours. Reds. Blues. Purples."

"I'm not like that."

"You are with me." He pulled down the cups of her bra and latched onto her already peaking nipple. He suckled strong enough to have her crying out. The sound escaped her into a gasp as he used his teeth. He moved his mouth to the other one as he released her bra.

Maggie threw her head back. Caiden's hands splayed across her upper back to hold her in place. She'd thought him a domineering ass who didn't like her. But he continued with his push pull and brought her closer. Then he stood up for her in the bakery. He wasn't what she'd first thought he was. Even after finding out she'd been a virgin, he refused to take it easy on her. But he had a gentleness now. Maggie didn't let that fool her. He had a scripted plan.

"I promised you I'd add some flavour this time." Caiden gripped her waist and stood her in front of him. He pushed at the elastic waist of her shorts until they fell from her hips. Running a finger down the front of her panties, he grinned.

"I want to see this covered in red. Bright, candy apple lace. Just so I can tear it off with my teeth."

Maggie breathed deep and slow. Her belly quivered, trying to hold in the air. Oh, this man was toxic.

"Stay there." Caiden planted his hands on her hips, setting her away from him. He stood and went into the cooler. Maggie shivered. He came out with a small container. She couldn't see what it was as his arm covered the label. He stopped at her shoulder, a mischievous grin reshaping his beard and face. "In my office."

She didn't move right away, stilled by the sight of him and the anticipation of what he was going to do to her. With his free hand, he turned her at the shoulder and nudged her toward his office. She heard a drawer open and close behind her as she walked. Inside his office, she turned around.

Caiden filled the room, not just with his size, but the way he commanded the space. Nothing compared to him. He brought something to life inside her. She didn't know how he did it—why it was with him she could speak out or stand here like this. Maggie hadn't considered becoming intimate with a man before Caiden showed up. He brought out every part of her that had hidden itself. And she was glad it had. If her past had destroyed those parts of her, she wouldn't have the chance at a full life now. Whether or not she stayed in Firebrook, Caiden gave her that gift.

"A tear?" Two steps, and he was in front of her and wiping at her cheek.

"I didn't know I was."

"Must have been thinking some awfully deep thoughts, nymph."

"A little."

"You can tell me about them later. Dessert is going to melt if we don't get to it soon." He set the container down on his desk and started moving everything off of it.

"That's cold." Maggie eyed the ice cream.

"You said it was your favourite dessert."

"To eat, not wear." Maggie's lips struggled to stay straight.

"You'll wear it for me." His voice dropped and his heat reached out for her.

"Is that so?" Maggie stepped back. The idea of the cold brought bumps to her skin, but the thought of Caiden licking it off her heated her core. Her panties dampened between her legs. Caiden stalked toward her now that the desk was clear. He opened the first three buttons of his shirt and pulled it over his head. Maggie's protests vanished. The muscles filled his chest. Between his dark beard and chest hair, he looked like he should work in the woods with an axe over his shoulder.

Maggie snorted. He probably did that often.

"Something funny?"

She shook her head. No way did she want him to know what she'd been thinking.

"Are you going to put yourself on the desk or am I?"

"What do you mean?"

"Exactly what I said. Dessert is going to melt if we don't get to it soon. On the desk."

She needed more than his words. Her feet didn't move. Caiden slid an arm around her and bent, lifting her under her legs. His arms cradled her, and Maggie lost her breath. A moment of being cherished she never thought she'd get.

He sat her on the desk and slid her panties off. Placing a palm between her breasts, he pushed. "Brace yourself on your hands. Back further."

Maggie lost her breath and her will to argue. Caiden's eyes crinkled and never left hers as he reached for the container and small melon scoop. She tensed as she watched every move he made. He lifted the small scoop of ice cream toward her breast.

Caiden flipped the scoop over and pressed the small amount on her nipple. Maggie gasped. Sheer chills and bumps spread over her chest. Caiden's free hand sat at her hip, holding her against the desk. He twisted the scoop and before he took it away, his hand moved inward. She tried to pull in air she couldn't find as his fingers found her clit. He stroked up and down on each side of the nub. Pressing the lever on the side of the scoop, he released the ice cream. His mouth was there to catch it as it slid off her. The instant heat of his mouth sucking back the cold made her legs quiver.

"Caiden." Maggie threw her head back as shock raced down her centre.

"Delicious." Caiden kept his hand working over her clit. Her hips moved, trying to reach a peak that was still too far away. "Ice cream always goes good with apple pie."

He took another scoop and flipped it over on her other nipple. Holding it there for a moment, he pushed his fingers down and slid two inside her.

"This hasn't lost any heat." Caiden curled his fingers as he turned the scoop before releasing the ice cream. His mouth followed, lapping it from the underside of her breast.

Maggie's hips bucked in time with the thrust of his hand. The next scoop didn't last as long. She didn't register the cold. Her skin heated, melting as if she were the cold cream herself. He took several more scoops for her nipples, the tops of her breasts, the hollow of her neck, and last a long trail down her belly. His tongue each time went from cool to hot and rough against her oversensitive skin.

Maggie's elbows gave out, and she struggled to keep herself up, but Caiden didn't let up. Lick after lick, scoop after scoop. She writhed on his desk, waiting for him to let her explode. Waiting for him to fill her.

"One more, little nymph." Caiden got down on his knees. Taking a small amount with just his finger, he looked at her from between her legs.

"No, please."

"Oh, yes. This is the sweetest part of you." He placed his cream covered finger over her clit. Maggie's cry was almost silent, and she tried to pull away. Caiden followed and latched onto her clit with his mouth.

The contrast, his strong pulls, and his curled fingers threw her into oblivion. Her orgasm came sharp and quick, spreading from her core to her limbs.

Forcing her eyes open, she rolled her head to look at Caiden. The green in his eyes darkened, and his hand moved to his jeans. Grabbing her hips, he pulled her to the edge of the desk, lining her up. He thrust in, scraping against her swollen flesh. Every nerve screamed it was too much.

But Caiden didn't go slow.

Her muscles ached from the previous night, being worked over again so soon.

"I don't know what I'm supposed to do with you." Caiden growled and tangled a hand into her hair.

"Seems you have that figured out at the moment."

Caiden chuckled and leaned forward. He nipped her bottom lip. "Smartass." Then he kissed her, claiming her mouth with his tongue like he claimed her body.

Maggie couldn't hold it back any longer. Her legs shook, and another powerful climax spiraled outward. Caiden's body vibrated. He released her mouth and buried his face in her neck, holding her head to the side by her hair. He bit down, piercing her flesh as he gave his final thrust, filling her with his own liquid heat.

She whimpered as the pain from his bite mixed with the pleasure.

"Caiden." His name was a whisper on her lips as she lost her strength. When she expected to fall to the desk, Caiden wrapped his arms around her back.

"I've got you, little nymph."

CHAPTER 13

Caiden held Maggie against his chest while he waited for her to rouse. He peppered kisses along her hair, jaw, and over her ear, keeping his touch gentle. God knew, he wasn't gentle when fucking her on his desk. He felt like an ass to treat her this way. She didn't deserve such an animalistic experience.

"I'm sticky." Her sleepy words mumbled against his chest.

"Yes, you are."

"That's not fair."

"You can pay me back later." He slid a finger under her chin and lifted. "I need to clean up." Caiden let her go, ensuring she could hold herself up. He replaced the lid on the ice cream and took a large label from his desk. He wrote on it so no one would use it for customers and stuck it over the cover and down the side. After putting his shirt back on and zipping his jeans, he took Maggie's hand and led her out of his office. He left her by the small table and returned the ice cream to the freezer. When he turned around, she stood while holding her shirt in the air with one finger.

"So, this happened." Her shirt was half wet from landing in the dishwater.

"Sorry."

"Are you, though?" Her squinted eyes and twisted features were made ineffective by her almost smile.

He wasn't, but he'd keep that to himself. "Here." He took off his shirt, then held it out for her.

"That's ridiculous."

"You're not walking out of here topless, and you're not wearing a wet shirt."

Maggie sighed and slid her arms into the shirt. Turning her to face him, he buttoned the top buttons.

"You look good in my shirt."

"You can't see me in your shirt." She bunched it up on her arms to keep her hands free, and the bottom went well below her ass. She slipped her shorts back on, but they disappeared beneath the plaid.

"I'll walk you home."

"Like this?" She stepped back and threw her hand down her side.

"Yes." He tried not to let his amusement free.

"You don't have a truck here?"

"Not here. If I can walk, I do. Don't worry, nymph. It's late. No one will be out."

"But now you don't have a shirt."

"I'm okay with that." Caiden placed a hand on her back and guided her out of the restaurant. He'd come in early tomorrow to finish cleaning up before any of his staff arrived. The sun still shone, but it had lowered behind the trees. The path sat in cool shadows.

"I need to thank you for earlier. I don't want to, but I need to." She'd have a hard time facing her issues and standing up for herself.

"Well, you're welcome. It's not often I serve ice cream for dessert like that."

Her lips twitched at his attempt to reduce the tension.

"I can imagine how difficult that was for you." She'd turned her head up to him and he couldn't help but steal a kiss. Letting her go, she turned her gaze back to the ground. "I meant what you did at the bakery."

"I know."

"I thought about going back to Alder Ridge after that."

"What did you decide?" His lungs squeezed. He hadn't realized how much he wanted her to stay. This wasn't looking good for him.

"I called them. But I couldn't ask for a ride. I don't want to go back yet."

Caiden breathed again. Chattering around the next bend in the path had him grabbing Maggie's hand and pulling her behind bushes.

"What is it?"

"Shhh. People."

"I can't hear them."

"You will."

Minutes later, two couples came around the corner. The girls giggled while gripping the arms of the guys, who looked down at them with indulgence. They either loved them or hoped to get laid. Or both.

"Millie and Jenny Sawyer with the Saddler brothers." Caiden leaned down and whispered into Maggie's ear. The teenagers were out on the path looking for privacy from eyes that would tell their parents who they were with. There weren't many mothers and fathers that approved of the Saddler brothers. Caiden grinned. There was a time when mothers and fathers hadn't approved of the Greer brothers either. Too many times angry dads had chased away him and Wyatt.

Maggie had a hand over her mouth, but amusement lifted the corners of her eyes. When she caught him watching her, she turned her set of greens on him. And just like that, Caiden's control slipped. He cupped her jaw and claimed her mouth. His cock lengthened and pushed against his zipper, as if he hadn't just spent himself inside her. Fucking her in the first place hadn't been the best idea. With each touch, he felt the pull to mate her again and again. Since biting her at the restaurant, she now had a matching mark on her opposite shoulder, one that was already healing into a crescent.

He forced himself to pull away from her. If he didn't, he'd lay her on the ground and fuck her again on the side of the path. He loved her sounds. There was no way he'd allow her to be quiet enough that no one would find them.

Her body flared to life to match his. Pulling her up, Caiden took her back to the path. Their steps had quickened to reach her cabin. A ringing in his ears blocked out the sound of their steps on the gravel. And it also blocked out the sound of the next person coming up the path.

Maggie skirted behind Caiden. Sam Tulk stopped when he saw them. Caiden stopped, too. Sam's eyes widened at Caiden's appearance, then he moved his head to the side to see Maggie.

"Sam." Caiden nodded, forcing politeness, and he took Maggie's hand to keep walking.

"Caiden. Taking advantage?"

"You need to mind your own business, Sam." Caiden didn't hide the warning in his voice or his eyes. He'd stopped beside the smaller man. Sam ignored Caiden and looked at Maggie.

"Miss Scott, you don't need to go with him. You need to be careful." He spoke to her like she was a confused child. Caiden was ready to erupt. A quick punch would shut the man up. But Maggie squeezed his hand, reminding him she didn't need to see that.

"I assure you... Sam... I only go where I want to go. Caiden is right. You should mind your own business." Maggie's voice quaked through her whole speech, but she'd tried so hard to deliver it with confidence, Sam may not have noticed. But Caiden did.

He had more he'd love to tell Sam, but he needed to get Maggie back to her cabin. Her hand chilled in his, pushing down his renewed need from their kiss. They would spend their night with him getting the whole truth of Maggie's past. Caiden wanted to put a stop to how the locals treated her. And that would start with learning her secrets.

HER HEART POUNDED. The beating on her chest matched the throbbing pulse in her neck. Being with her would tarnish Caiden's reputation. He wouldn't take advantage of someone like that. And she couldn't let that happen.

Maggie left Caiden at the door to the cabin. "Wait here."

"I won't."

"Please. I'll just be a minute to change out of your shirt and then you should go." Maggie turned toward the ladder to climb to the small bedroom, but Caiden grabbed her wrist and pulled. She spun back, landing hard against his chest.

"I like my shirt on you. And I'm not leaving. It's time we talked."

"I don't want to talk."

"Don't care. I need to know." His precise tone stilled the air, and Maggie's lip quivered. She pulled it between her teeth to stop the movement. Shutting her eyes, she pushed against his chest. Surprise had her stumbling to catch herself when he let her go. She hadn't expected it to be easy to get away from him.

"Caiden, you don't need to know. People look at me differently when they know things. I've built an almost normal life in Alder Ridge. My friends there only know part of what I've been through because they've been through it with me."

"Been through it with you?" Caiden stalked toward her, a frown darkening his face, setting his bright eyes in shadow.

Maggie rushed around the back of the couch. "No. I don't want to tell you."

"You'd rather I listen to the rumours and theories of the locals?"

"No." Anyone else believing those things, she could deal with, but not Caiden. Not the one person who saw her—saw her past all her damage.

He tried to walk around the couch, but Maggie kept pace to create the circle.

"You should go. You don't deserve the accusations that Sam just threw at you. They'll only grow from there." They continued to circle the couch.

"You should stop moving away from me." A predatory smirk tightened his lips, and the shadow fell away from his eyes. They flashed, but only for a second. A warning that he was coming. Maggie paused. He wouldn't give her a choice.

"Caiden, please. I've enjoyed my time with you. You've helped me without intending to. But I think my stay in Firebrook is over."

Faster than she expected, Caiden used one hand on the

back of the couch and lunged over it. She startled, the back of her knees hitting the coffee table. His arm skated around her back, catching her before she fell.

Maggie hung in the air, at his mercy, with no purchase on her feet. Her hands landed on his arms. The muscles flexed beneath her fingers. He held her there, and everything slowed. Her heart rate increased, but his thumped loud in her ears as an intermittent beat to create a melodic rhythm. Heat seared her back where a single hand splayed and controlled whether she fell or found her feet. His face hardened. Flared nostrils pulled in a deep breath. Tilting his head, he lifted his hand and ran a finger over each mark on the sides of her neck.

"No, little nymph. Your stay here isn't over." He pulled her up and lifted her off the floor. Stepping back, he sat on the couch and arranged her so she straddled his lap. His hands landed on her hips like heavy weights. She tried to lift up, but he held her in place. "Now talk."

Being on his lap, her eyes were level with his. There was no way to hide anything while she talked. She wouldn't be able to skim through details and keep her emotions in check. He'd read it all on her face. "I'll talk, but let me sit beside you instead."

"You had your chance to talk your way. Now, it's my way. Start from the beginning, Maggie." He softened his baritone. The sound ran like smooth fleece over her skin, coaxing her to trust him.

She closed her eyes and opened her mouth to start.

"Eyes open, nymph. This is important. No more hiding."

He'd cracked her shields before, and now he tore them away. He saw too much of her. She allowed her eyes to open, but they settled on his jaw instead of his eyes.

"Tyrone was my step-brother. I was young when our

parents married. He was a lot older than me. My step-dad was great. We were all so happy for a while. I don't know when things changed. It happened so slowly. I'm not even sure how, but over time, I said less and less when he was around. When I said something he didn't like in front of others or to him, he'd threaten me. Not to physically hurt me, but he'd threaten my toys, my friends. He'd threaten to do something wrong and then blame it on me to our parents. He'd wait for me outside the school, hiding, and listening to my conversations. It took me a while to realize it, but he used to wait until I left then talk to my friends, twisting the things I'd said, especially if they were about him, but he'd twist them to make it look like I lied all the time. Sometimes, he made it seem like everything I said was a fabricated story altogether, like I lived in another world in my own head. I stopped talking most of the time. I was very careful with what I did say."

Caiden pushed her hair back from her face and let that hand slide down her neck, her arm, her thigh. His heat soothed her and helped her to keep going. She hadn't yet reached the worst of it.

"When he graduated and moved away from home, I had a bit of freedom. Without him in Firebrook, I could make friends again. And I did. I pushed some rumours away. People shrugged and let it go. But after Tyrone's first trip back, he crushed everything. And he crushed me. He said he had a plan and wanted me for it. He made me a deal. Do as he said, and he'd stop the rumours. I did what he said, but he never stopped the rumours. He only fed them without me knowing. I couldn't understand why friends had stopped talking to me or started treating me differently. Some would talk to me at school, but would no longer invite me to go anywhere. I even had a date. Just one. He said he didn't listen to gossip. But Tyrone came back to town that same night and came looking for me. The guy never spoke to me again."

"What was the deal? What did he make you do, Maggie?"

"He made me fight. He taught me and trained me, but never taught me enough to beat him. The bruises and marks he left on me from sparring with him were never visible."

"Why didn't you ever tell your parents?"

"I tried, a few times. They never quite believed me. Tyrone hid it so well and sometimes even convinced them I was upset about something and lashing out at him. I had to stop trying or I would have lost the last two people I still had with which I could be me."

"Keep going." His thumbs drew circles over the tops of her thighs.

"My step-dad passed away suddenly from a work accident. My mom went a few years later. He took me away from Firebrook then. He refused to let me attend the funeral or tell me what happened to her. I still don't know how she died. I've been afraid to find out."

"We can help you if that's what you want."

"I'm not sure." There'd always been a part of Maggie that suspected Tyrone of killing her mother. She didn't know if she wanted the truth. All she needed to know was that her mother had been taken long before her time.

"There's still more," Caiden coaxed.

Maggie nodded. "That's when he started the underground fighting ring that the news exposed last year. I was his first fighter. I watched so many women come and go. I fought against all of them. When they didn't perform, lost too much, or became difficult, Tyrone killed them—well, he had one of his hired security kill them. The last two years, Holly and Ezaray were there too. Zachary came looking for Holly, to rescue her. The doctor," she had to remind herself again he wasn't one of the bad guys, "Garrett, helped him. Asher and Nathan had come, too. They helped all the women they rescued get home. I didn't have a home to come back to. I asked to go with them to Alder Ridge."

"The news said they never found Tyrone and are still looking for him. Do you know where he is?"

"He's dead." Maggie squirmed, trying to free herself. Caiden latched back onto her hips.

"You're not going anywhere, nymph."

Caiden had listened, but Maggie didn't want to see if he believed her or not. She meant it when she told him he'd helped her. It felt good to be around him. She was vocal, a little brave. And being desired by someone was a high she never wanted to let go of.

"Maggie, stop struggling." He didn't need to raise his voice to snap out a command. His hands tensed and moved from her hips to her waist. Maggie peeked up and gasped. Fury dashed through his eyes. "How did he die?"

"I didn't see it. I'd passed out. But I think Zachary and the others killed him."

"Good. Although, I wish I had been there."

Maggie's body drooped as her muscles warmed and her shields fell. He believed her.

CAIDEN HELD MAGGIE, keeping his hand still, so he didn't hurt her with the fury running through his blood.

"You haven't had much of a life, little nymph." He hoped the sneer on his lips as he spoke didn't scare her.

"No." Acceptance came through the matter-of-fact response.

"This is your start. And you've had to jump back into the past."

"I had started a life in Alder Ridge." Pulling her cheek between her teeth, she tilted her head.

"But is that what you wanted?" She hadn't looked happy there.

"What do you mean?"

"As a kid, what did you want to do? Where did you want to live?" What would her life have been like if Tyrone hadn't interfered?

"Get out of Tyrone's reach. That was all. After that, I could go anywhere and do anything."

"Well, here you are." Caiden spread his hands to encompass the world for her to take. They landed back on her hips, enjoying the shock that zinged between them.

Her eyes widened.

"You hadn't thought of it that way, had you?"

Maggie shook her head.

"It didn't seem like life was going anywhere for you in Alder Ridge. Not with all of them coddling you. Do they treat Holly and Ezaray the same way?" He already knew the answer.

Her little nose scrunched up. "No. They don't know everything, but they know Tyrone was my step-brother."

"They're imagining the worst." He hadn't known Tyrone and sure didn't know how he'd treated the women. Imagination based on the news reports was all he had. Some of the others in Alder Ridge had seen what she'd been through first hand. Of course they would imagine the worst.

"Yeah. I never told them. I only wanted to move on."

"Doesn't look like you're able to do that." Maggie hadn't been living while he'd been there. She'd tried.

"Not unless I left Firebrook and Alder Ridge."

Caiden ignored his lurching stomach. Moving on is what she had to do, and keeping her wasn't an option. But he was already in too deep not to help her. "Maggie, I don't think you can move on until you face it. And you need to do that here. Stay a while. Prove to them you're strong. You'll prove it to yourself too."

Maggie sagged, her muscles releasing any energy they had left now that their conversation was over. "I don't want to. But I think you're right. The only time any part of myself shows through is with you. Why is that?" She tilted her head up, wide eyes pleading with him for an answer.

He didn't want to tell her there was a fated connection between them he intended to break. It was possible that connection gave her some instinctual trust in him that allowed her to be herself. Caiden hoped there was more to it than that. Whatever would help her was a good thing. Her being his mate didn't matter.

Maggie's tongue traced her lips. Caiden groaned. "I don't know why, nymph."

Her breathing sped up and her hips moved under his hands, sliding her centre along his already hard cock. She froze when he growled. But he didn't want her to stop. Using his grip, he moved her back and forth, letting her feel it all.

"Time for a shower before I fuck you again. I'm sure your body needs a break. I haven't been easy."

"I never wanted easy."

A rumble rose in volume and he stood, lifting her with him. Stalking to the bathroom, he dropped her into the shower. He stripped them of their clothes before turning on the water.

Maggie braced her hands on the wall to steady herself.

"We're just washing, little nymph."

"If you say so, grizzly." Her mocking tone said she didn't agree. Caiden breathed deep through his nose. He would control himself.

Nudging her under the water, he took the half step back that the small shower allowed and leaned against the wall, crossing his arms over his chest. "Wash up."

"You're not helping?" She tilted her head to the side. Shadows still danced in her eyes from retelling her past. She was looking for a reprieve. He hated to deny it. For now.

"No."

Her flirty expression diminished, and she reached for the soap. Ah, fuck. Her body must be sore. He needed to give her a rest. Caiden promised he'd make it up to her. Later in bed. No, tomorrow. Tomorrow night. She needed rest.

His mind swirled with what he'd do to her the next time they came together, and he'd missed watching her wash. He realized she'd finished when she moved toward him with a soaped up loofah.

"No. You get out. I'll wash myself."

She pretended to think about it, then shook her head. "No." She moved the loofah up and down his chest, then outward to his sides. Maggie covered every inch of his upper body, even reaching behind him to get as much of his back as she could when he refused to cooperate and turn around.

Caiden saw her intent too late and missed catching her when she dropped to her knees in front of him.

"Stand up. Now."

No answer came from her—not a look, not a shake, not a word. She only ran the loofah up over each leg until they were coated. The last thing she paid any attention to was his erection that hardened to painful proportions. She dropped the loofah and, with soapy hands, ran them up and down his cock.

"Maggie." It should have been a warning, but her name came out as a prayer.

"I've never done this before."

"Good." He didn't want to imagine his nymph, his mate, on her knees in front of another man. He didn't want to think of the men that would come after him, either. But that's what letting her go would mean. Be with her now, but she would belong to someone else.

Her hand shook as she moved it lower to cup his balls. His head smacked against the wall. Her light touch and slow strokes were driving him mad. Just as he was about to put an end to it, Maggie stood and pulled him under the water. She waited while the soap slid off him.

Caiden reached around her to turn the water off, but her small hand landed on his wrist. Her fingers only wrapped half-way around him. He narrowed his eyes. He couldn't take any more of her torture and still keep his control.

Maggie dropped to her knees again and engulfed him in her mouth. He let out a low roar and threw his hand out to the far wall to catch his balance. Leaning forward created a new angle. Her head tilted back and his cock slid into her throat.

Small hands squeezed his thighs. Her nose flared open and pulled in air. She'd figured that out quickly. With effort, Caiden straightened to give her room to work. The heat was too tempting to leave.

Maggie moved her head back and forth, taking him to the back of her throat each time. After a few strokes, she used her tongue along the underside.

So tentative. So slow. So tortuous.

Both fully under the spray, the water hit his front and slid downward, colliding with Maggie. He slapped one hand against the wall beside him and the other formed into a fist. He couldn't take over, take this from her. She trusted him and had the confidence to show it. Ripping himself from her and demanding they take a break would hurt her. Would hurt him, too.

Her suction pulled, straining for his climax. Her tongue and teeth only made it easier for the animal in him to rise. He could break her, and it surprised him he hadn't already. He hadn't been gentle, and he wouldn't be now.

"I'm sorry, nymph." His hands fisted in her hair. Taking control, he tilted her head back further and reared over her, thrusting deep. Gripping his thighs, she tried to hold herself up, but it was the hold he had in her hair that kept her in place. She relaxed her jaw and breathed shallow breaths through her nose. Her eyes watered and he filled with primal satisfaction.

"Swallow, Maggie."

Caiden exploded, keeping his eyes locked with hers. He stilled at the back of her throat and watched her work his pulsing cock. With each pull, he grew more sensitive. He groaned, not ready to release her. But he was spent.

Pulling free from her mouth, he helped her stand and held her under the water against his chest. His heart pounded, and a mating chant ran through his blood. Caiden didn't want to let Maggie go. Not now. Not ever.

CHAPTER 14

He knew. Everything. And he didn't push her away, make excuses and run out the door. Caiden hadn't even offered sympathy. Anger, yes. But he told her of her own strength, giving her courage to continue on with him. To continue on here in Firebrook, at least for a little while. Maggie would have to return to Alder Ridge, eventually. And soon. When she did, she would demand better for herself.

Caiden had left before dawn, kissing her neck to say goodbye. She hadn't opened her eyes, only moaned as he nipped her skin and whispered in her ear that he'd see her later.

After she'd showered and dressed, she checked her phone to see a message from Caiden.

Get yourself some breakfast. Come to the restaurant if you have to.

It wouldn't be easy to continue to face the public here, but that's what she was going to do. She knew her truth, and that was all that mattered. What happened to her throughout her life with Tyrone was none of their business.

Maggie called Kayla and then Mr. Whitehall to tell them she wasn't heading back to Alder Ridge right away and would be available in town for anything they needed. Kayla asked her to meet her within the hour to go over the official offer put in by the tenants. Then she messaged Caiden.

I'll get breakfast in town.

Her phone dinged as she stepped out the door.

Raise some hell, little nymph.

Maggie grinned at her phone. She wouldn't purposely cause trouble, but she understood what Caiden meant. Don't back down. Don't stay quiet.

Kayla offered to meet her at Bella's Bakery, stating it was much better to go over contract details with caffeine and sugar. Maggie agreed, preparing herself for a similar episode to the day before. Keeping her head up, she walked through town. Hiding behind sunglasses, she could look where she wanted and not have to worry about averting her gaze from the locals. Most ignored her, some even smiled as if passing by anyone else in town. But there were a few who made their opinions clear in their expression. The same mix of sympathy and sneers.

Kayla already sat at a patio table outside of the bakery. Two coffees and a small white box sat on the table.

"Thank you for meeting me here instead of the office. I try to get out of it whenever I can, so when I find clients who like to discuss over coffee, I jump at the chance." She pushed the coffee closer to Maggie and opened the white box to reveal four different flavoured scones. "I didn't know which you'd like, and I'll eat any of them. They're my favourite."

"Mine, too. Thank you." Maggie smiled back and reached for a scone.

"I lie to myself about how much I come here. I say it's once a week. It's not." Kayla pulled out a scone.

"Your secret is safe with me. This has always been my favourite place in Firebrook." Because of her mom.

"Do you remember when we were kids and it was only Bella working here?" Maggie hadn't been friends with Kayla growing up, but they knew each other as children. "That woman could be stressed and flustered and she'd still stop and greet every customer that came in."

"I remember. She always handed out scones for my mom and I before we could order." Bella had been her mom's age. She'd taken over the bakery when the previous owner died, but couldn't afford to hire any staff. Her husband helped her when he could, but this place was all hers. Even while raising her two daughters. Town members pitched in when they could and eighteen months after taking over, Bella hired her first employee.

Kayla placed her hand over Maggie's that held her coffee. "I'm sorry about your mom. Dealing with this must not be easy."

"Being here isn't easy." It should be her mother and the house that made this difficult. It wasn't. And that wasn't fair that yet again her time for grief was stolen. "But I barely remember the house. It isn't the source for memories of my mom."

"Let's get to it, then. Once I told the tenants you were willing to sell, they were quick to come back with their offer and conditions before I discussed a list price with you." She flipped through the first couple pages to find the right number to point at. "This is their offer. They've based this on the sale of other houses in the neighborhood and the report from the inspection. I still have our inspector booked, but they hired their own about a month ago. So, this offer comes with conditions." She flipped the page and pointed to a list.

Maggie read them over.

"The inspector pointed some of these out and others are things the tenants themselves have asked the previous landlord in recent years to fix or replace."

Panic bubbled low. Maggie didn't have the capability to do these repairs or the finances to see them through.

"They'd like this done before finalizing the sale."

"What happens if I don't meet some or all of these conditions?"

"You don't have to accept the offer. You can come back with a counter offer."

"Oh. Okay."

"Are there any of these conditions you are willing to meet?" Kayla took a sip of her coffee and looked at her with patient eyes.

That was the problem. It wasn't a matter of if she was willing. She couldn't. "Do I have to come back with a counter offer right now?"

"No, of course not. You can take this and look it over. But for now, how about I show you the rest of the contract and what a counter offer would look like?"

Maggie sipped her coffee while Kayla talked on. She absorbed every bit of information she could. It would make it easier later when she called Shaye to ask her for advice.

So engrossed in their conversation, Maggie hadn't noticed the two women at the table behind her until they'd finished and Kayla had left. Their whispers hovered while they stared.

"I'm happy to see you selling the place. That couple deserves to have their home." A woman a few years older than Maggie sat at another patio table. Her friend sitting across from her leaned forward.

"You'll be free to leave town again once the sale is final. Accept whatever offer they give you."

"Why would selling the house mean I'm leaving?" She didn't have to leave. The money from the sale could buy her her own place. Wherever she wanted.

The two women reared back.

"Maybe you two can talk some sense into the poor girl." Sam Tulk, the man she and Caiden ran into on the way back to her cabin last night, stopped at the women's table. "She needs to leave town for her own good. Caiden Greer is taking advantage of her."

"Poor girl? You mean she…" The woman looked at Sam and wobbled her head.

"*She* is right here. And I can make it all clear to you and anyone else who wishes to discuss either my mental abilities or my loyalties. I am neither of those. Not a single word spread about me through this town is true and never has been. All three of you, and anyone else who wants to join you, can take your opinions and shove them up your ass." Maggie spoke with perfect calm and clarity, and even ended it with a smile. She closed the box on the last scone and held it with the papers against her chest. With her coffee in her other hand, she forced easy steps as she walked away.

Clapping and a whistle sounded from some of the other tables. She saw two of the three full tables sending her approving nods and applause. She may have spoken with clarity and calm, but her voice had risen. Letting out a sigh, Maggie left.

If she allowed herself even a minute to think about what she'd just said, she'd give herself the shakes. As soon as she was back in her cabin, she called Shaye and asked her about the offer and what she should do for a counter offer—not giving herself even a moment to dwell on what just happened. She was strong, and she needed to act like it.

"Maggie, if you can't meet any of those conditions, then you can't do it. I would go back with at least the same amount and no conditions. But give me a little bit to do some market research to make sure they're offering a fair price."

"Thanks, Shaye."

"No problem, Maggie. I'll call you back later today."

She hung up. With the need to keep herself busy, she went in search of Wyatt at the main lodge. She needed to discuss payment for the cabin. It didn't matter they intended it to be free. She wanted to give something.

Wyatt was behind the main lodge. He swung an axe over his head and down, splitting the log to fall in pieces to the ground. Maggie called out while he had the axe angled toward the ground.

"Hello?"

Wyatt lifted his head and a smile that Maggie didn't think his brother was capable of split his face. "Miss Maggie. What can I do for you?" He put the head of the axe against the round stump he'd been chopping on and leaned on it with one hand on the handle.

"I was hoping you had a minute to talk, but if you're busy, I can come back later." She didn't want to come back later. She wanted to keep doing something to occupy her mind.

"Not too busy to stop and talk. Is something wrong?"

"No. I just want to settle on a payment for the cabin. As much as I appreciate it, I can't accept it for free."

His smile vanished, and his eyes narrowed as he lifted

his chin. His lips pursed beneath his beard. Maggie fought the urge to squirm as he studied her.

"I'm not sure when I'm going back to Alder Ridge. I don't need to stay here and it doesn't feel right to stay here for free when it isn't necessary."

"No. I can't accept anything for it. That's what the cabin is there for. Try not to worry about it, Miss Maggie." His lips twitched, pushing away the seriousness with which he'd studied her.

Maggie wanted to argue further, but she had nothing to counter him. "There must be something I can do as a thank you."

Wyatt opened his mouth to answer, but a deep roar from inside the trees cut him off. He tensed and spun toward the sound. A second roar joined the first. Wyatt searched the area.

"Go get Caiden." His deep voice matched his brother's. "Now." Wyatt toed off his boots and ran into the woods.

Panic had leapt off Wyatt in waves and hit Maggie in the chest. She bolted away from the lodge and hit the path from between the cabins. She ran, harder than ever. Her lungs seizing. It was up to her to get to Caiden in time. But for what, she didn't know.

"Okay, everyone. We've got two orders of the salmon sandwich and two deluxe bison burgers." Caiden pinned the order up on the board. The day was beautiful and with it came a new arrival of tourists that morning, which made the lunch rush busy.

Caiden's only warning was a waft of Maggie's scent before the back door opened, slamming against the wall. He whipped his head around to see her wince at the sound and try to catch the door to bring it back.

"Maggie?"

"Something's wrong. Your brother needs you."

"Jay, you're in charge." Caiden abandoned his kitchen, ushering Maggie out the door. With no one around, he gripped her shoulders. "What happened? Where is he?"

"I don't know what happened. We were behind the lodge and we heard two roars. He told me to come get you before he ran into the woods."

The pairs had called for them. Caiden would get to them faster if he shifted and ran through the woods from here. "Go back to your cabin or go into town. Don't come near the woods." He pushed her toward the path and turned himself to the trees. But Maggie gripped his arm to stop him.

"No. I'm coming, too."

"No, you're not." He pointed down the path and pulled his arm from her grasp. Inside the trees, he took a moment to make sure no one was around. He started stripping when he sensed Maggie behind him. "Go home, nymph. I don't know what's out there and I don't want you getting hurt."

"I'm coming, Caiden. Like it or not."

He hid his clothes and faced off with the tiny redhead. Her eyes flamed and strength held her body upright. The change in her since he'd met her gave him a glimpse of the woman she should have been all along. And fuck, was she ever fierce.

"Go back now, Maggie."

"No. Grizzly." An infinitesimal shake twined as she used her name for him. She took a solid step forward. "Shift. I'll follow."

"You're too slow, and you'll get lost."

"Then I'll ride on your back. I'm sure you can carry me. Hurry up, Caiden. You're wasting time arguing with me."

Caiden ground his teeth. Gripping her chin, he forced her head back to meet his eyes. "You do as I say and stay where I put you. And you don't wander off on your own. Got it?"

"Got it," she whispered. He took a moment to enjoy her reaction—her heated eyes, her quickening pulse, and her body leaning toward his despite his harsh grip.

Caiden released her and stepped back, letting the magic pull from his core to reshape his body. He groaned when his bones popped and joints realigned. Less than a minute later, he landed on the ground on four paws. Crouching low, he waited for Maggie to get on his back. He growled quick and sharp to get her attention when she drifted toward him, still in awe from watching him shift.

Snapping out of it, she climbed onto his back and wrapped her arms around his neck. Even with her tight grip, Caiden didn't run at full speed for fear of knocking her off. But they made good time through the trees. As he got closer to the lodge, Caiden slowed. Lifting his nose in the air, he searched for Wyatt and the others. He found their trail and stalked after them.

What's going on? He stayed standing to keep Maggie on his back. If they needed to move, he didn't want to waste time for her to get on. She straightened and held onto his fur.

They think they saw the hunter. They chased after him for a while.

That was dangerous. Caiden eyed the pairs. They could have gotten shot.

His gun wasn't loaded. He was staking out this spot and sighting in the rifle. He hadn't been here long.

So he'll be back. Can we track his scent?

Maybe. He's masked it. It will take some time to track him down now that he's back in town.

Just as long as we do before he goes on another hunt.

Caiden crouched down to let Maggie off. Then all four bears spread out, searching the ground and trying to find the hunter's scent to make sure they recognized it the next time they came across it. Maggie stayed close to him. They found three different spots he'd settled in. Scrapes on the bark of trees and bent bush branches were signs of where he'd set his rifle, let alone the smell of the gun. His scent was faint, coated with cologne. Caiden couldn't recall anyone in town that used something that strong. But his natural scent was there, difficult to pinpoint.

Getting frustrated with finding nothing more than the last time they searched, the four of them met back at the initial site.

We need to set a trap. Caiden didn't want any of them getting hurt. Or chance Maggie getting hurt in the crossfire. The stubborn nymph that refused to stay behind.

Agreed. You two stay on this side of his sites. He's pointing to the water in each one. Stay above here if you see him, but don't let him out of your sight.

And don't let him see you. It went without saying, but Caiden felt better giving the reminder.

"There's something here." Even speaking to each other in this form seemed quiet. So when Maggie spoke, all four heads swung toward her.

She crouched down. A clunky chain chimed off her fingers. Colour flashed as it swayed back and forth. Maggie stood and held it in front of her, using her other hand to cradle it. It couldn't be what Caiden thought it was, but his denial didn't stop him from shifting.

His breath heaving in and out of his nose was the only sound filling his ears as he picked up the charm bracelet from Maggie's palm. He ran his thumb over the blue lily charm—the last one he'd given her. A Laura Lily, he'd called it. The bracelet had been missing since Laura was attacked. She'd worn it that day, but when they recovered her body, it wasn't there.

Caiden had given her the charm bracelet when they were fourteen. Each year, sometimes twice a year, he'd added a new charm. He'd only ever looked at Laura as a friend. A good one. One of his best friends. He'd never realized how deep her feelings went for him.

Where had this bracelet been all these years? And how the hell did it end up here? The sight of her attack was at least three kilometers south.

Caiden closed his fist around the charms and looked up at Maggie. Her bright, innocent eyes were like a slap to the face. He was going to hurt her, too.

"It's time for you to go back to Alder Ridge." Coldness slowed his words. The same coldness that seeped into his chest, warring with him. No matter what he did, he'd hurt her. Sending her away now would just make the pain a little less. But he hadn't expected the pain that assaulted him as he told her to leave.

Maggie staggered backward. "That's what you think, grizzly." Then she turned away and walked toward the cabins.

"Maggie," he snapped. "I told you not to wander off."

"Then you shouldn't have told me to leave."

Caiden growled and stalked after her, but she ran as soon as his feet moved over the ground. She was surprisingly quick as she hurdled over bushes and some fallen trees. Her body angled to move herself around trees that were in her way. Caiden shifted and gave chase—his four paws closing the distance between them. A new thrill at chasing his mate gave way to a primal instinct. He was so messed up when it came to her. It was a wonder she hadn't told him to fuck off a long time ago.

Only a few feet ahead of him now, she jumped another fallen tree. Caiden intended to catch her, but what he would do with her when he did, he didn't know. Pack her in the truck and drive, or lay her out in her bed and bury himself inside her.

STUPID. Just as she'd accused Asher and the others of lacking bear smarts, here she was running from a grizzly bear. She'd forgotten the animal he was. Maggie had been so adamant to follow Caiden into the woods. All she knew was that she couldn't leave him.

Surprising pain blew up in her chest when he told her it was time for her to leave. She'd already promised herself that no one would make her decisions for her again. She'd leave Firebrook when she was ready, and not because he thought he wanted her gone. If he didn't want her near him, then fine.

But as soon as his growl hit her in the back and the sound of his heavy steps from his bare feet followed, her own need to get away forced her to run.

Bad idea. She no longer had a man coming after her, but a bear. A bear that had devoured her in the most delicious ways. And yet, had just tried to order her out of town.

Something about that charm bracelet spooked him. Enough to change his mind about her.

Her lungs hurt, but she kept going, weaving around a skinny tree.

Caiden bolted up beside her and spun the back end of his body around. Dirt flew in the air from him skidding in a stop to cut her off. His lips around his snout lifted. A predator trapped her.

Maggie lurched forward, planting her feet to keep from colliding with Caiden. She turned her shoulders to carry her weight and bring herself upright.

Pain, burning and slicing, hit her upper shoulder. The air flew hot past her ear. Three identical roars echoed from behind them, and Caiden's delightful sneer lowered. He stepped forward, gripping her shirt in his teeth. Pulling her forward, he broke her fall with his body.

Maggie swung her leg up and gripped his neck. Turning her head, she saw blood coating her arm. The moment had shot her with adrenaline, recognizing danger before she'd known what it was.

Caiden turned and ran toward the treeline, toward the cabins. His paws thundered over the ground. Another shot sounded off, but it didn't land near them. Roaring followed. She hoped none of those were roars of pain.

He landed on his belly and nudged her off. Shoving her in the back, he shifted.

Maggie kept her eyes off in the distance behind them, rather than moving forward.

"I told you to get moving."

"No, you pushed me." Her arm had turned numb.

"Same thing, nymph. Now, go." He planted a foot in front of him to urge her forward.

"What about you?"

"I'm right behind you."

"You're naked."

"Go!" His voice wasn't his own.

Maggie ran to her cabin, but didn't go inside. She stopped at her door and waited for him. He surged through the trees and ran to the cabin.

He wrapped an arm around her waist and lifted her inside.

"The bastard shot you."

"He wasn't aiming for me." All she needed was the reminder for her arm to scream out.

"Sit." He commanded her, yet he put her in the chair himself. Retrieving a first aid kit from the bathroom, he crouched in front of her.

His eyes changed as he cradled her shoulder in his hands. They smoldered and swirled, echoing the pain she felt in her arm.

"It's just a graze, but a deep one. You don't need stitches though." He opened the kit and pulled out some cotton pads. Pouring one of the liquids from the kit, he avoided eye contact. "This is going to sting."

He dabbed around the wound first before cleaning the inside. He was right. It stung. But it wasn't the worst she'd felt.

Maggie winced, but controlled it. The only difference between now and the past two years was the person treating her.

She'd always blocked out Garrett, lumping him in with her brother and the handlers of the underground organization. But she couldn't block out Caiden.

One hand held her under the arm, lifting it away from her body and keeping it where he needed. Warmth from that touch spread, calming the sting and joining the pain. His thumb drew slow circles, giving her something to concentrate on. Otherwise she'd concentrate on his nearness, his kindness, the gentle way he cared for her, and the way he rushed her out of danger when he should have been chasing after the hunter. But what good would thinking about those things do when he'd told her to leave Firebrook?

Whatever they had was over, as far as he was concerned. But she wouldn't leave on his terms.

Maggie wanted Caiden. At least for a little longer. She wouldn't expect forever. But she found companionship, giving her strength to continue to move on.

"This doesn't hurt?" He paused and frowned up at her, making eye contact.

"I've had hundreds of injuries like this. I barely feel what you're doing." She could block out the injury and the pain, even if Caiden's nearness was all consuming.

"So you'd fight, and they'd fix you up?" He finished cleaning the wound.

"Garrett did."

Caiden's spine straightened, and he lifted his head. Every muscle coiled with a tight threat.

"He blackmailed him." Maggie rushed to explain. "Garrett helped us escape."

"I'm going to need more than that, but it can wait." His focused went back to her arm.

"You'll have to ask him, anyway. I don't know what Tyrone had against him."

Caiden grunted and opened a bandage. Placing it over her wound, he used butterfly tape to hold it in place. With it so high on her shoulder, wrapping it wouldn't work.

"Where was he shooting from?"

"Opposite side from where we thought he'd be. I have to go help the others. You stay here. Don't go anywhere and don't open the door for anyone." He didn't point his finger at her to declare the order, but it shot from his eyes instead.

"Why would someone come looking for me?"

"I don't know. But until we find him and figure out his goal, you aren't to step foot in the woods again."

"Caiden, I'm not..."

Caiden gripped her neck and pulled her close, slamming his mouth down over hers. The intense exchange leaked frustration. But it didn't lack the heat that lived between them. "Shut up, little nymph." He whispered against her lips.

Her half-lidded eyes watched his brighten as they looked over her face and landed on her shoulder. After a low growl, he left the cabin without another word or a chance for her to argue. Staying out of the woods would be safer for both of them until they caught the hunter. Not that he gave her a chance to point that out.

Fine. She wouldn't follow him into the woods, but she wouldn't sit here and wait for him like a trained woman.

CHAPTER 15

Caiden checked the area after stepping out the door of Maggie's cabin. With no one around, he darted back to the woods and shifted. He needed to find the others. But they found him first.

We lost him. He must have been close to the treeline on his way out.

Saw an opportunity and took it. Caiden thought of what the hunter would have seen at the time he took the shot. He saw a grizzly bear chasing after a woman. That wasn't enough for Caiden to forgive the guy. He shouldn't be out here scouting the area to begin with. *Did you find where he was at the time?*

Yeah.

Caiden followed Wyatt and the pairs. The ground wasn't packed down like the others, but the scent was stronger. Just as he thought, it had been a shot of opportunity. An opportunity Maggie gave him. He should have forced her to stay behind. This is what happens when Caiden is responsible for someone. They get hurt.

The kiss before he left her had been a goodbye. It had to

be. If she wasn't involved with him, then she wouldn't be in the line of fire.

Desire had raged through him as he fed the passion. Each touch, each kiss, each time he entered her body, their bond grew. He didn't know what letting her go would mean, or if it was possible at this point. But he had to try. For her. The reminder of Laura was all he needed to convince himself.

We need to get the scouts in place. Make an ambush easy the next time he comes out. Less chance of someone getting hurt.

Agreed. We'll set up a rotation. Huck nodded.

Be careful. Wyatt bumped the other bears. *I'll talk to Beck and the other wolves.*

Caiden went back toward the restaurant to retrieve his clothes. Then he needed to check on Maggie.

He poked his head through the back door to see how the restaurant was doing. He'd left in the middle of a lunch rush. They seemed to have it under control, so he left, saying nothing. He ended up running the path back to Maggie's cabin. Not bothering to knock, he opened the door.

The air was stilted. Maggie wasn't there. The cabin didn't have many rooms. The main level, the bathroom, and the loft.

"Maggie?"

No answer. He checked the bathroom, then climbed a couple steps on the ladder to make sure she wasn't asleep on the bed. Where the hell was she? He'd told her to stay here. Why couldn't the woman listen?

The hunter hadn't come this way. The cologne he used to mask his scent was strong enough for them to track back into town. He hadn't come near the cabins. But Maggie could have crossed his path in town.

Muscles throbbed and his insides convulsed. Caiden

spun around in the void cabin. He hadn't even claimed her as his mate, and he was already getting her in trouble. He'd lost her before he ever had her. There wasn't time to dwell on what he'd do to her if he found her.

He stopped at the lodge to get Wyatt's help. Her scent filled his nose, the fan from the air conditioning unit blew it at him. He paused and sighed, one long breath that dispelled the urgency, calming the convulsing panic. Turning his head, he saw Maggie and his sister sitting together in the main lobby with coffee in their hands.

"What the hell do you think you're doing?"

Dakota snapped her head around, but Maggie only brought her coffee to her lips. She took her time with the sip, holding it in her mouth for a moment before bringing her cup back down to her lap. "Having coffee. Want some?"

"I don't drink it. It's disgusting."

"Says you." Maggie took another sip.

"What are you doing here?" Caiden closed his eyes, hoping to find patience instead of letting his anger out on the mutinous nymph.

"I already told you. Having coffee." Her placate posture pissed him off.

"I told you to stay in your cabin."

"And I didn't listen." Her stubborn chin lifted, baiting him.

"Clearly." His upper lip lifted to stretch out the sound.

"She's safe here too, Caiden." Dakota stood and blocked his path to his mate.

"Stay out of this, Dakota. Time to go, Maggie."

"No." A calm tone flew from her contradicting the anger in her eyes.

"Yes. You have packing to do. I'm taking you back to Alder Ridge tonight."

"That's not your decision to make." Now he heard her voice break.

Caiden side-stepped his sister and towered over Maggie. He pried her coffee from her hands and set it down on the end table. Cupping her chin, he leaned her back and followed the motion. One hand braced on the back of the couch, he pushed until she slouched against the cushions.

"That's where you're wrong. This has gone too far and the best decision is for you to leave." The words scraped painfully over his raw throat. Deep down, he didn't want her to leave, and he didn't want to be the one to take her back. But taking her back would keep her safe. Claiming her as his own or not, she was still his mate, and the need to protect her pounded in his chest. He couldn't say he didn't understand her need to defy him, but he wouldn't excuse it when it kept her safe. His mate was getting far away from him.

"YOU WILL NOT INTIMIDATE ME." A lie, a terrifying lie. But the intimidation didn't reveal itself in the form of fear. It was more like anticipation. He may say he wanted her to go, but raw heat simmered along his skin. Caiden was just as torn about them as Maggie. "You are not taking me back."

"Maggie, I'm trying to keep you safe. He shot you, in case you forgot."

"I didn't forget." While the burn was only a low hum to her as she had so many injuries like it before, she still felt the pain and the pull to her skin when she tried to move. "I'm not going back to sit on my hands waiting to hear if you got the hunter or if the hunter got you."

"Too bad."

"Who did the bracelet belong to?" Maggie softened her tone.

Caiden released her chin and shoved off the couch.

"None of your business." He turned his back on her.

"I'm making it my business." Maggie gave his own line back to him. He reached in his pocket and kept his hand there. His pocket and hand muffled the light clink of the chain.

The front door opened, and Dakota ran toward it. Caiden didn't look up from the floor, but Maggie saw Dakota push on her other brother's chest. "Why the hell can't I go in my own lodge?" Wyatt's grumble moved further away.

"You've been hot and cold with me since we met, that's fine, but that bracelet made you want to drive me from town. Why?"

"Having feelings for me will only get you hurt one way or another. You need to go home."

"I'm not leaving simply because you say so, grizzly."

Caiden spun around, and Maggie had to step back from his gaze. His locked jaw reflected the pain swirling through the green of his eyes. "You don't understand. And you're not going to because you need to leave."

Maggie didn't think he was aware of the pain he exuded. Or aware of his surroundings—he didn't budge when Wyatt and Dakota sneaked back inside. They watched their brother with a sympathy that was painful even to her. Sympathy wasn't a good gift like some thought. She didn't want people's sympathy, and she couldn't imagine a man like Caiden wanting it, either.

"Let's go, nymph." He reached for her, but Maggie stepped back. She let a smile play on her lips, intent to calm the storm brewing inside him.

"No. I'm not leaving town until I'm ready. If you want to stay away from me, that's fine. But I'm staying."

"You don't know what you're doing."

"You could tell me." She allowed everything to drop for that one moment, just enough to show him he could trust her.

"No."

Maggie shrugged and sat back down on the couch. Reaching for her coffee, she looked back at Dakota and Wyatt, hoping they wouldn't side with his brother out of pity and kick her out of the cabin. Wyatt cocked his head and left the building out the back door. Dakota poured more coffee and stood to the side, waiting to see what her brother would do.

Maggie had no logical reason to stay or to push against Caiden, but she grew stubborn roots around the man. And she wasn't ready to pull herself free.

THE SAME WOMAN he'd met only weeks ago didn't stand in front of him now. Each time she spoke, a new flicker brightened in the fire at her core. And he loved her fire. Unless she threw it at him and stood her ground. She was beautiful when she did it, but he needed her gone. His mate needed to leave. Her heart wasn't safe from him. Hell, his heart wasn't safe. He loved her spark and sass, and he was falling in love with her.

It was already too late. But he had to try.

He fingered the charm bracelet in his pocket. Laura had been in love with him and she'd been so young. Maggie hadn't experienced this side of life. As far as the concept of love went, she was still sixteen.

"I don't do relationships, Maggie." Caiden didn't miss the pinch in her eyes. She bowed her head and covered it with a sip of her coffee. If he wasn't so in tune with her body, with her emotions—if he couldn't feel them like they were his own, she might have fooled him.

"That sucks for you." Maggie tilted her head to the side. "I didn't ask for one."

"I'm trying to send you home so you don't get hurt."

"I can handle a little hurt."

"Bullshit."

"Screw you, grizzly." Quiet anger seeped over the rim of her mug, but she controlled her body, keeping herself still on the couch.

"I've hurt someone before. I don't want the same thing to happen to you."

"The owner of that bracelet."

"You don't deserve that."

"I'm sorry you feel that way, but it isn't your decision to make."

"Now isn't the time to stretch your independent muscles, nymph."

She pinched her lips between her teeth. Her gaze locked on his while she set her mug down. Her pupils narrowed, showing off the bright green. Face to face with the part of Maggie he loved, Caiden swallowed, surprised that nerves pushed down on his chest.

"I am not leaving Firebrook until I'm ready. I'm on my own just as I should be and these *independent muscles* aren't something to practice with. With me, you can't decide if you're hot or cold. Until you can, keep your indecisive ass to yourself." She sidestepped around Caiden and left, passing a wide-eyed Dakota on the way.

Once the door shut, Wyatt appeared in the back door. "Smooth, brother."

Caiden ignored his siblings. The last thing he wanted was to evaluate his past with them. The bracelet in his pocket made him see Maggie as Laura. Caiden gave his little nymph a head start, then followed. She stalked on the gravel, even her angry steps light and careful. He kept himself far enough back and to the side that she didn't see him. As soon as she closed her cabin door and didn't venture into the woods, he turned to go back to the restaurant. Where he intended to spend most of his time until Maggie returned to Alder Ridge.

CHAPTER 16

Maggie tried to return to her routine she had in Alder Ridge, minus the job. She contacted the realtor with her counter offer on her mother's house. She didn't have the funds or resources to meet any of their conditions. The sale had to be as is. But Shaye researched the market, and their offer was a fair one without doing the renovations they requested. That had been two days ago.

And two days was all it took for Maggie to get bored without a job.

There'd been no sight of Caiden since their fight in the lodge. She still had a bandage on her arm, but it was healing exceptionally well. She considered leaving Firebrook, now that he kept his distance. But Maggie knew there was more that she wanted from her time here. So what if he didn't do relationships? She'd never asked for one and hadn't been hoping for it either. But she gained so much for herself by being with him. Maggie didn't want to let that go. Not yet.

That left her back where she was when the hunter showed up and she got shot. Asking Wyatt how she could compensate for her stay at the cabin.

"I'd love to have someone fill in at the front desk of the lodge. I'm still trying to get some of the cabins ready, but we have a lot more guests already showing up."

Maggie pinched her fingers, using the pain to dispel her panic at taking a job that dealt with the public. But at least they would be tourists and not locals. "I can do that."

"I could also use someone to help with a few errands from time to time when Dakota finds herself busy."

"Oh. I don't know how to drive."

"What?"

"I never learned."

"Well, Miss Maggie. It's time you did. If you want to, of course."

Maggie nodded. Driving hadn't crossed her mind, not since she was a teenager. She'd been so focused on maintaining her routine in Alder Ridge, she hadn't considered learning something new.

"Okay." Wyatt waved at the main building. "I could use you at the desk today and tonight I'll give you your first driving lesson."

Maggie went inside and settled behind the desk, taking the time to find everything. Wyatt gave no instructions on how to do the job, but it seemed straight forward. Answer the phone, record reservations, answer questions once she found out the answers for herself. Odd excitement filled her at the thought of learning to drive. Although she wished it had been Caiden that insisted on teaching her. Maggie wouldn't turn down Wyatt's kind offer, despite him being the wrong brother.

Only two of the reservations that afternoon required her to find out information for them. The rest, she already knew. Firebrook would be full of activity for the season. Maggie longed to be part of it. There was a home here for her she never had a chance to love. A love for it grew inside her now. But if she were honest with herself—it wasn't just a love for the town. Caiden rarely left her thoughts.

There were many reasons to stay, but Caiden was at the centre. He believed her feelings to be childish. She'd let go of childish infatuation a long time ago. Developing a relationship hadn't been what she wanted, and she believed it was too soon. She'd watched her friends fall head first and fast after finding their freedom. Maggie had different priorities. But her uncontrollable connection to Caiden and her desire for him dug roots in her soul—alive, real, and thriving.

As if she'd summoned the mountainous grizzly with her thoughts, he walked in the front door.

"Wyatt, I need help with repairs at the restaurant. My…" Caiden stopped and slammed the door shut behind him. "What are you doing back there, little nymph?"

"Working."

"Working?"

"If you have a problem with that, talk to your brother." Maggie finished transcribing the reservations she'd written in the paper ledger to the computer system. Since she wasn't familiar with their system, it was more efficient to write the information down and transcribe while no longer on the phone with guests.

"Are you ready, Miss Maggie?" Wyatt walked through the front, smiling wide at her and Caiden.

"Ready? For what?" Caiden may have asked his brother, but he looked at her. She didn't answer. He wanted distance between them. Maggie would keep that distance for as long as she could. When he didn't get an answer, he turned to give Maggie his back and talk to Wyatt. "I need some help at the restaurant if you have some time."

"Give me about an hour or two."

"What are you doing?"

"Miss Maggie is getting a driving lesson," Wyatt announced proudly.

"A what? From you?"

Maggie put the computer to sleep and walked out from behind the counter and past Caiden. She tried not to feel his heat or pull in his woodsy scent. She tried not to flex her hand with the need to touch him. She tried to push him away with her thoughts, hoping there would be enough coming off her to make him take a step back. Instead, his hand snaked out around her waist.

"Why do you need a driving lesson?" He spoke low. The deep hum warm against her cheek.

"To fly, grizzly." She kept walking. His hand slid off her. He kept the contact to the last fingertip, ensuring the sensation of his hand wouldn't go away soon.

His muscles ached. His body hummed with the need to shift often, but they'd agreed to stay out of the woods for a while, unless it was their shift to keep watch. Each day that passed with Maggie spending time with his brother and not him tightened the pain. The distance was his own doing, not hers. He couldn't blame her for trying to make him jealous, if that's what she was doing. But jealous he was—of Wyatt. Caiden wondered if she felt the same pain as him. It grew like a monster trying to take control. He heard it roar at night when he wanted to rest. The animal side of him agreed. He needed his mate.

The thought of the hunter helped push aside the need for Maggie. Frustration mounted with no more sign or scent.

They couldn't find the cologne he'd used to mask himself in the woods. He'd hand-picked it to cover his tracks.

Scouts roamed the woods. They often rotated shifts with their pairs. After talking to the wolf shifter pack outside of Firebrook, some offered help as scouts. The threat of the hunter looking for shifters had been enough. With Noah, Tavis, and their pairs, they had more than enough scouts to stay vigilant. The hunter wouldn't slip past them next time. If he'd only go back to the woods. If he didn't show soon, Caiden was prepared to use himself as bait to draw him out.

Caiden had his suspicions about the hunter. He didn't believe the guy was looking for shifters. Only for Caiden. Laura's bracelet being found wasn't a coincidence. Caiden searched for that bracelet himself after Laura died. But if the hunter was looking for Caiden, then he also knew what Caiden was. Which would put all the shifters in the area in danger.

Caiden left the restaurant, deciding to take the rest of the day off. He hiked to the lodge, intending to talk with his brother, convincing him to let Maggie go, and evict her from the cabin. She'd completed the sale of her mother's house. She wasn't safe here, not until they dealt with the hunter.

Their dad's old beater farm truck lurched back and forth in the middle of the road in front of the lodge. With the windows down, Wyatt's instructions filtered out. And so did the satisfying scent of apples and spice.

Caiden ripped open the driver's side of the door. "I'll take it from here, brother."

Maggie fumbled with the shift and the pedals, making the truck lurch once again. He kept his grip on the door and followed the forward movement.

"Shh. Breathe." His own body calmed now that he was within touching distance of his mate. His exhalations hushed out of his nose, the sound coming from the back of his throat.

Caiden hadn't noticed Wyatt leave, only that the passenger seat was empty.

"Stay calm, little nymph. Don't watch the gauges, just feel the truck, and listen. She might be old, but she's vocal." Once Maggie's breath matched his, he shut her door and went around to the other side. "Smooth transitions on the pedals and ease her into first."

He rested his arm across the back of the bench seat and ran his fingers up and down the side of her neck. Her pulse jumped, but soon evened out when he didn't stop or change the pattern. She did as he told her, this time her work on the pedals easier. When she reached the end of the lane without incident, she put the truck in reverse.

"Has Wyatt been making you go back and forth on the lane?"

"Yes."

Caiden closed his eyes instead of letting loose the curses and choice names for his over-patient older brother. "No. Put your signal on. We're turning right."

"We're going into town?"

"Yes." He kept the same movement of his hand up and down the back of her neck. Now that he touched her, he couldn't stop.

"There are a couple things wrong with that."

"Oh?"

"I suck. And I don't have a license or even a learner's permit."

"You don't." She'd only been nervous. "And that doesn't matter. Go." They'd worry about getting her a learner's permit another day.

"I'm going to cause an accident," she muttered, but put

her right turn signal on, anyway. The highest speed limit in town wasn't over sixty kilometers per hour. It would make for a sweet and simple driving lesson. "Can you hear the change in the engine?"

"I think so."

"You should be able to feel it too."

"Yeah." She nodded, her eyes darting from the road to the truck and back.

"Time to shift gears. Smooth on the clutch and put it into second."

Maggie rounded her lips and blew out quickly when she made the move without an issue. "That wasn't bad."

"No. It's not hard."

"It was back there."

"Why was Wyatt teaching you to drive a stick?" That had been the last thing Caiden expected to find.

"Because I asked him. My step-father had one. He promised to teach me one day."

"Ah." They drove down the centre of town, Caiden giving hints when she needed to shift. He realized the date as some of the shop owners carried tables across the street to the town park. The annual summer fire festival was in a few days.

"I forgot about this." Maggie's whispered words sounded more like she was making a wish. "I was ten the last time I went to the festival." With the road now clear in front of them and Maggie watching the people setting up booths, the car behind them honked, holding in the horn for dramatic effect.

Caiden growled. He didn't like being disturbed from the view of his mate, lost in time.

MAGGIE TIGHTENED her hands on the wheel and turned her attention back to the road. The horn blaring behind them stopped, but when Maggie lurched and had to try again to get going, the horn blared again.

"Maybe you should drive us back."

"No. He can wait. If it's an emergency, he'll pass you. Ignore him." Caiden's fingers massaged her neck. Points of heat dripped down her spine. The sick ache in her stomach that had plagued her since he walked away from her melted. She hadn't expected permanency from him, seeing their relationship as a way to keep moving forward. But the way her body reacted to him screamed that this was more. Now that he was no longer ignoring her, she felt the truth. She loved him.

Maggie tried again to get the truck moving, pulling in the calmness he fed her. But her realization shocked her system, keeping her on edge. "I'll try again later. I can't do it right now."

"Don't let cowardice out, my mate. You can do this."

"Cowardice?" She dropped her hands and turned toward him, ready to point out the true coward between them. But the rest of what he said echoed in her mind. Her anger vanished and her lungs seized. "What did you call me?" She quieted her voice, afraid of what he'd say.

Caiden's lips flattened and his eyes flashed. "Nymph."

"Nope. No, you didn't."

"I did." His brow raised, as if trying to convince her to go along with the lie.

"Why would you call me that? What does it mean?"

"Nothing. It means nothing."

Maggie watched every move Caiden made, searching for a tell. And he had many. A ticking jaw, a storm in his eyes, and a low hum coming from his chest. Mate. He was part animal, part nature. Just as the shifters in Alder Ridge were. The quick relationships of her friends made sense. Holly and Ezaray hadn't latched onto men for safety after the escape—at least she'd thought it had been for safety. They were mates. In a flash, Maggie reevaluated everything that had happened between her and Caiden. He'd known all along what she was, but fought it.

Her hands shook as she stumbled out of the old truck. Once she stepped around to the front, the guy behind them zoomed past, veering to avoid oncoming traffic. Traffic that slowed to watch Maggie pace the pavement in front of the truck.

"Maggie, get in the truck. I'll drive us back." Caiden reached for her shoulders, but she twisted away from him.

"How long have you known?"

"Known what?" His eyes were rarely wide, but right now he looked like a trapped animal.

"Don't play stupid, Caiden. You're not."

"Maggie." His low warning didn't stop her.

"Okay, next question. Why didn't you tell me?"

"I didn't want to hurt you."

"Because you plan on sending me back to Alder Ridge." Maggie lifted a hand to the throbbing mark on her neck, changing the gesture at the last minute to rub her shoulder. "It isn't nothing, is it? These haven't gone away."

"I'm so fucking selfish." Disgust twisted his features before his eyes flared while staring at his marks. "I don't want those to disappear, proof that you were once mine. But I can't do this. You have to go back."

"Selfish? I'd say. You can add idiot, arrogant, domineering, stubborn, secretive." She ticked each off on her fingers.

"Keep going, nymph. You're missing all my good qualities." His eyebrow curled upward.

"Good? Lying isn't a good quality."

"I've never lied."

"Are you really stupid enough to claim that omission isn't lying?"

Caiden straightened, acceptance squaring his shoulders.

"Why?" Maggie had to swallow to hold back the emotion drowning her voice. "Why get close to me at all?" She didn't allow that question to reach the onlookers. "You've planned on pushing me away from the beginning. So, why?"

"I didn't have a choice. I couldn't resist you. I love..." Caiden choked, his eyes bulging. Taking a step back, he cleared his throat. "Your sass. Your snark."

"Now who's the coward?"

"Get in the truck, Maggie."

"No. I'll walk."

Caiden gripped the back of her neck. "In the truck or I'll put you there myself."

Maggie didn't weaken as he plunged his hand into her hair and pulled. She heard the gasps from the surrounding crowd, but didn't care. Their opinion didn't matter. "Tell me the truth. Here and now. What am I?"

"Don't ask questions you won't like the answers to. Are you going to get in the truck on your own?"

"I'll answer yours if you answer mine."

"I'm not playing around, nymph."

"Neither am I, grizzly. I wear your marks. So, what am I?"

"You're my mate." She didn't recognize his voice. He sounded more like an animal than man. The force of those three words hit her in ways she wasn't ready for. The power behind them setting her world to rights. "You're infuriating."

"Apparently that's what you love about me."

Caiden growled—his upper lip curled. Maggie glimpsed

a sharp canine before he lowered his head and kissed her. Each time they came together was otherworldly, but this had meaning behind it, even if he wasn't ready to admit it. His lips firmed and his beard rubbed against her. When his tongue plunged into her mouth, she lost her balance. For a fraction of a moment, the only thing holding her up was the grip he still had in her hair. He wrapped an arm around her waist—his limb creating a solid bar.

A fresh buzz of need drowned the murmurs of the crowd. It had only been days since they'd been together, but to her aching body, it had been years. Her core throbbed, her pulse thumped. His erection throbbed against her. Maggie let her hands trace up his arms. Feeling bold, she pressed her fingers against his skin, tracing each muscle until she reached the back of his neck. Caiden tilted his head and deepened their exchange. Sweet excitement simmered like a slow storm.

Releasing her hair, he slid his hand down around her ass and lifted. He stalked to the passenger side of the truck and put her inside. "You don't understand what you're getting yourself into." He nipped her lip, then swung her legs inside.

"And you've underestimated this."

Slamming the door, he glared at the crowd. Once they moved, he went to the driver's side. A quick U-turn put them back on the road to the lodge. But that wasn't where they stopped.

"Caiden?"

"No talking."

They went inside her cabin. He stood away from her. Each time she opened her mouth to talk, he held up his hand to stop her. His newly shaped eyes raked over her. Maggie felt as if he saw beneath her clothes. He'd already seen it all—clothes didn't matter anymore. So why did she gasp and her skin shiver when he reached out and gripped the hem of her shirt?

All harshness from the argument in the street had left his face. Encompassing heat and determination replaced it. She could feel what he was going to do to her. The images flashed through her mind. He grinned with a sinful expectation that showed off his growing canines. Those things would bring her to her knees. And she didn't mind the thought of going to her knees in front of Caiden.

Time paused intermittently with each piece of clothing that hit the floor. Her shirt, then his. Her shorts. His jeans. Standing naked, he claimed her mouth again while his hands claimed her body. His imprint seared her skin. Boneless in his arms, she concentrated on his wandering fingers, opening further to him when he traced her ass and dipped toward her centre.

He slipped his fingers inside her, but it wasn't enough. She wanted more, needed more. She needed him to see what was between them. If Maggie saw it through her filtered vision, then he could, too.

"It's going to be now, nymph." He spoke against her lips and removed his fingers. Lifting her under her ass, he carried her to the ladder. Maggie latched onto his shoulders, preparing for him to climb, but he set her on a rung. He buried himself inside while she was still trying to get her balance. Her moan cut off into silence. Every sensation exploded from where they joined to fill her head, her heart. With the time spent apart, it multiplied. But it was all so clear. Mates. It was why he'd pulled her onto the deck at Asher's. It was why he kissed her, touched her, claimed her. But it didn't explain why he continued to push her away. Not again. She'd get the truth from him.

He thrust hard, grinding against her clit. Maggie met his eyes. A few weeks ago, their intensity would have scared her. Now it was what she craved.

Maggie was floating, climbing, falling, flying—ecstasy that held her on a precipice. Each stroke of his cock gave her something more. She couldn't hold back. Not from her climax, and not from him.

"Caiden. I love…"

"I know, little nymph." He set his forehead against hers. "I can feel it. But please, don't say it."

Keeping the words hidden didn't make it less true, but she'd give him this, for now.

With a tight grip on her hips, Caiden angled her, tilting her against the ladder. Her hands left his shoulders to grip the wood. She tried to pull back, to reduce the overwhelm on her body. His cock hit a spot that released rhythmic shocks.

"You can't get away from it, mate." Like the promise that it was, his words set off an explosion. Maggie rocked against him while clinging to the ladder. Her thighs tightened around his hips, holding him against her. She feared if she released him, he'd push her away again. Maggie wouldn't accept it so easily next time. Not now that she'd found love this true.

CHAPTER 17

Caiden rode her climax. He feared what he'd do when he stopped. She loved him. He was too late. And he loved her. But he wouldn't admit it. Caiden wasn't so sure he could let her go anymore. But what pain would that bring to them?

Her heat contracted around his cock. He didn't stop, thrusting into her next climax. Burying his face in her neck, Caiden allowed himself to follow. Despite his weakening body, he didn't let go. She slumped against him and he used all his strength to hold them there, together and connected.

"Caiden." Her sleepy whisper beckoned him.

"Not yet."

He moved his hips, eliciting groans from each of them, both oversensitive from the effects of orgasm. But with his legs on the verge of collapse, Caiden changed his grip to wrap an arm around her waist and climbed the ladder.

Laying her in the bed, he considered taking her again. He was ready. He would never not be ready. But as she looked up at him, he sensed her question before she spoke.

"Why? Why do you push me away?"

"I've never wanted this… this connection."

"What happened to the girl who owned the bracelet? And who was she?" Maggie ran her hands down his face. Caiden settled beside her, resting on one arm and pulling Maggie down on his chest.

"A friend from high school. Her name was Laura." Caiden hadn't recounted these events since the week it happened. "We were close, but only friends. At least on my part. I suspected she had feelings for me a few times, but I ignored them and things would always return to normal. I didn't think continuing our friendship the way we were would do any harm. I gave her that bracelet, and each year I gave her a new charm on her birthday or other special occasions." Caiden didn't pause. If he was laying all this out, he wanted to do it quickly.

"She came to me one day and laid out her feelings. I never knew they were that strong. I felt horrible that I couldn't return them. I just didn't see her that way. Laura didn't hold back. And I let her talk. When she finished, I sat her down and told her I didn't feel the same way. I tried to be gentle. She was important to me and the last thing I wanted to do was hurt her. But that's what I did. She ran off, straight for the woods. I let her go, knowing she only needed time.

You know that wind that shows when I shift?"

"Yes."

"It showed up only minutes after Laura left. A warning. By the time I got to her, it was too late. She'd run in the path between a mama grizzly and her cubs, startling them all. The mama took offense. I'd shifted as soon as I was far enough into the woods. I attacked the bear and scared her off, but it was too late. Laura was gone."

"Oh, Caiden. I'm so sorry."

"She was precious. I miss her."

"It wasn't your fault. But this isn't the same situation. Stop pushing me away."

"I'm going to try. Every time I try to get rid of you, I'm beyond happy when you push back." He wasn't ready to give promises. He'd admit to himself he loved her, but that's as far as he'd go. A lifetime of boundaries and feeling guilty for Laura falling in love with him wouldn't be easy to break. "You should get some sleep, little mate. Before I decide against giving you a break."

Maggie nipped his chest, then her lips moved over his skin when she smiled.

Caiden closed his eyes as she settled against him. He was trapped, stuck with a mate he wasn't supposed to have.

MAGGIE DROVE the old truck to the town centre with a load in the back. Caiden sat in the passenger seat and Wyatt drove behind them. They had enlisted the brothers to help build a few new stands and repair old ones. They also provided their own that included maps of the trails and info on safety in the area.

Caiden spent the past two nights in her cabin with her. He kissed her after walking her to the lodge and leaving for work. Eating breakfast in bed, laughing at each other, showering together, all little things that made her ridiculously happy. A normal life. One her past couldn't touch. Maggie felt hope. Caiden hadn't made her any promises, but they were together. Maggie didn't need to push him. They both knew they loved each other. That was more than enough for now.

Maggie parked the truck and turned the key. Lifting her

hands like she surrendered, she waited for the truck to protest, telling her she did something wrong.

"Good job, nymph." Caiden hadn't had to instruct her the entire drive.

"Thank you." She tried to keep a straight face, but her cheeks hurt as she beamed at him. His returning smile was full of indulgence and love, even though he wouldn't admit it aloud. Maggie saw it, felt it. An odd instinct had grown between them. They could read each other.

The wound on her arm had healed. No way did she believe that was normal—for a wound that deep to heal in only days. Being a mate had magical perks.

Caiden opened the tailgate and pulled out the planks of wood. Maggie grabbed his toolbox and followed.

The day heated without a cloud in the sky or a breeze. Dakota lent Maggie some clothes to work in—old baggy overalls and a camisole. She was glad for the breathing room in the clothes. With three booths built, Caiden passed her a can of paint and a brush.

"We'll paint all of them grey then the owners of the booths can paint what they want on them."

"Okay." She paused before moving to the first booth they built.

"Is something wrong?"

Maggie spun around, stopping when she saw Caiden's toolbox. "Nope." Searching through the top compartment, she found the flathead screwdriver she needed to pry open the can. She grabbed a nail and stuck a hammer under her arm. Maggie turned her head over her shoulder to grin at Caiden. He nodded and moved off.

Tuning in to the people working around her, she set a steady pace and lost herself in the job. She listened to an older couple argue over which side of their booth to put the cotton candy and where to put the barbeque. The argument didn't last long. He soon said, "Of course you're right, dear," and kissed her on the head.

"Oh, stuff it, you old goat."

Maggie outright laughed, holding the back of her free hand against her nose when she felt a snort trying to escape.

A group of teenagers pushed wheelbarrows of wood to the centre for the bonfire, muttering complaints as they passed.

"Maggie Scott?"

Maggie turned her head and saw a middle-aged woman standing with her hands clasped in front of her. Taking in her position, Maggie stood. "Yes."

"I'm Bella Boone. I own the bakery. Have for almost twenty years." Bella tilted her head and her eyes turned downward.

"I know. I remember you."

"I remember you too, and your family. You used to come in with your mother. I heard how my staff treated you last week. I want to offer my sincerest apologies. I don't understand it, and I'm ashamed of my staff."

"Thank you. That means a lot." Bella had been the face of the bakery when Maggie had been a child. This was the first she'd seen her since returning to town.

"You let me know if you have any more trouble the next time you come in."

"I won't." Maggie smiled softly. "It will just take time for some people."

"You're a mighty strong young girl. Especially if you're taking on one of the Greer brothers." Bella's brows rose in one motion, and her lips flattened into a low smirk. She walked off. Maggie went back to painting the last arm of the booth. The hope she'd felt for her future grew more with the acceptance of even one person. She didn't need it, but it helped and would go a long way to making life easier for her if she stayed in Firebrook.

Lifting the can of paint, Maggie moved on to the next booth. Caiden had finished building the last one and was now helping with repairs to older ones. She remembered some of these booths. So much stayed the same over the years. She looked forward to the weekend to take part in the festival.

"You missed a spot, little nymph."

Maggie turned around, putting herself right in line with Caiden's paint covered finger that swept over her nose.

"No, grey doesn't suit you." He stepped closer.

"Funny. What colour do you think would be better?"

"Red. Blue. Something bright and bold." With a gentle hand cupping her jaw, he kissed her. His tongue licked along her lips as if searching for a taste. She felt his focus, his concentration on keeping the kiss simple. With the paintbrush still in her hand, she lifted it to tap the side of his neck. He didn't jerk away, only smiled against her lips. "Do you think the colour suits me?"

"No. Green is definitely your colour." Maggie tilted her head back and kissed him. "I need to get back to work before the paint dries."

"Yes, you do." He released her. "Are you looking forward to the festival?"

"I am. I hadn't realized how much I missed it until I saw them setting up."

"What used to be your favourite part?"

"The bonfire. And the marshmallows. I made myself sick off them almost every year." Maggie scraped the excess of the brush and continued to paint. "What's yours?"

"When all the tourists leave and even most of the locals. Some of us keep the fire going all night."

"I like the sound of that."

"I thought you might." Caiden tugged on a curl that fell from her bun, then left. She watched him go, enjoying the delicious thoughts that crossed her mind. He had a fine body, and it was hers to explore.

She pulled her attention from him, a smile still playing on her lips. But the sensation of being watched made her pause. She tried to look around, but no outward stares of people stood out. Maggie took the paint and moved to the other side of the booth, hopefully putting her out of sight. She hadn't felt that odd shiver since Tyrone first took her away to his fighting ring.

CAIDEN HAD to tamp down Maggie's emotions that ran through him. Her excitement and wonderment as they walked through the festival were simple to handle, but her trepidation grated. She still worried how others would treat her, despite many already acknowledging her as an equal. He had to admit, he saw some looks and heard some whispers, but they would die off with time. If she stayed here.

He'd struggled after telling her about Laura. The guilt he felt was real and still there. It didn't matter it wasn't his fault. He knew that. Always had. But he missed her most days. Maggie didn't push him to let her go. She only asked that he stopped pushing her away.

He had. He accepted the idea of a relationship. The chance of her getting hurt scared him. And with the hunter searching for him, the risk was greater. But now that he'd let her in, he saw a future. His imagination created portraits and landscapes, snippets of a happy life. Caiden wanted it. He held the images in suspension, for now.

They'd arrived at the festival with Wyatt and Dakota. The Bearbrook Cabins booth didn't need to be manned. It only contained brochures and a few free souvenirs. Wyatt joined the crew building the bonfire, and Dakota found Bonnie and friends. Caiden held Maggie's hand and took her to each booth, only stopping when he felt her heart jump. They played a few of the games and ate as much food as they could.

The Firebrook Festival was a tradition they all treasured, a time when locals came together and showed the outside world what it was like to be part of this community. Despite their judgment toward Maggie, they were usually a friendly community. And the longer Maggie stayed, the more the whispers receded to gatherings behind closed doors.

Music played, people danced, and alcohol appeared when the sun set. Hours of festivities that wound down to a small portion around the bonfire.

A couple played their guitars and their daughter sang. Caiden took Maggie's hand, pulling her up from the log she sat on.

"What are you doing?"

"We're dancing."

She laughed. Caiden held her against him, leading her through the quick steps. Wyatt grabbed Bonnie Boone and swung her around on the grass. That was all it took for people to pair off. Only a handful still sat, clapping along with the music.

Noah swooped in and stole Maggie, laughing as he danced her away. Others followed his lead and before long they were passing partners around like it was a game. Kayla, Bonnie, and Dakota snatched Maggie and pulled her into a middle circle before they all spun around and found new partners. Even Tavis was pulled up from the logs to dance.

He'd seen Maggie smile before. He'd even seen her laugh. But he hadn't seen this much joy light her eyes. Her skin flushed and her head swiveled, watching him, their feet, the other people dancing. When she looked at the musicians, the fire reflected in her eyes, flickering in a dance of its own.

His chest hurt, a spreading ache that took over his body. It was all for her. His mate. The one he loved, but couldn't admit it.

The music changed—the family switching to a slow tune, altering the atmosphere. It seemed like the fire moved to match the new air.

Caiden reclaimed Maggie and didn't let her go. Her laughter slowed, and she looked at him. He moved them in slow circles, swaying in a way that allowed their bodies to rub against each other. Her softness cradled his hardened body. He realized they wouldn't be staying the night by the fire like he usually did.

Her breathing quickened despite their slow pace. Her fingers tightened on his shoulders. The need to join didn't come only from him. He felt it from her. Could smell the desire pooling between her legs. Caiden could carry her off then and there, but he waited. He kept them moving, building the anticipation between them. The marks on her neck called to him. A song pulling him deeper.

The music stopped and couples returned to the fire, but Caiden didn't let go or move with the group. He kept Maggie against him and moved his hands to roam her body. One splayed over her back, keeping her in place, and the other tensed over her hip.

"I'm ready to get out of here."

"Me too." Shallow breaths pushed her breasts against his chest. She gripped his upper arms. Caiden tilted his head and devoured her lips. The softness against him forced to calm himself, slow the kiss and tune into her emotions. No emotions other than love for him surfaced, but he felt the sensations he caused inside her. His blood echoed hers.

Whistles and calls pulled his attention away, but he didn't release her mouth. Ignoring the crowd, he cupped her ass and lifted her against him. His cock searched for her heat, despite the barrier of clothes and the mostly drunk audience behind them.

He broke the kiss, only to watch where he was going as they left the festival. The need and desire were too strong to wait to get back to her cabin. The warm night had a bright sky of stars and an almost full moon. His restaurant was closer on this side of the lake. He walked there, passing it to go into the woods.

"I need to be inside you, Maggie."

"Make it quick, grizzly."

Caiden chuckled and set her down on a grassy hill. When he started on his clothes, she pulled at hers.

"You're not the only one who can't wait."

On his knees, he moved up her body, stopping between her legs on the way. He lapped at her wet centre. A few quick pulls on her clit, and he covered her body, thrusting and filling her. Maggie cried out, but Caiden slapped a hand over her mouth. They were alone. No one nearby, but with the festival and the amount of drunks roaming the town, he wouldn't take a chance of someone finding them.

"You need to be quiet, little nymph."

"No promises."

Caiden took her wrists and lifted them above her head. Holding her in place, he pounded into her, reaching for a peak he couldn't find. Thankfully, the grass was soft beneath them. He gave no mercy as he claimed her body. His teeth lengthened. He checked their sharpness by running his tongue over each of them.

Her heat clamped around him, sucking him back in each time he pulled out. Her body quivered, ready for release. Release for both of them was held back, frozen in place.

"Caiden." Maggie cried out his name. The animal in him growled with satisfaction. But neither of them moved closer to climax.

The breeze rose around them, warm and gentle. Maggie opened her eyes to meet his, then looked beyond him. Caiden turned his head and saw his wind. The translucent green danced with the same seductive motions they had by the bonfire.

Words floated through his mind, and the need to speak pounded in his throat. Maggie's lips moved, struggling with the same sensation.

Bound and blessed. A mate's promise. A vow, a chant, a promise of commitment, of responsibility. His lips moved, ready to say the words.

"Bound..." Caiden fought it.

"Blessed..." Maggie started her own. He heard the promise running through her mind as clearly as he heard it in his.

The wind hugged them, the colourful magic filling them.

Caiden growled. A promise like this would make her irrefutably his—his responsibility to protect, to keep safe.

"No!" His roar cut off her words and broke the chant in the air. He let go of her wrists and pushed himself away. The wind shattered. It faded into broken pieces. Caiden stood and looked down at his mate.

Pain flashed over her features. The flush in her skin drained, not only from her cheeks, but it slid down her body. She braced herself on her hands, closing her legs and pulling them to the side.

"Caiden? What happened?"

"Nothing happened."

"That wasn't nothing."

"It doesn't matter. But whatever that was, won't happen again."

Caiden backed away from her. She shivered on the grass, hurt by him. Just as he predicted.

CHAPTER 18

"What are you saying, Caiden?" Her wrists ached from his harsh grip and her core throbbed from him tearing himself away. She'd heard the words, felt something amazing run through them. They'd joined, not only physically, but emotionally. His heart pounded as if it had been inside her own chest. The words still echoed in her mind, wanting to be free. She understood them. She had to admit, it was too soon for that kind of promise, even for her, but she had trust in what this was, trust in Caiden that everything would be okay.

"It's wrong. The wind, Fate, whatever controls this—it's wrong."

Maggie reached for her dress and pulled it over her head. Caiden didn't move. His chest heaved and his muscled bulged, tension pulling him apart. "I don't understand. How could it be wrong?"

Caiden's eyes lowered. Darkness took over the beautiful green. His jaw set as he straightened his shoulders and clenched his fists. Shadows covered them both, the moon's glow barely breaking through. Maggie looked up. The same green wind that enveloped them spread out above them.

"Caiden?"

"I won't be responsible for anyone."

Pain, followed by searing heat, filled her ears. He ripped himself from her, broke the bond forming between them because he didn't want the responsibility. That's all she was to anyone. Someone to look after. She thought it had been different with Caiden. He pushed her, argued with her, made her better and stand on her own. But as soon as things got too real, he was just like everyone else.

"I am no one's responsibility." Maggie didn't recognize her own voice. A lowered feminine snarl full of bite and power. She slipped on her sandals and left, stalking past him back toward the festival, abandoning the rest of her clothes. Not intending to join the others around the fire, but in the hope it would keep Caiden from following.

He vibrated when she passed, the shock of his anger lashed out at her arm.

"You have to understand."

"Oh, I understand. You're just like everyone else."

When he started after her, despite being naked, Maggie ran. Once she broke into the street, he stopped—she assumed for his clothes. Maggie ran until the festival was in sight. After that, she walked and hoped Caiden wouldn't catch up before she made it back to her cabin. On the road to the lodge, she turned around. Bright green eyes glowed in the dark. He watched, but he didn't follow.

Maggie shook her head. Why bother following her if she wasn't his responsibility? Because he cared. He more than cared. He loved her. But allowing the feeling to live was too much for him. Maggie deserved more.

She allowed the tears to release inside her. She wasn't

numb, but letting them out to the world she wouldn't do. Grabbing her phone off the table, she stared at it, knowing she needed to call someone to come get her. Who was the question. They all cared for her and she knew by calling one, she was calling them all. They may be a family that coddled her, but they cared. She called Ezaray, guilt plaguing her over the late hour.

"Hello?" Zachary's sleepy tone answered her friend's phone.

"Hi. I'm sorry. Is Ezaray there?"

"Maggie? What's wrong?" Zachary's words didn't slur. They came out sharp and alert.

"I should have waited until morning. I didn't need to wake you."

"Do you need to come home?"

She didn't have a home. For a short time, Alder Ridge had been home, but Firebrook had taken its place. Until tonight. "Yes. I need a ride, though. I'd like to come home tomorrow."

"Are you okay? Are you hurt?"

"I'll be fine." With time.

"Okay." Solid security settled through the line. The same as he'd been when he rescued them from the fighting ring. He'd promised to be there to help her whenever she needed. She needed him, them, now. "We'll be there in the morning."

"Thank you. Goodnight."

Maggie locked the cabin door before taking a shower. She smelled like Caiden, and the last thing she wanted was to sleep with his imprint.

There wasn't only pain from losing him coursing through her. She'd fallen in love with Firebrook again and had been looking forward to making a life here. Even if things hadn't worked out with Caiden, she never imagined being ripped apart so harshly. All because of some stupid notion he had. She could take that kind of opinion from the locals here, the people she didn't care about, but not from him.

Maggie didn't have the strength to make it up the ladder to the bed. She crashed on the couch and hoped to get some sleep before she needed to pack. But struggling for a couple hours was all she could take.

It didn't take her long to pack. Her single bag had grown to two. Half of one contained the gifts she'd bought for Holly, Ezaray, Gwen, and Shaye. Dressed and ready to go, she still had hours to wait. Zachary didn't say what time they'd be here, only that they'd come for her in the morning. Maggie laid down on the couch again and tried not to think about Caiden. But the bearded grizzly wouldn't leave her mind.

His aversion explained his behaviour toward her, and losing someone so special under those circumstances gave him the aversion to commitment. Not because he didn't want to commit, but he didn't want to take on the responsibility of a person and lose them. Understanding his reasons didn't excuse him.

After tossing and turning for a while, Maggie sat up. Her stomach rolled, nausea welling up. A headache formed at the base of her skull. Shaking it off and taking a deep breath, she went to the kitchen to make herself some tea. She needed to rest, to calm herself.

Leaving with Zachary and the others was the right thing to do. Maggie didn't deserve to be treated like a burden. But the thought of not going back to Caiden physically hurt. Bile burned as she prepared herself to leave.

She couldn't fix him. If Caiden wouldn't see her as a

capable equal on his own, as she thought he had, then Maggie couldn't change that.

Maggie closed her eyes and tilted her head on the back of the couch after sipping her tea. Holding the hot mug between both hands gave her a sensation to focus on. She'd rather the heat of hers and Caiden's bodies, but the tea would do.

Someone knocked on the door. Maggie jumped, then winced as her tea spilled, burning her hands and lap. She assumed it was Caiden and didn't move to answer it. Going to the kitchen, she grabbed a towel to dab at her legs.

They knocked again.

Maggie frowned. Whoever it was, was persistent, but it didn't carry the determination of the bear shifter she knew.

"Who is it?"

Another knock answered.

Disappointment clanged when she didn't hear Caiden's rough voice saying, "Let me in, nymph." Maggie gingerly walked to the door and opened it a crack. Sam Tulk stood on the other side.

"Sam?"

"Miss Scott. Maggie. May I come in?"

Maggie held the door tight, keeping it open only an inch. "No."

"Please. I need to speak with you."

"It's still very early. Can you come back in the morning?" The sky had only begun to lighten with the sun just below the horizon. Hopefully, by the time Sam thought to come back, she'd be on the road to Alder Ridge. He made her skin crawl. Something wasn't right with him.

"This is urgent." Sam shoved the door open from her grasp and stepped past her into the cabin. He shut the door and blocked her way. "You have to come with me."

"No, I don't." Maggie braced a foot back. She'd fight her way out of the cabin if she had to. Right now, he only seemed deranged, desperate. His hands shook when he stepped to the side to peer out the window.

"It's for your own good."

"Lots of people believe they know what's good for me. They're wrong and so are you."

"You'll be safe from him. Come with me now."

"You need to leave, Sam." Maggie's muscles tensed, ugly memories instructing her body. She may hate the ugly beings, but right now they were right to take control.

Sam's fidgeting stopped. His body stilled, and when he lifted his head, he seemed to grow. "You are coming with me one way or another."

Maggie hid her readiness with her hands still at her sides. Sam reached for her arm. She swung that hand up and out, blocking his hold. His brow quirked, and he tried again. She blocked, but he didn't wait to make another attempt. Maggie blocked him effortlessly. Pulling her leg up, she managed a quick front kick to dislodge his balance, putting some distance between. She settled into a stance that felt too comfortable for her.

"Leave now and leave me alone."

He shook his head, and pity filled his eyes. "No, I won't do that." His tone thickened with a modified pout. Then he came at her. His longer reach gave him an advantage, but she held him off, giving her time to study his movements and posture. He wasn't trying to fight her. He was trying to grab her.

Maggie managed a punch across his jaw. She threw another one to the throat as he turned his gaze back to hers. He choked and anger flared. He took punch after punch, but reached for her shirt before she jumped back. Pulling her forward, he wrapped an arm around her shoulders when she lost her balance.

"Stop fighting me." He squeezed and got her feet off the ground.

"No." Maggie reared her head back and slammed it forward on his chin. His roar echoed, then faded to a hum when pain fired in her temple and the world went black. Blackness used to be a haven for her. This time, it terrified her. Now that she knew there were people in the light that cared about her. Even if one of them was an idiotic grizzly bear.

CAIDEN PUSHED THE PAIN, the ache, and the bile down. It would all pass. But the need to shift, to roar into the wild and let his animal free, almost controlled him. He'd seen Maggie go into her cabin. That was the last of his responsibility to her. Over the past few days, he'd let go, let her get close and allowed their connection to grow. Staying silent hadn't changed it.

Dim, grey light shone through the windows when Wyatt came home. Morning was near.

"What the hell happened?"

"What are you talking about?" Caiden didn't lift himself off the couch.

"I saw Maggie walk through town last night. Hell, I smelled her. So did Noah and Tavis. She smelled different. She has since you two got together, but last night was strong."

"What do you mean?"

"She smelled like a shifter."

The mates in Alder Ridge had that odd wild scent, but

missed the full animal. The wind, the bonding of the night before—that must seal mates together. They'd at least started the process. "Fuck."

"What did you do?"

Caiden should get mad at his brother for assuming he'd done something wrong, but he was right. "I've broken it off with her."

"Why?"

"You know why." Caiden closed his eyes and threw his arm over his head. He didn't need to hear a lecture from Wyatt right now.

"No, I don't. If this is about Laura, you're wrong. You know that."

"I don't want to go through that loss again. And this time would be worse. I didn't love Laura the same way I…"

"The same way you love Maggie? Then it's already too late. You're the one putting yourself through that loss right now. You're in pain." It surprised Caiden that Wyatt recognized that.

"I'll go through it now and it won't hurt later."

Wyatt's humourless laugh reached him. "You're an idiot. I'd bet she's in just as much pain as you. Probably more because she isn't a shifter."

"And not yet a full mate." Guilt assailed him. "She'll be fine with time."

"Don't make me hurt you, Caiden." His big brother tone wasn't quite the same anymore. A genuine threat flowed behind it. "What happened to Laura was rare and had nothing to do with your feelings for her. Maggie isn't Laura and you aren't kids."

"I won't be responsible for her getting hurt."

"Listen to yourself! Don't you see the irony?" Wyatt slammed his hands on the back of the couch.

"Time just needs to pass. I won't be responsible for her." Caiden's deadened monotone rasped against his throat.

"I doubt she'd let you, anyway."

"What?"

"That seems to be the exact situation she's escaped and I can't see her allowing anyone to take control of her again."

Her words flashed back at him. She wouldn't be anyone's responsibility. There hadn't only been anger in those words, but disappointment—in him. He'd been harsh. Ripping himself away from her was bad enough, but his reason implied he believed she needed someone to watch over her. Caiden had to make this right. She needed to know he wasn't like everyone else.

"I'll talk to her in the morning."

As Caiden lay on the couch for the last hours of the night, the pain in his chest and stomach worsened. Panic set through his blood, but he ignored it. It rose only because he let her go. He should be with her now, taking them both to unimaginable heights of pleasure. Caiden rubbed his chest, pressing hard to push away the pain.

The sun made its appearance, piercing his heavy and sensitive eyes. He ignored Wyatt in the kitchen when he went to shower and dress. He'd stop at Maggie's cabin on his way to the restaurant and make things right—offer help to get her back to Alder Ridge.

"Good luck," Wyatt called as Caiden shut the door.

Taking the day off sounded like a good plan. He'd check in with the scouts about the hunter. But he'd rather get lost in his busy kitchen. There were more distractions there to keep his mind off his mate.

Caiden knocked on the door and waited. He listened, but no sound came. Knocking again, he kept it gentle. He didn't have the right to demand her anymore.

He cleared his throat, trying to dislodge the burning pain still searing his chest. When he knocked a third time, and she didn't answer, Caiden turned the knob. It wasn't locked. The emptiness encased him the second he stepped inside. The cabin was clean. The bed upstairs made, and her bags missing. She'd already left.

His stomach rolled and his chest inflamed. Rubbing the pain away, Caiden left. He didn't give himself a chance to pull in her scent one last time.

The cabin shook as he slammed the door.

He stopped on the gravel. Wyatt and two others walked up from the main lodge. Caiden frowned when he saw Zachary and Nathan.

"What are you two doing here?" Not the most polite greeting, but Caiden didn't care.

"We're here to pick up Maggie. Your brother said she's staying here." Zachary's smile wasn't really there, only politeness toward someone who fucked up.

"She called you?"

"Yes. A few hours ago. We left right away."

"Is she waiting in your truck?" Caiden looked behind them. They'd already gotten her. They had no reason to come back here, unless they wanted to lay in on Caiden for hurting her.

"No. We're here to pick her up." Zachary pointed at the empty cabin.

"She already left."

"Not with us." Nathan's low tone shed light on the danger this meant.

Caiden rubbed at his chest again. Why would she call them to come get her, but not wait for them? Caiden spun around, his eyes on the trees. She wouldn't go in there alone, not with the hunter around. But somehow, Caiden knew that's where she was.

THE ARROGANT, deranged, knob-headed, twat. Sam dragged her through the woods. Maggie allowed her feet to fumble and catch on anything she could. She would not make this easy for him.

She'd woken up sitting on the floor of the cabin by the door. With her wrists and feet tied, and also tied together, she was immobile. Sam had cleaned up the mess from their fight, and he cleaned the rest of the cabin. He'd walked past her, carrying her bags. Looking around, it had been as if she'd already left town. Would Caiden believe it when he came looking for her?

He'd kept her bound, but allowed for slack between her feet for her to walk on her own. But she wouldn't be throwing any more kicks to Sam's gut. What were the odds that life would deal her another kidnapping? Inwardly, she shrugged. This was mild compared to what she lived through. Except for the gun he had slung on his back. The rifle. Sam was the hunter after Caiden. She'd laugh at the absurdity of it all if he wasn't out to kill the man she loved.

Sam had been quiet since she woke up back at the cabin. She needed to get some answers from him.

"What do you want with me?"

"I don't want anything with you. I'm saving you from him. You'll see that. But you also make good bait. I'll let you go when this is all over." He believed he was doing her a favour.

"Bait? You're setting a trap?"

"Yes."

"For who?" She needed as much information from him as possible.

"Caiden and any others of his kind I come across." He knew. Maggie wondered how much he'd seen.

"His kind?"

"Don't play dumb. There's a side of him that is a monster."

"Why Caiden?"

"He killed her." Sam's strained voice lowered when he dipped his chin to his chest.

"Killed who?"

"Laura. The girl I loved." Laura had loved Caiden, but Sam loved Laura.

Finding the charm bracelet after all these years hadn't been a coincidence. This was all about Caiden's past. But why did Sam think Caiden killed her? "I don't understand."

"You don't have to. Just know that the monster in him won't hurt you."

"He didn't kill her."

"You don't know what I saw." A raw rasp carried the words. "Enough." He yanked on her upper arm. Maggie tripped, this time not on purpose. "Keep leaving a trail. I need him to know right where to go."

Sam wasn't stupid. He'd seen her stumble along, breaking branches and leaving tracks.

"It's a shame you got caught up in this, but you'll be better once you move on."

"Untie me."

"Why?" He narrowed his eyes.

"I want to show you how well I can't take care of myself." Maggie had enough of being managed.

"I admit, you surprised me when you fought back at the

cabin. You must have been working with your step-brother after all."

"I was the prize fighter. Untie me and I'll show you." She didn't care if he knew the truth or not.

"Maybe you're just as evil as he was, but I'm sure he must have forced you—at least at first. You'll find your way again." Maggie wanted to bang her head against a tree.

"This won't work. Caiden won't come looking for me. He knows I planned to leave town."

"It might take him a little while, but he'll come."

The only solace Maggie had was that she'd already asked Zachary to come. She hoped he brought others. They'd helped kick some bad guy ass before. They'd do it again.

Hairs on the back of her neck stood to attention. Something hid in the woods. Eyes flickered. The scouts. They'd tell Caiden. And Caiden would run head first into Sam's trap. Maggie turned her head enough that whoever was watching could see her lips and read what she said. Mouthing the words *it's a trap* over and over, she kept her eye on Sam to know when he was looking.

Sam's trap wouldn't work. There were too many scouts in place to track him and to warn Caiden. Maggie may have been about to leave Firebrook, leave Caiden, but she would do what she could to keep crazy Sam from her shooting the grizzlies.

CHAPTER 19

His skin crawled and his bones popped. The bear side of him could find his mate within minutes. If her trail led to town, he'd terrify the tourists and annoy the hungover locals. Caiden's instincts knew she wasn't in town.

Nathan set his hand on Caiden's shoulder. "Control it. I assume we're here to get Maggie because something happened between you two. If you shift now, you won't be able to shift back. Trust me. I couldn't fight it and I was stuck for a few days. You need to control the shift, for now."

Caiden twitched. The urge was strong.

Green eyes flashed in the treeline. They all ran. Wyatt shifted to speak with Huck. They waited. Caiden's nerves popping, impatient snaps through his system. Wyatt shifted back, but stayed on the ground, ready to allow the animal free.

"Sam Tulk. He has Maggie. She mouthed the word *trap* to the scouts."

"Sam? I don't get it." What the hell did he have to do with this? Sam had always been aggressive with Caiden, ever since they were teenagers. Teenagers. "Laura." Sam had a crush on Laura. It had devastated him when she died. Things still didn't add up. Was this some form of vengeance on bears for her death? This was a lot simpler than he'd thought. The man was after bears, not Caiden—not shifters. But why take Maggie?

"He's not hurting her. He's using her."

"It won't work. These woods are ours. And we have enough scouts out there to spot whatever trap he thinks he's made."

"How many scouts?" Zachary lifted his face to the trees.

"Five at one time and taking rotations. Right now, two grizzly pairs and three wolves, one shifter and two pairs. We follow, track their scent and meet up with the scouts as we go. We'll catch up and pull his trap on him." Caiden took control. An odd calm infused in him. He still twitched with the need to shift, but his mate needed him and he would rescue her. This time, he wouldn't be too late.

"We can track better if we shift." Zachary eyed Caiden.

"First, what happened between you and Maggie?" Nathan stepped in front of him.

"Not your business."

"No, it's not. But my mate left. She wouldn't stay with me. Wouldn't allow Fate to control her life. I shifted and had no control. So, do you have control of yourself?"

Caiden didn't, but he'd have to, to save Maggie. He had to trust that Fate and the magic would allow him to shift if needed. "I will."

Nathan nodded. "Then let's go."

Wyatt shifted, and Zachary stashed his clothes. Winds rushed through all of them.

Caiden's nose twitched. He picked out Maggie's scent. Sam's was there. He recognized it now. The strong cologne still stuck to parts of him or his gear, but it didn't overpower.

Sam wanted Caiden to recognize him this time. That wasn't all he wanted him to recognize.

Sam and Maggie had hiked toward all the spots Sam had sighted in. They never stopped. But at each one, he left behind something small. Caiden recognized each one. A necklace. A hair pin. A tiny trinket box. All of them belonged to Laura. It seemed Caiden wasn't the only one that blamed him for Laura's death.

MAGGIE WORRIED as they passed the last sight being watched by the scouts. She'd spotted them all along the way, recognizing Caiden's and Wyatt's pairs. She hadn't met the wolves before.

"Where are you taking me?"

"A place where I have the advantage." He moved them up the river until it came to a narrow section. His grip on her arms as he tried to get her to cross didn't bruise, but the firm grasp was undeniable.

"I can't cross with my feet tied. I need to jump."

"Your feet will have to get wet."

"I don't know how much further we need to go, but I won't be able to hike well in wet sneakers." It would be uncomfortable. Comfort wasn't what she worried about now. If she could get him to free her legs and keep them free, she could either run or at least be useful when the time came.

Sam narrowed his eyes. "Behave, Miss Scott. I don't want to hurt you again. I intend to help you when this is over." He knelt in front of her and untied one ankle. He left the rope attached to the other like a leash. It was that leash that kept her from kicking him in the face to land on his ass in the water. Sam wrapped the free end around his hand. One quick yank and she'd fall.

Sam hopped across, keeping his arm outstretched and low with a grip on the rope. Maggie paused, hoping inspiration would hit with a way out of this. Nothing. She bent her knees and jumped. She rocked forward on her toes.

Sam crouched and reached for her ankle.

"Please don't. That hike looks steep."

He sighed. "No. I can't chance it. You don't believe me. You'll try to stop me."

Keeping her tied up wouldn't prevent that. "Keeping me tied will only slow us down."

"He wouldn't have found us so soon. There's plenty of time."

That wasn't true. Even if Caiden hadn't discovered her gone from the cabin. The scouts would have told him by now. Sam thought he was leading Caiden to a trap, and that it was only Caiden he would face. But there were at least seven shifters and pairs. More if Zachary and whoever he brought were already here.

"Why are you doing this?"

Sam stood after retying her ankle. Grabbing the slack between her wrists, he pulled. "I already told you."

"He isn't a monster."

Sam rounded on her and snarled, his upper lip vibrating furiously. "I loved her. I tried so many times to get her to see me, but all she saw was Caiden, positive that when she told her friend how she felt, he would feel the same. I knew he wouldn't. I tried to warn her so she wouldn't get hurt. But I never expected him to hurt her like that. Such a senseless murder."

"There was no murder."

"What the hell would you know? A child at the time who couldn't lift her eyes from her own feet."

"I'm looking now." Maggie mirrored Caiden's threatening lilt. Her voice would never go as deep, and she'd sound ridiculous trying. But her tone caught Sam's attention. Her confidence surprised him. Shaking his head, he turned and pulled her behind him.

"No more talking."

"I spent a lot of years silent." Completely silent for some. "I don't want to do it anymore. You're wrong. Whatever you think happened, you're wrong."

"Don't make me hurt you, Maggie."

"I'm not making you do anything. You don't have to do any of this and you didn't have to take me. This is all on you." She wouldn't carry anyone's blame.

He stopped and pulled another length of rope from the side of his pack. Shoving it at her face, he wedged it between her teeth. He leaned in while tying it around the back of her head. "Shut up." His heavy consonants slammed against her ear. "I'm killing Caiden Greer. And if there's a chance, I'll take out his brother, too. You're going to want to close your eyes when the time comes."

Maggie bit the rope to stop from screaming in his face. The material was rough on her tongue and cheeks. Fighting a gag, she had no choice but to follow when he kept moving. She couldn't watch him kill Caiden, or Wyatt. The only thing that kept her upright was the number of scouts and help they had. Sam's trap would fail.

They climbed higher. More and more rocks protruded from the ground.

"Use your hands." Sam pushed her in front of him. A short rock wall stood in front of her. Panic welled. This wasn't where they needed Sam to be. Maggie climbed, and the sight of a small clearing backing onto a larger rock wall brought her down to her knees. They had the numbers, but Sam had an advantage. There was only one way to come at him, and that was head on. He wouldn't get out of this, but he would kill someone before they got to him.

Sam pulled her to her feet, then set her against a large rock. Untying her hands, he pulled them behind her back. Adding more rope, he tied it around the rock. When he finished, Maggie tried to pull out of it, to stand. Tying her around a rock that she could stand over seemed silly, but when she pulled, pain lanced her shoulders.

"You're only going to hurt yourself. You're tied to the ground."

And facing the one way to reach them. The one way Caiden would come for her.

THIS WON'T BE that simple. Beck, an alpha of the wolf shifter pack, met them on the other side of the river.

Why? As they had continued to follow their tracks, passing all advantageous locations, dread grew in Caiden.

They hiked up, and he's backing onto a rock face. He's making a last stand, or he's only expecting you, and maybe your brother.

Where's Maggie?

He has her arms wrapped around a rock and tied to a ring in the ground. I don't think he intends to hurt her. He believes he's doing this for her own good. But he gagged her a while ago when she tried to convince him otherwise.

That's fucked. Nathan growled behind them. But Nathan didn't know what the cause of all this was. It surprised Caiden that they hadn't asked. Sam thought Caiden was going to hurt Maggie. But Caiden didn't understand why.

I need him to talk before we stop this—in case he gets hurt, but I want to avoid that, too.

I don't want anyone who isn't a shifter knowing about us. Beck stepped closer, an almost threat pulling at his fur.

I understand. But we'll have to find another way to deal with him if we can.

He's the one who shot you? Zachary stood on a fallen tree.

Yeah.

It's your call. Zachary nodded. Beck's narrowed eyes didn't look like he agreed. *They may lose the wolves' help toward the end of this.*

We'll do what we can. Caiden turned toward Beck. *Let's go.* So much for them springing the trap.

Beck took the lead, but none of them needed to follow. The scent and trail were clear. Sam wasn't hiding.

They skulked below the rock face, silent and hidden from view. They stilled to listen. Harsh breathing cut off by groans and muffled words. Rough rope scraped against metal. A man's sigh and the shift of the metal of a gun.

"Make all the noise you want, Maggie. It won't matter. He knows how to find us and he has one direction to reach you."

Caiden looked up. There was more than one way. They could jump down over the rock. It was high and wide, but not impossible. Sam's tone rang with pure confidence in his plan. Coming in from behind would also put Maggie in the line of fire. He realized Sam didn't intend for this situation to last long. He'd shoot the second Caiden poked his head over the rise to reach them. It would be over in seconds. Then what would he do with Maggie? What would happen when he realized she wouldn't keep her mouth shut? Unless he counted on no one believing her. Maggie had better connections than Caiden with the shifters in Alder Ridge. By the sounds of it, this wasn't their first round with someone like Sam. He wouldn't get far if he succeeded in this.

I'm going up the front.

He'll shoot you on sight.

I didn't say I was going the whole way up. I want answers. Give me time to get him talking. Someone needs to get behind him and free Maggie without him hearing or seeing you.

I will. Zachary stepped forward.

Hold on. Beck moved between Caiden and Zachary. *You can't go in as a wolf.*

Why the hell not?

I don't want anyone to know there are wolf shifters in this area. If Caiden insists on letting him live, then he's going to believe there are only bears.

I'm not from here.

Doesn't matter. If he sees a wolf, it will give him reason to believe there are wolves here. We put a lot of effort into staying hidden.

Fine. I can't argue with that.

It wasn't as if Caiden wanted people to know about him and his brother and cousins, but he wouldn't harm someone over it. They'd deal with that concern when they crossed it.

Caiden nodded to Zachary to go ahead. Beck turned around.

My wolves and I are going to step back. He closed his eyes and tilted his head down. *We won't leave. We'll stick around in case things go really bad, but if Sam is going to make it home tonight, I don't want him to see any of us. I'm sorry.* Beck's fierce eyes met Caiden's from lowered lids. A leader looking to protect his people.

I understand. I'd rather he didn't know about us either, but the damage is already done, it seems.

Beck nodded and left, the other wolves following him. They climbed out of sight, but Caiden still felt their presence. He looked at his brother and their pairs. *Get as close as you can and be ready to leap in if Zachary needs help.*

Caiden crouched at the bottom of the rise and waited for everyone to get in position. They called out to each other without the worry that Sam would hear them while communicating as animals. Caiden pushed everything away. Maggie needed him, and she needed him in control.

The shift was difficult. The magic struggled to get free. It had hurt to push her away, to let her go. There was more damage than he realized. But he had no choice. Forcing the magic forward, he suppressed the roar of pain—until the shift finished and his groan let loose.

"Come on up here, Greer." The sound of the gun moving, his grip shifting, preceded Sam's call.

"Let Maggie go."

"I will. And I'll make sure she gets help. After you can't hurt her."

"I won't hurt her." No one needed to make a sound for Caiden to hear the *bullshit* from each of them. He hurt her. And he would fix it. The pain without her had been unbearable. The only reason he could put one foot in front of the other and calm himself in this moment was because she was in danger.

"You would have done to her what you did to Laura."

"What did I do to Laura, Sam?" Caiden kept the top of his head below the edge, but he was ready to leap over when he had the chance.

"You tore her apart!" An unnatural scream for someone of Sam's size flashed outward from the rock face like a sheet carried on the wind. Maggie's movements stilled. No more muffled whimper or scraping rope. Zachary must have made it down.

"You'll have to be more specific. How did I tear her apart?" Caiden hurt Laura, but they were kids.

"In the literal sense. You're a fucking monster."

"I don't understand."

"Get up here, Greer."

"Sam, help me understand." Caiden wouldn't show his head until he had Sam's twisted story.

"I saw the whole attack. The claws, the blood, the teeth. You tore her apart."

"You watched the bear attack her?" Caiden hadn't seen the whole attack, but he'd seen enough.

"I watched *you* attack her! I ran to help her and by the time I could see her again, you sat there naked with her in your arms. Feeling bad about what you'd done doesn't absolve you of it."

"Why do you think I attacked? It was a bear." He saw it in pieces and put them together.

"I've watched you for years. You go in the woods, then you're nowhere to be found, but a big ass grizzly is always around."

He'd never watched Caiden shift, but he'd put enough together. "Why didn't you say something after the attack?"

"Who would believe me?"

"Sam, I didn't attack Laura. That bear wasn't me. You're forgetting what the investigation said. The bear was a mother and there were signs of the cubs around. I saw them myself, Sam. It was an accident. Laura ran between the cubs and their mother."

"Lies. Lies you told to cover your ass. She never would have been there if it hadn't been for you."

"Why do you think I cried over her body for hours?" He

needed to yell at the man. The urge was there, but pain clawed at the words so they came out in shreds.

"You won't make me feel bad for you now. I loved her. But she loved you."

"I know, Sam."

Gravel crunched. "Your turn, Greer." Sam moved to the edge and shot without aiming. He cocked quickly for the second round while he aimed. He might have gotten him too while he'd pulled back and moved away from the first shot if it hadn't been for the female battle cry.

CHAPTER 20

She kept a sharp gaze on Sam the second Zachary jumped down from the upper cliff. Bending his legs with his landing, he hadn't made a sound. Ropes scraped more against her skin as he'd worked the ones around her wrist. Maggie listened to every painful and guttural word both Sam and Caiden said. They both hurt over the loss of Laura, and they both blamed Caiden. Even faced with the truth, Sam wouldn't sway from his goal.

Maggie worked on the gag while Zachary started at her feet. He pulled her up and to the side. They could climb down as long as Sam stayed occupied talking to Caiden. He'd held the gun ready for so long, but now that Caiden was close, he also held it up. His body so tense, he'd shoot before he was ready. Caiden and Zachary weren't the only ones here. Anyone could get hurt. But Caiden was his sole focus.

Zachary pulled, but Maggie's gut said not to look away from Sam. Her stomach dropped when Sam took long, harsh steps toward the edge. She struggled in Zachary's arms, but he overpowered her. Sam reached the edge and shot without looking.

Maggie threw an elbow into Zachary's gut. His hold loosened, but not enough. Turning her aim, she threw the next elbow up into his chin. He groaned, and she broke free.

Sam readied himself to shoot again, only seconds on the heel of the first. Maggie screamed, terror and fury ripping from her heart. Sam straightened. Maggie charged and ran into his back. He lurched forward and fell over the edge. Maggie lost her balance, swaying, before a patch of loose gravel slipped under her foot.

"Maggie." Zachary's growl reached out like his hand, but he didn't catch her. Her entire body scraped and hit against the jutting rock. She had enough clarity to wrap her hands around the back of her head and bend her elbows forward, protecting herself from a head injury. But the rest of her body took a solid beating.

Maggie held in her screams on the way down, but not her groans when she landed. Lifting her head was the only movement that didn't cause pain. Taking stock, Sam had dropped the gun and rolled to his feet. He fell over the rocks rather than slid down them. In hindsight, Maggie should have jumped with him.

Caiden stood tall, but ready for an attack. He'd moved himself between Sam and the gun. Maggie gritted her teeth as she propped herself up on her elbows. She didn't know what damage the fall had done to her body, but it hurt like hell. She'd take the pain if it meant this would be over. With Sam unarmed and surrounded by shifters, this would end soon.

Sam snarled and reached for his back. Steel flashed from the spotty sun rays that made it through the trees. He held a knife. Not some small pocket survival knife, but a six-inch long, wide blade that curved to a devastating tip.

Maggie smothered her cry when she pushed up from the ground—years of practice kept her silent. Zachary appeared by her side and helped her up, but her feet flew forward to run to Caiden. He was quicker and wrapped an arm around her middle and held her against his chest with her toes barely touching the ground.

Sam's eyes wavered away from Caiden, noticing Zachary.

"Let me go." She begged him, her voice filled with unshed tears.

"No."

"Then you have to help him." Maggie searched for others and saw Nathan, naked and leaning against a nearby tree with his arms crossed. "Help him."

"We will if he needs it. But you need to stop struggling before you hurt yourself further. That was a nasty fall, Maggie."

"He's going to hurt him, or kill him."

"Caiden doesn't look worried."

And he didn't. Caiden's eyes narrowed on the knife. Maggie watched each muscle tick into place down his bare torso and legs. A magnificent creature with enhanced abilities against a crazy man with a knife. She had full confidence in Caiden, in her mate, but that didn't stop her from worrying.

"I'd rather not take any chances." Maggie struggled against Zachary, trying to step away from him, but her legs weakened and her back protested. Zachary had to pull her up to keep her off the ground.

"You're hurt, Maggie. No more moving." His growly command was as authoritative as Caiden's. And he was right. The pain didn't dull to an ache. It exploded through her body and billowed out her pores.

"This all ends now, Greer."

"You're right, Sam. It does." Caiden's firm response resonated with sadness, a resignation that Maggie felt inside her. Caiden had a storm brewing in him with its own war.

Sam's grip on the knife tightened and he lunged forward. Maggie screamed at him to stop, and once again tried to escape from Zachary. Her kicks to his shins and elbows to his gut had no effect this time. He was ready for her, and the pain in her body muted her strength. All she could do was watch the man she loved fight.

CAIDEN DODGED SAM'S ATTACK. From the corner of his eye, he saw Maggie struggle against Zachary, relieved he kept a good hold. *Keep her there, wolf.* He felt every bruise and injury in her body.

"Sam, listen to yourself. This isn't right."

"I've had almost twenty years to listen to myself. I know what I saw."

"You saw a bear attack her. You saw me holding her. What else?"

Sam frowned. "I know what you are. I've followed you for years."

Caiden didn't react. He'd never shifted with anyone close enough to watch. Sam may have masked his personal scent with cologne, but not the fact he was near. "And what did you see when you followed me?"

Sam tensed and lifted his arm, slashing downward. Caiden stepped to the side and kicked Sam in the ribs. The man growled. "You'd go into the woods, and your brother, then four bears would always be nearby. I've always figured your brother to be a monster, too. But he never killed anyone."

"There're bears in these woods, whether I'm in town or out for a hike. You know that, Sam. There's more than bears. Part of living here."

"No. No, one of those bears is you!" He lunged again with a straightforward motion. Caiden slapped the knife away, but he'd gotten close that time. Maggie's whimpers carried through him with the breeze.

"What you're saying is crazy."

"But I'm not crazy."

"You are." Maggie screamed from Caiden's left, pulling against Zachary's arms.

"Then why the hell are you all naked?" Sam wavered the knife to gesture toward the three shifters, then steadied it back in Caiden's directions.

"Summer's hot," they said in unison. There wasn't a good explanation for it, but they all spouted the same reasoning.

"I shot you and you went missing." He wagged the knife like a finger. "Everyone thinks you left town the day I shot you. And you brought her back." His chin jutted to the side.

"Shot me? I haven't been shot." Caiden forced confusion into his brow and risked taking a moment for his eyes to wander his body instead of watching Sam.

"I shot a bear."

"You shot a bear. Not me. I wasn't in the woods the day I left to get Maggie."

"I saw you go into the woods!"

"I'm sorry. You didn't. I left town that day to get Maggie. I was going that way on an errand for Bearbrook Cabins and Brian Whitehall asked me to give Maggie a ride." Caiden didn't believe he'd change Sam's mind, but he hoped to confuse him enough that Sam could let it go.

"You were missing. It was more than a day trip. I shot you and you disappeared." It was like reasoning with a child.

"The nymph didn't want to leave." Caiden cocked his head toward Maggie. "It took days to convince her she needed to come back."

"I'm right."

"Sam, I'm not a bear. I didn't kill Laura. And you didn't shoot me."

Sam crouched down, his arm shaking with the might of his grip on the knife. He wasn't giving up.

"Put the knife down." Caiden strived for calm authority.

"No. People might not believe me, but I'm still going to make you suffer." Sam shot forward with an attack. Caiden moved to block him, but he faked his approach and sliced into Caiden's side. He didn't suppress his unnatural growl. Maggie's cry interrupted his concentration. She fought against Zachary with renewed energy. Caiden pushed the pain down and focused on Sam, but he was too late. Sam aimed, and Caiden had only enough time to move to keep the knife from driving through his ribs. Instead, he made another deep cut across the side, slicing to hit bone.

Nathan appeared by Caiden's side, splitting Sam's attention for only a moment. Both his sides throbbed with heat while blood dripped from the wounds. Caiden was Sam's only goal. He tried to bypass Nathan. Caiden stood ready, but Nathan twisted and threw a punch. He hit hard across Sam's jaw as the knife reached only an inch from Caiden's shoulder. Sam's head snapped back and he fell to the ground. His body lay still, but his chest moved up and down.

Nathan took the knife and threw it for it to stick high in a tree. Out of sight, out of reach.

Zachary wrestled Maggie over to him.

"Stop struggling, nymph." Caiden faced his mate and darkened his voice, expecting her to listen. He should have known better. Her struggles increased until Zachary let her go. She winced against the pain as she pulled her shirt off. She panted while yanking at the collar of the fabric, but nothing happened.

"Tear this." She held it to the side for Zachary. But Caiden snatched it from her hands and ripped it in half. "Sit." Maggie pushed on his chest. He felt the weakness in her body from her own injuries. If it made her stop moving, he'd do whatever she told him to. He sat and leaned against the rock. Maggie placed one half of the torn fabric against one cut and lifted his hand to put over it. Then she covered the other gash, but used her own hands to stop the bleeding.

"They're not deep, mate. I'll be fine in a couple hours."

"Don't call me that."

That was what he intended to call her, because he wasn't letting her go anymore. But before he could convince her, he had to deal with Sam. Caiden looked at the still body on the ground and fought with what he should do with the man. Misguided, grieving for almost twenty years. Caiden couldn't hurt him. But that left them with the risk of exposing the knowledge of shifters.

PAIN TRIED TO SUFFOCATE MAGGIE, pulling her ribs and skin inward to crush her body. But she still had the ability to move. She'd help Caiden. Holding her shirt to his wound, she looked at Sam on the ground and then at Nathan.

"If it was that easy, why didn't you step in sooner to help?"

"I didn't think he was stupid enough to get stabbed." Nathan shrugged. Neither he nor Zachary seemed concerned that Sam had hurt Caiden.

"Oh, he's stupid. He didn't even need to come after me." Her gaze switched to the man she was going to leave. "You should have just stayed away. He wasn't going to hurt me. He only wanted you. You could have sent Zachary and Nathan in to get me when he gave up and moved me."

"We don't know that he wouldn't hurt you, despite what he said. Desperate men don't know what they're going to do."

"You don't want me. Why the hell would you come after me?" The blood slowed between her fingers.

"Why do you think? Mate."

Maggie scoffed. Mate. He came because some urge forced him to.

Wyatt made his appearance from the trees where he'd watched the whole thing. She figured it had been smart to stay out of sight of Sam. Caiden tried hard to convince him he was wrong. There was enough absurdity to his claims that most wouldn't believe him. It may cause doubt in some, but with time it would pass. Caiden and Wyatt were too important to this community.

"I told you not to call me that."

"Too bad. Maggie, you need to see a doctor."

He was right, but she wouldn't stick around for him to take her. She'd call for Garrett to examine her. "So do you. Since you have all this to take care of, I'll leave."

He gripped her wrist in an unyielding hold.

"You're not. You need to go to the hospital. I can feel all your pain, little nymph."

"Too bad." She threw his words back at him before punching his arm to loosen his grip. A groan ran through her as she leapt to her feet and out of Caiden's reach. "You have a brother to look after," she said to Wyatt before turning to run back to the cabins. Every step shot a ripple of thunder through her body. She just needed to make it to the cabin. Sam had hidden her bags nearby before dragging her into the woods. If she found her phone, she'd call Garrett. Once she reached Alder Ridge.

"Maggie, stop." Caiden's voice almost stopped her. "Go after her." Footsteps followed.

She pushed her body, assuming the increased pain meant she was putting distance between whoever was coming to get her. But someone plucked her off the ground in seconds. She landed against Wyatt's chest.

"You're hurt pretty bad, Miss Maggie."

"Leave me alone. They need your help."

"And I'll come back once you're settled."

"Settled where?"

"With the doctor. Caiden will be there as soon as he can."

"He told me to leave. So, I'm leaving."

"Whatever you say. But not until we get you taken care of."

Maggie fell silent, and Wyatt hiked through the woods. The walk was gentle, but she realized Wyatt adjusted his hold over the rougher terrain so as not to bounce her around. The pain settled in, drawing her into a sleepy darkness. She forced her eyes to stay open.

Wyatt stopped and set her down. "Wait here a minute. I need to get my clothes." He pulled a pile from a bush and dressed, pulling his shirt over her instead of his. After slipping on his boots, he lifted her again. Maggie didn't protest. As long as Caiden wasn't coming after her, she'd escape.

Wyatt didn't stop at the lodge like she expected, and he didn't put her in his truck. He walked straight into town and stopped a block from the street to the lodge. Shouldering open the door, he wedged them inside to the sterile air-conditioned air.

"I have a patient for Doc Matthews."

The receptionist jumped from behind the desk and waved them through to a room.

"If she needs to be at the hospital instead, I'll take her now."

"He's just finishing up with another patient. I'll get him in here right away."

"I don't want to be here." Maggie said to Wyatt once the receptionist left.

"I'll send Caiden down as soon as I get back there to deal with all of this for him."

The doctor walked in. "What happened?"

"She took a fall down some rocks while out for a hike. She's pretty banged up, but I'm not sure how bad. She's reluctant to go to the hospital, so I brought her here first."

The doctor shook his head. "The hospital would have been the better choice. But I'll look. Can you get the shirt off her?"

Wyatt winced, but pulled it up. The doctor looked, his fingers gently prodding. "I don't think anything is broken or any internal damage. These are some serious bruises forming, though. I'm going to run some scans, and she'll need pain medication and rest. Looks like this could have been worse."

"Thanks, Doc Matthew."

"Where's the blood from?" The doctor nodded toward Maggie's hands.

"No hers."

The doctor raised his brows. He shrugged when Wyatt didn't explain further. Wyatt nodded to the doctor, then lifted Maggie's chin. "Caiden will be here soon. Stay put." His demand didn't mean much to Maggie. She waited, giving Wyatt enough time to leave the building before speaking to the doctor still poking at all the vital locations.

"Are you sure there's no serious damage?"

"I can't be sure, but I would be surprised if there was. Sit tight. The nurse will come in and get you ready for the scans."

The doctor left. Maggie didn't intend to be here for the nurse. Every part of her felt weighted, pain pulling her to the ground, as she put Wyatt's shirt back over her head. Holding herself straight, she walked from the examination room and past the receptionist as if the doctor had given her the okay to leave. Maggie didn't know if anyone noticed, because she kept her eyes on the door. In the heat and the sun, she allowed her body to droop. Maggie refused to wait for Caiden to show up. No matter how much she wanted him to wrap her in his arms. He didn't see her any differently than the others—a burden.

CHAPTER 21

"What do we do with him?" Zachary grabbed Caiden's hand to pull him up from the ground. Not that he needed the help, but he wouldn't turn away a friendly gesture. Especially when it was Zachary and Nathan he'd have to go through to keep Maggie here.

"There are two choices. Turn him over to RCMP and hope that our story sounds more convincing than his. Or we give him one hell of a warning and hope he keeps his mouth shut and doesn't try again." Caiden only spared a quick glance at Sam before his eyes followed the path Maggie and Wyatt had taken.

"You warn him off and keep a close eye on him." Beck showed up through the trees, but didn't come any closer. If this was Beck's decision, a warning wouldn't be the only thing dished out to Sam. Sam took this too far, but he didn't deserve to be harmed. And by going to the RCMP with two stories to make his look crazy, they'd be doing to Sam the same thing Tyrone and the locals of Firebrook did to Maggie.

Caiden nodded at Beck and watched him leave. He

listened to the wolves run hard back to their territory. "He's right. Let's carry him back and find our clothes." This would take more time than he'd like, but it needed to be dealt with. Now.

But his mate couldn't wait.

How had he been so stupid to let her go? To hurt her the way he had? And even while attempting to tend to his wounds, she had a final look in her eyes, a final tone in her words.

"Let's get this over with."

Nathan pulled Sam up and lifted him over his shoulder. Zachary carried the gun. They hiked until they met up with Wyatt.

"Where's Maggie?"

"At Doc Matthew's. He's running some scans. She should still be there when we're done here." Wyatt had grabbed their clothes on his way back and passed them out. "You good?" He eyed Caiden's torso.

"Yeah. I'm good. Bleeding has almost stopped. They're healing." He felt the urgent pull of his skin coming together. "Is she okay?"

"The Doc thinks so. He'll send her to the hospital if the scans show anything and let us know."

Once they were all dressed and had stashed Sam's gun and all of his gear, they tried to wake him up. He hadn't stirred the entire hike to the river. Splashing him with the icy mountain water did the trick.

"What..."

"I'm going to make this quick, Sam." Caiden didn't have to force the threat into his voice. Just thinking of what he'd put Maggie through was enough. "You've got this wrong. All of it. And you need to remember that, or you'll hurt innocent people. Laura's parents, for example. Just as you hurt Maggie today."

"Maggie can fight. She was working with her brother."

"Another thing you've got wrong. She was his first *victim*. I advise you to put this behind you, far behind. There are good people that will suffer if you don't." Caiden lowered his shoulders and crouched down in front of Sam, who still sat on the ground. "I miss Laura, too. I'm sorry you've lived all these years thinking I killed her. Go back and review the details again. You're wrong. Laura wouldn't want any of us dwelling like this. Move on."

Caiden waited.

"Sam, I need your word before I can leave you alone and I've got places to be."

"Or what?"

"We'll make sure you find a new home." Let him imagine what he would from that threat. "You realize I could also turn you over to RCMP and press charges, don't you? This is the best deal you're going to get. And I'm doing it for Laura."

At the mention of Laura's name, his eyes shot darts, but his body relaxed. "Fine."

"Good. We'll be keeping an eye on you, Sam." Caiden stood and left with the others.

He needed to find his mate and take her home. He stopped at the lodge long enough to change his clothes, since the last of the blood from his wounds had soaked through his shirt. Taking a quick look, the bleeding had stopped, but the wounds were still raw. Not much longer and they'd be scarred lines fading to nothing.

Stepping into the doctor's office, Caiden walked straight to the desk. "Where is Maggie Scott?"

The receptionist frowned. "We assume at the hospital instead."

"The hospital?"

Doc Matthew walked out. "Caiden. What are you doing here?"

"I came to see Maggie. Wyatt told you I'd be here."

"She isn't here. She was missing when the nurse went in to prep her for the scans. I assumed Wyatt had come back and changed his mind, taking her to the hospital instead. I tried calling him, but there was no answer."

Caiden's stomach dropped, and it took all his strength not to tear through Doc Matthew's clinic looking for her.

"I take it Wyatt didn't take her to the hospital."

"No," he growled.

The Doc shook his head. "She must have sneaked out."

Caiden nodded and left before he scared anyone inside. His mate was missing. Twice in one day. He'd laugh if he wasn't so worried she was hiding while dying from her injuries.

Zachary and Nathan waited outside the clinic while Wyatt had gone back to track and follow Sam.

"She's not here."

"How?" Zachary pulled his hands from his pockets and pushed away from the building.

"She must have left on her own."

"Anyone else in town have something against her and would take her?" Nathan spoke low.

"I don't think so. Most of them have learned to accept her, if not befriend her." And the rest left her alone. There wasn't any rising panic like there'd been that morning when Sam took her. He had to believe she was only being stubborn and trying to escape without facing him again.

They checked both her cabin and the lodge. There was no sign of her and still no sign of her belongings.

"Split up. Take two trucks and start at opposite ends of town. It isn't big. She'll stand out." With her red hair, she couldn't hide. And she wasn't back in the woods. They would have scented her.

Caiden waited for Zachary and Nathan to drive away before he chose his direction. But the two men paused when they got in the truck. A hand waved out the driver's side window, beckoning Caiden to follow. Zachary pulled out and did a U-turn. He stopped one block away at the clinic. Stepping out, they waved Caiden over. Zachary pointed to the back seat with his thumb. Caiden shuddered with relief, and part of him wanted to laugh at her attempt at being a stowaway in the very ride she asked to come get her.

He opened the back door, and his tiny nymph sat on the floor with her knees tucked against her chest. Pain shone in her eyes as unshed tears. She was hurting herself by trying to escape. As curled up as she was, they wouldn't have seen her, only smelled her.

"Maggie."

"Just let me go home."

"I will." He didn't tell her that her home was now with him. "But you need to see the doctor first."

"Don't make this harder, Caiden. I'll see the doctor when I get to Alder Ridge. Dr. Matthews said he was sure I was fine."

"You didn't let him run the scans to make sure." Zachary poked his head around Caiden. "Out."

Caiden controlled his growl as she took Zachary's hand to get out of the truck.

"Please take me home now." Maggie kept her eyes down.

She could have been asking either of them to take her, but she wanted Zachary to drive her out of Firebrook.

"After the doctor gives you the okay." Zachary pulled her inside the clinic. That's as far as Caiden would allow another man to touch his mate. He took her other side and lifted her into his arms, stopping for a moment at the desk to raise a brow at a wide eyed Doc Matthews.

"This way." Caiden followed him to the back of the clinic.

"Let me go, Caiden."

"Never, nymph." He nipped her earlobe before setting her down on the examination table. Maggie closed her eyes, shutting him out. He needed to prove how he felt about her. To prove that he wouldn't let love slip away.

Doc Matthews gave her the all clear. She walked out of the clinic on her own two feet, feeling better after some pain killers from the charming doctor. Maggie went straight to Zachary and Nathan, putting herself between them and away from Caiden.

His low chuckle was far from humorous. "You're not going with them, little mate."

Maggie whirled on him with the fire in her eyes that burned his lungs. "You haven't listened, have you? I am no one's responsibility and I will not be controlled."

"I wouldn't dream of trying."

"You made yourself clear when you tore your body from mine and then again when you only came after me because I'm a burden."

"I never considered you to be a burden." Caiden lowered his chin, and the truth tumbled past his lips. But that didn't matter. He didn't want her, he didn't want anyone. She wasn't in the state of her life to change people.

"I'm not doing it anymore, Caiden. No more hot and cold. I'm going home."

"Yes, you are." A single quirked brow was her only warning. He bent and lifted her against his chest. She yelped and tried to move out of his reach, but both Zachary and Nathan stood motionless behind her.

"We'll wait." Zachary and Nathan leaned against the truck and turned to a conversation between themselves. But she saw the spark in their eyes and tilt of their lips.

"Put me down."

"No."

Maggie bucked against him, trying to dislodge his balance. She didn't care if she fell to the pavement, as long as she could leave him behind. The warmth of his hold hurt too much.

"If you don't stop, I'll have to throw you over my shoulder. I don't want you getting hurt any more."

"Not your problem, remember." Maggie growled between her teeth, then turned her head. If kicking and bucking to get from his hold wouldn't work, then maybe biting would. Opening her mouth, she bit hard into the tough flesh of his bicep.

His growl ran along the side of her body as it grew with intensity the longer she held on. He tucked his head in her neck, and his sharp canines ran along her skin. "My bite is bigger than yours, little nymph. Let go." Caiden pressed lightly with his teeth.

Maggie gasped. Heat and arousal seared her body, but so did a fresh renewal of loss. He threatened her now, but those teeth would never again sink into her flesh and mark her.

Reaching the lodge, he walked behind the building and set her down.

"I was wrong."

Maggie paused.

"I panicked. I've never seen you as a responsibility."

"But as someone you needed to be responsible for if we stayed together. That's enough. I won't do it again."

"There's nothing I can do to change that, Maggie. As my mate, I feel responsible to keep you safe and happy. That's an instinct I can't let go."

"But you did let it go." The pain of him pulling away from her snapped all over again. She didn't deserve this, not from someone she trusted, loved, been wholly intimate with.

Caiden fisted her shirt at her side and pulled her against him. Maggie leaned back, pushing on his chest. "I was wrong. I've been wrong for years. I couldn't let go of what happened to Laura. Not until I felt what I was giving up with you. The pain of being without you was unbearable." He dropped to his knees—the top of his head under her chin.

"Caiden?"

"I never wanted to push you away or let you go. I was stubborn. And foolish. Part of me still believed Laura got hurt because she loved me."

"That's ridiculous."

"I know. I always have, but that belief had buried itself deep." The green in his eyes glistened. "You're mine, nymph. Don't take yourself away from me."

"What happened in the woods? The wind. The words. What was it?" Maggie's hands fisted in his shirt at his shoulders.

"They were vows. A promise. I think we've been mating

since I first bit you. That was what would have sealed us together."

"How can I trust it won't scare you again? I've been cold for too long, grizzly. I don't want any more from you."

"No more cold. Only heat, little nymph. And a lot of it." His fingers flexed around her waist. Maggie gasped, pulling in desperate air. She didn't want to be pushed away again, but neither did she want to continue living without him. This was home now. He was home.

Caiden swallowed and blinked. The shine in his eyes turned to a deep storm.

"This is it, Maggie." He stood and lifted her with him. The pain killers had kicked in so his tight grip on her ass didn't register as more than a minor bruise. He stalked toward the lodge, but stopped. "Tourists," he mumbled under his breath. Turning, he took them into the woods.

Maggie held back. She wanted to touch him, kiss him. But all she remembered was lying in the cool grass alone.

Trees blocked them in, creating shade from the sun except for a few rays that cast a sensual glow. Maggie didn't want there to be something in the air. She didn't want to fall again. Caiden had dropped her just as she let go.

"I won't pull away again, nymph." He cupped her cheek and let her slide down his body. She hadn't tried to hide her uncertainty. "I can already hear the call, the vow, the promise. It means so much more than it seems. It was terrifying when I wasn't ready. But Maggie, I am now. There was so much pain for both of us when I pushed you away. I won't cause that again. I won't live without your fire in my life. I love you."

"Caiden." The pieces of her shattered heart floated in her chest—a tingling sensation across her chest. "You can't order me around, or control what I do. I'm not a responsibility."

"I will keep you safe and you'll do what I say in any situation that needs it, but I will never hold you back."

Maggie lifted her hand, touching his lips, he nipped then kissed it away. Fire lanced through her, and her heart settled into place. She heard the same calling, vow. The promise of mates. "I love you, too."

Caiden sighed with a growl and captured her lips. The kiss was the only demanding part of him. He claimed her mouth as he'd already claimed her, but his hands were gentle over her body as he peeled away their clothes. The breeze rushed in, but it soon warmed as it lifted her hair and tickled the back of her neck.

"I never had a chance from the moment I caught your scent in Alder Ridge. I'll never let your fire die, my little nymph."

That promise settled into her soul, igniting a life she deserved, they both deserved. They'd burn bright together. Her promise, her grizzly, her fire.

EPILOGUE

Caiden held his mate against his chest. Leaning against the picnic table, he lined her up between his legs to make them comfortable. Zachary and Nathan had stayed in Firebrook for the night. It gave Maggie the time to rest and for Caiden to organize things at the restaurant before they all came back to Alder Ridge. Two days of a full house with shifters and their mates helping Maggie pack hadn't given him much time alone with her.

Except the nights.

With the mate bond sealed, she was healing quicker than normal, and Caiden took advantage—claiming her over and over. They made the trip here to get her things without thinking. But in the quiet hours of the night, they'd decided to live in the cabin while they built a home of their own.

Caiden had never realized he was missing this kind of happiness.

"Don't think we won't come visit." Ezaray leaned against her mate. Zachary's hand curled around the back of her neck.

"I'd love that. You have all done so much for me. Part of me is sad to leave."

"Only part?" Shaye lifted a teasing brow.

"Oh!" Maggie jolted from his arms. "I have gifts for you guys."

Caiden let her go. The women followed her back to his truck, where they'd tied all of her things down in the back except for a single bag up front.

"She's changed." Zachary watched after the women following Maggie. "She's brighter, she bounces."

"She speaks up," Asher added.

"That's a lot of change in only a few weeks." Garrett tilted back his beer. As soon as they all heard what happened, the doctor examined Maggie for himself, and each day since.

"She didn't change. She just never let it out." Caiden had seen it in her from the first moment. And she hadn't hidden it from him.

Maggie passed out small gift bags to the other women. Asher and Gwen hosted a farewell barbeque for her, and Caiden intended to leave for Firebrook as soon as it was over. This was a lot of people. However, he enjoyed getting to know the other shifters more. They made good allies, good friends. They looked out for each other. Caiden didn't mind being a part of that.

He didn't think his brother would either. Wyatt had called earlier to report on Sam. He'd been keeping quiet and to himself, avoiding work and only leaving for necessities. That morning, Wyatt noticed a sickly darkness to his face. They intended to watch the man, even talk to him, so he didn't fall into some sort of depression. What he'd done, and tried to do, was unforgivable, but it came from almost two decades of misguided grief. They wouldn't make him live another two decades with the same misery.

Maggie came back with several arms wrapped around her. Caiden counted the shifters and their mates. That could be a lot of visitors. He made a mental note to talk to Wyatt about adding more cabins. They booked solid every summer all summer. They'd benefit from more availability, anyway. But those cabins could wait until he and Maggie had their home built. Near the restaurant and the lodge. There was the perfect clearing at the edge of the land they owned. He'd show it to Maggie first thing tomorrow.

Caiden pulled his mate closer as they passed around fresh drinks. He let love in, and everything that came with it. He'd never let his nymph go.

Garrett Daly had always worried about Maggie the most. There had been a time where she didn't speak at all, and he couldn't help but imagine the trauma she must have endured to silence her entirely. Although she'd also been the best fighter. Maybe Tyrone had cared for his sister in some twisted way. Maybe he only valued the power he had over her.

She deserved the most out of what freedom could give her. And she got it. Bold and bright, Maggie captured the attention of everyone there when only a few weeks ago she attempted to blend in. Her happiness was a great gift. Not only to herself, but to Garrett and the others. They'd all wanted what was best for her.

But not everyone had left Tyrone's grip free and happy. So many women over the years had come and gone—killed for not being good enough or not carrying enough value to bring in money. They used some as collateral.

Garrett never would have worked for Tyrone if he hadn't had to worry about his sister's life. Before they killed Tyrone, he'd told Garrett his sister was dead. He couldn't accept it. Since the escape, he'd been searching. If he didn't find his sister alive, then he'd at least find out what happened. He needed closure.

He'd hit some dead ends, but a lead finally surfaced.

Garrett wouldn't have this chance if it weren't for the people around him. Happy, mated, and all conquered trials of their own. Garrett took a step back. They deserved this time. He didn't.

He made his exit, saying a silent farewell. With his own mission to conquer, he hoped he could return to his friends. He wouldn't be happy and whole, but that didn't matter. Being part of Tyrone's organization, even under duress, blackened his soul. There wouldn't be a happy ending for him, but there could be for his sister.

And he was going to find her.

Join my newsletter to receive special content, the most up to
date information on releases, and special promotions.
http://bit.ly/sarahurquhart

Also, visit my website at...
http://www.authorsarahurquhart.com
... to see my full book list.